THE BROKEN BRIDGE

The

Broken

Bridge

Philip Pullman

Alfred A. Knopf · New York

Manufactured in the United States of America
10   9   8   7   6   5   4   3   2   1

Library of Congress Cataloging-in-Publication Data
Pullman, Philip, 1946–   The broken bridge : a novel / by
Philip Pullman.   p.   cm.
Summary: Over the course of a long summer in Wales, six-
teen-year-old Ginny, the mixed-race, artist daughter of an
English father and a Haitian mother, learns that she has a
half-brother from her father's earlier marriage, and that her
own mother may still be alive.
ISBN 0-679-81972-X (trade)
ISBN 0-679-91972-4 (lib. bdg.)
[1. Identity—Fiction.   2. Family problems—Fiction.
3. Wales—Fiction.   4. Artists—Fiction.   5. Blacks—
Fiction.]   I. Title.   PZ7.P968Br   1992   [Fic]—dc20
91-15893

THE BROKEN BRIDGE

ONE DAY in the school playground they'd said, Eeny, meeny, miney, Mo', Catch a nigger by his toe, and they'd all looked at Ginny and laughed. They called her Eeny Meeny after that.

In the bath she told Dad to wash her harder.

"Why?" he said. "You're as clean as a whistle."

"I'm dirty," she said.

"You're not dirty, silly."

"But I'm not the same as them. I want to be the same color. They call me Eeny Meeny."

"You're the right color for you, and they're the right color for them," said Dad.

She wanted to say, Well, why is it right for me to be different from everyone else? Even Dad was white like them. But he kissed her and wrapped her in the towel and dried her hard, and she couldn't talk till she'd forgotten what she was going to say. They stopped calling her Eeny Meeny, though.

3

1

The Visitor

ONE HOT DAY toward the end of the summer term in which Ginny had her sixteenth birthday, she got home from school to find Dad already there, talking to a stranger. Normally he didn't get home till six or so, by which time she'd have done her homework and peeled the potatoes or made a salad or prepared whatever else they'd decided to have for supper. He hadn't told her that he'd be home today; she heard voices as she came through the kitchen, and her heart beat nervously for a moment.

She found them in the living room. Dad was looking preoccupied, and there was a woman in a suit, who smiled and held out her hand to be shaken, so Ginny automatically shook it.

"This is Wendy Stevens," said Dad.

Wendy Stevens was big, or fat actually, Ginny thought, with lots of blond hair elaborately waved like a country and western singer's. Her suit was dark blue, and she wore blusher and eye shadow, and her forehead was gleaming with the heat. When she spoke she smiled at the same time. She was very friendly, asking Ginny about school and hobbies and sports and fashions and pop music in a way that, after five minutes, began to make Ginny feel puzzled and rebellious. Dad had gone out to the kitchen; Ginny could tell he was relieved to get away.

Finally she said, "Who are you anyway? Are you a friend of Dad's?"

"No, I work for the Social Services Department," she said. "Not locally. In Liverpool."

"Are you a social worker?" Ginny was suspicious at once.

"Sort of. Why? Don't you like social workers?"

"I don't know any," she said. "Why are you asking me all these questions?"

"Just getting to know you," said Wendy Stevens, smiling.

"Well, you won't find out much by . . . I mean, sports and fashion and pop music . . . It's not *me*, really."

"Your dad's told me about your hobby."

"Hobby?"

"Drawing. Painting."

"That's not a hobby," said Ginny severely. "I don't want to be rude, but . . . what are you doing here anyway?"

"Does it worry you?"

"Yeah. Are you checking up or something?"

"What would I be checking up on?"

"Dunno. Anything."

"What sort of things?"

This was a stupid game, Ginny thought. Then something came into her mind and made her shiver: there'd been a case in the news recently where the social services had been criticized for failing to remove a child from the care of her father, who'd been abusing her. And there'd been another case where they had split a family up, and it turned out that the father hadn't done anything at all. . . . But was that why Wendy Stevens was here? Did they think she was being abused? Did they think that was more likely to happen where there wasn't a mother? Would they take her away from Dad?

She stood up and moved to the window that overlooked the tiny front garden and the fields leading down to the sea. You could never tell. She didn't know how much power social workers had; they seemed to be able to take children into custody whether or not the parents objected. But it was ridiculous. They couldn't believe that Dad was doing anything like that to her. It was impossible.

"You look as if you've seen a ghost," said Wendy Stevens. "Am I that bad?"

The door opened, and Dad came in with a tray of mugs of tea and some biscuits. There *was* something the matter; Ginny could tell. She wanted to get out and go down to the beach, but she thought she'd better stay and show there was nothing wrong between her and Dad. If Wendy Stevens could see that everything was normal, she might go away and leave them alone.

So Ginny sat down again, passed the biscuits, talked about school; and presently Wendy Stevens looked at her watch and began to put away the papers Ginny noticed for the first time. She had a cherry-red plastic briefcase with green canvas webbing at the corners; a tattered sticker on it said SUPPORT THE MINERS.

"Nice to meet you, Ginny," she said as she stood up. "Hope we see each other again."

She shook hands. Ginny smiled and nodded, and cleared the mugs and plates away as Dad went out with the woman to the Renault 5 parked in the lane.

"What did she want?" Ginny said when Dad came back. "She was asking all kinds of questions. All stupid ones, about pop music and stuff. Patronizing."

"How d'you know she wasn't my new girlfriend?" Dad said.

" 'Cause you've got better taste."

He smiled, but there was still something wrong. He went to the sink and started washing the mugs.

"But what *was* it?" Ginny said again.

"Oh, it was some nonsense. . . . D'you remember when we lived in Liverpool?"

"Was that the basement where you slept next to the fridge?"

"Next to the fridge? Oh, no, that was Hammersmith. When we lived in Liverpool, the Social Services helped out when I had to work late. There was a sort of nursery place. And Wendy Whatsername worked there, so she remembered you."

"But did she come all this way just to see us again?"

"No. We're not that famous. She was on her way back from a conference in Aberystwyth and just dropped in to say hello. Nothing important."

Oh, yeah, Ginny thought. But she didn't say it. Instead she wandered back to the living room, took out her schoolbooks, and began the last French homework before her exam.

APART FROM art, French was her best subject. She considered it to be her native language, her mother tongue, her mother's tongue. She'd never learned it from her mother, who had died a week or so after Ginny was born, but Ginny was proud of it all the same; just as she was proud of her mother and the color she'd inherited and the exoticness in her blood. Her father was English, white, but her mother had come from Haiti, where they spoke French and Creole, so Ginny applied herself to French with love and ardor: it belonged to her in the way that Welsh belonged to the other kids at school. Ginny had to learn Welsh too, and she did it conscientiously, but it felt cramped and alien. In French she was at home.

So normally she'd have worked at this exercise with pleasure, maybe imagining the day when she, speaking French perfectly, would be studying art in Paris or seeking out long-lost cousins in Haiti; but not today. Something was wrong. Dad wasn't telling the truth.

She gazed at the line of sand dunes a mile or so away, wondering if someone had told the Social Services that Dad was abusing her. She thought it must be that. One of the neighbors? But on one side lived Mr. and Mrs. Price, a retired stationmaster and his disabled wife, and on the other side were the Laxtons and their bed-and-breakfast. . . . Of course not. They were good people. Ridiculous. She went back to the French, listening to the sounds of Dad in the kitchen, the radio, the knife on the chopping board, the kettle boiling.

GINNY'S DAD owned his own business, setting up computer systems for offices and factories and advising people how to run the ones they had. He'd never remarried after Ginny's mother died. Now, at the age of thirty-seven, he looked as if he came from an earlier time; without being ridiculously handsome, he had the sort of looks that film stars of the thirties and forties had had. He had a beard, and if he put a spotted handkerchief around his head, a gold ring in one ear, and a dagger between his white teeth, he could have played alongside Gene Kelly in *The Pirate*, which Ginny had watched on TV over Christmas.

He and Ginny were close, almost like brother and sister, like equals. He was proud of her, proud of her talent, proud of her diligence; and she was proud of him, of his energy, his attractiveness. He had many girlfriends. Ginny used to think of them as the breakfast ladies, because sometimes she'd come down to breakfast and there would be a strange young woman she'd never seen before. She thought they just came for breakfast until she realized that they stayed all night, but she didn't realize why they stayed all night until much later, when there was only one of them. She was called Holly, and she stayed six months, and Ginny, feeling that they ought to be respectable, wanted to know if she and Dad were going to get married. But shortly afterward Holly left.

Ginny didn't feel jealous, because Dad always included her in things. When he took one of the breakfast ladies out for a meal, Ginny came, too, and learned to be sophisticated. When it was another's birthday, Ginny chose a present for her. And she and Dad talked about them: how Annie loved to gorge herself on fried bread and bacon, how Teresa hardly ate anything, how Mair used to sing hymns in the shower.

They were all white, of course. Not that Ginny expected Dad to have a black lover just because Maman had been black—in this part of Wales there were hardly any black faces to be seen—but when things were difficult, that was part of the difficulty. It was always there, being a black person in a white world, from the time she'd first become aware of it: Eeny Meeny—she grew hot at the thought. But it hadn't been urgent. Well, it wasn't urgent now, but she was sixteen, and though she thought she was pretty and Dad told her she was pretty and though her friends reassured her too, nevertheless, boys . . . well, they were cowards anyway. Which one of them would want to mark himself out from the rest by going out with a black girl? She knew that was how they'd feel. She guessed that was why no one had asked her. And if they did ask, they'd resent her for making them feel like that, so there'd always be other feelings mixed up with the relationship. She'd put the thought aside, into the darkness, but it hadn't gone away; she could sense it there, awake, and one day she'd have to deal with it.

"Supper's ready," Dad called.

"I'm not hungry," she said quietly, but she went anyway.

"Dad, what *was* she here for?" she said over the grilled lamb chops and salad.

"Nothing. Just passing."

"But this isn't the way to Liverpool from Aberystwyth."

"She might be going somewhere else for the weekend. Who knows? Who cares?"

"I thought she was stupid."

"I expect she noticed," he said.

"What d'you mean?"

"Well, you're not very tactful, are you?"

"Me?"

"You were looking at her as if she was poison."

"I wasn't . . ."

"Well, it probably doesn't matter. I don't suppose she'll come again."

"She had a load of papers all spread out. Was it something about me?"

"No, of course not. D'you want to finish the salad?"

After they'd eaten and she'd washed the dishes, she went out and wandered down the lane toward the beach. The house stood between its two neighbors in this little side lane off the road that led down to the sea from the main route along the coast. Inland, on the far side of the main road, a range of great grass-covered hills, not quite mountains but as high as hills could get, rolled endlessly away out of sight; but on this side, the seaward side, there was a space of magic and beauty, Ginny's realm, her kingdom, her queendom.

It was a mile wide: all the land between the main road and the sea. There was a grassy field below the road, then the lane with her house, then more fields, then a railway line, then another field and the sand dunes and the beach. To the right there was a parking area and a little shop, and a tiny trailer park that you couldn't see from the house; and to the left there was an estuary, where a little river, which only a few miles back in the hills was tumbling swiftly among rocks, spread itself out wide and slow through a tidal lagoon. Beyond that there were more dunes and, at the very edge of the horizon, an airfield from which tiny silver planes occasionally took off, to skim over the sea and vanish. Everything from the airfield to the trailer park, from the main road to the edge of the sea, was Ginny's.

She owned it, first, because she knew it: during the years they'd lived here, she'd wandered all over this gently sloping margin, this halfway place between the hills and the sea. She owned it because she'd drawn it, from the insects on the dry-stone walls to the decaying church half-buried in the dunes to the little bridge that carried the railway line over the estuary. And she owned it, finally, because she loved it. Everyone who entered this kingdom became a subject of hers without knowing it, owing her allegiance, paying her invisible respect. Nothing bad was permitted to happen in Ginny's kingdom; she was in charge; she saw to it.

So now as she wandered down the lane she looked over everything, inspecting the landscape as if it were a guard of honor. The ancient round stones in the walls, gray and lichen-covered, the grass in the fields, brown and dry from the weeks of hot weather, the coppery sun, still with an hour or two's light to shed before sinking into the sea—it was all in place, all as it should be.

There were still quite a few people on the beach, though some of them were beginning to pack away their sandy picnic boxes and their wet towels and their gritty, oily suntan bottles and make stiffly for the parking area. Ginny wandered along the soft sand to the right, above the rock pools where children were still crouching, intently fishing for little transparent shrimps, for crabs and starfish. The late golden light tinted everything evenly, benevolently, and the sea folded neat little waves quietly over onto the flat sand.

"Ginny!"

It was a stage whisper rather than a shout, and she couldn't place the voice, but then a lazy hand went up on the slope of the dunes to her right.

"Andy! What're you doing back?"

She threw herself to her knees beside him, too pleased and happy to do more than grin. Andy was two years older than she was, which was a lot, of course, and he'd left school the previous term and gone away somewhere. In the whole school, his had been the only other black face. He was mysterious, glamorous with a kind of evasive magic, half spirit, half con-man. He was much darker than Ginny, both his parents having been African; but he'd been adopted by a white couple in the town eight miles to the south, and that gave them something else in common: looking black, they'd each grown up feeling white.

Ginny had only got to know Andy properly in the past year or so, and then he'd vanished. And now he was back, and she was so happy she didn't know what to say.

"How you doing, then?" he said, lying back with his hands under his head. "You got a boyfriend yet?"

12

"Shut up," she said. "I don't want a boyfriend. Where you been?"

"In Bristol," he said. "Catering college. I know it all now. Mayonnaise, wine, carbonnade de boeuf, opening sardine tins—I can do anything."

"Has the term finished or something?"

"No. *I* finished. I might go back sometime, learn a bit more, but I got a job in the Castle."

"The Castle?" There was a battered little ruin in the town a mile or two up the coast, but Ginny had no idea that anyone worked there.

"The Castle Hotel. In the kitchen. It's a right laugh. Carlos, the chef there, he's got all kinds of scams, all kinds of rackets going on. . . . I'm getting a trailer, how about that?"

"A trailer? Aren't you living at home?"

"Well, that got a bit dodgy. They don't know I'm back. No, me and Dafydd Lewis from the garage, we're going to share this trailer. We're putting it in old man Alston's field just back there."

Ginny had never seen Andy's adoptive parents, but she'd heard that they were elderly and strict. If Andy was going to be living just behind the dunes, everything was going to be wonderful, brilliant. She knew the field he meant: it belonged to the richest man in the county, who owned factories and garden centers and printing plants. Dad had done some work for him. He was having a house built in the field, but not very quickly. Every few weeks some men would drive down in a truck and unload timber or bricks or drainpipes and go away again, and by the time the workmen arrived to do something with them, half the materials would be missing. No one seemed to mind.

"Does he know?" Ginny said.

"What, old man Alston? He won't know. Oh, we'll have

some good times this summer, Gin. You wait and see.
. . . Aye, aye, watch out!"

He rolled over onto his stomach, facing away from the beach, and laid his head on his hands.

"What?" Ginny looked around to see who he was hiding from.

"Bloke down there with a leather jacket," Andy muttered. "Big belly on him."

The man was plodding through the sand below them. He was heavy-looking, and the leather jacket he wore added to his bulk, but the most remarkable thing was his head. It seemed almost inhumanly large, the features coarse and blunt like a giant's, and everything the same sandy color: lips, eyebrows, thin greasy hair.

"What's he doing?" Andy said.

"He's stopped—he's looking the other way—now he's going up to the parking lot. There, he's gone. Who is he?"

"Joe Chicago," said Andy, rolling over again. "Gangster, he is. From Aberystwyth."

Ginny found herself giggling at the idea of a gangster called Joe Chicago coming from Aberystwyth. Andy shook his head.

"You can laugh," he said solemnly.

"Where's his gang, then?" Ginny said.

"Oh, he hasn't got a gang."

"But that's what gangster means—having a gang!"

"Yeah, maybe. But he's a soloist."

"Why's he after you?"

"Oh . . ." He shrugged, and for the first time in Ginny's experience, Andy looked embarrassed. The expression sat so strangely on his face that for a moment she mistook it for fear. But no, she thought, not Andy, he wouldn't be afraid of anything, surely?

The moment passed like a small cloud drifting over the sun, and then Andy was sitting up again as if nothing had happened.

"Hey," he said, flicking her knee, "you want a job?"

"After the end of term, yeah, I wouldn't mind. What sort of job?"

"In the Yacht Club. Angie Lime needs someone in the kitchen and setting the tables and that. I said I might lend a hand meself, but you know, I'm a busy man, I might get overstressed. Could be fatal."

Anyone less likely than Andy to die of stress hadn't been born, she thought. "Okay," she said. "I wouldn't want you to run the risk of that. Is it every day?"

"Evenings. Six till eight. I'll tell her, shall I? I'm going over there later. Doing the rounds, you know, visiting my flock, giving them their little touch of Andy for the day."

"Yeah. Tell her. I'll go and see her myself. That's great!"

The Yacht Club in the estuary wasn't a club at all, it was the Harbor Restaurant, but the Welsh were inventive with names. Angie Lime was only called that because her husband's name was Harry. Consequently, he wasn't Harry Williams, his real name, but Harry Lime, as in *The Third Man*, and she was Angie Lime. They'd had the Yacht Club for a year or so. Ginny and Dad had been there for a meal; it was small and friendly and bistro-like, and Angie was a good cook. It would be fun working there. It would be fun having Andy around. Everything was good suddenly, everything was fun, everything was as it should be in her mile-wide kingdom by the sea, as the last visitors trudged up through the soft sand toward their cars and the waves kept falling neatly and the sun sank toward the edge of the world in a welter of blood-red sky.

"DAD? You know Andy?"

"Andy Evans? I saw him today. He was talking to Dafydd in the garage. Why?"

"Well, he said they needed someone to help in the Yacht Club, in the kitchen, right, and I said I'd do it. In the evenings."

"What, the whole evening? Aren't I going to see you at all?"

It was late. Dad was lying in the hammock in the hot night, with something by Mozart playing very quietly through the open window and the underside of the leaves lit up above him by the floodlight at the base of the tree. He often lay in the hammock. Sometimes he slept out all night. Sometimes she joined him, bringing her mattress and duvet out under the stars. It was going to be hot enough for that tonight, but there was a distance between them now, after Wendy Stevens's visit.

Ginny reclined the deck chair to its limit and sat down, not far away, gazing up at the canopy of leaves, the lightest viridian against the velvet black.

"Only from six till eight o'clock," she said.

"Well, that sounds all right. D'you want to?"

"Yeah. That's why I said I would."

"So you did. How much are they going to pay you?"

"I don't know. I haven't actually spoken to them yet."

"Counting your chickens again," he said.

"Well, maybe."

They sat companionably, without talking, for a few more minutes. The Mozart tape came to an end and clicked off.

"You ought to have your Walkman on," she said. "Then you wouldn't have to keep getting up to turn the tape over."

"I don't have to. I ask you nicely, and you do it for me."

"You reckon?" she said, getting up.

"No worries."

"D'you want the other side?"

"No. Chopin Nocturnes. The Rubinstein one."

She went in, found the tape, set it going.

"I still think it'd be easier with the Walkman," she said, outside again.

"I don't want to shut the rest of the world out. I want to hear the music coming quietly from a distance, with all the night around it. As if you're hearing it through the open windows of a great house across a lake . . ."

"Yah! Pretentious twit!" she said, but the image secretly delighted her, and she pictured it to herself, composing the scene in her mind like a painting. She could see it taking shape; her imagination worked effortlessly, taking what it needed from every memory she had of classical buildings, and lawns, and light reflected off dark water. Unlike memories of people, memories of things came easily to her; she had only to think of an object or a place to find it before her, correctly textured, three-dimensional, casting shadows. There were a lot of things about herself she didn't know, and one was how rare this gift was, though she was beginning to sense it.

She lay back in the warm night, in the magic circle of light under the old tree, with Chopin coming faintly across the imaginary lake, with her beloved father close by, and felt unbearably rich. She loved him so much. The world was so full, so strange, and she and Dad understood each other so well; this was how it should be forever.

2

Rhiannon's Sister

ON THE FIRST afternoon of the summer holiday, Ginny's best friend, Rhiannon, came to see her and told her something strange.

Rhiannon lived in the town a couple of miles up the coast, where her parents ran a café called the Dragon. Ginny liked them; Mr. Calvert was a bouncy, eccentric man given to sudden enthusiasms, such as sailing or playing the guitar, which he'd take up and pursue passionately for a few months and then suddenly drop, whereas Mrs. Calvert was patient and sensible. Ginny enjoyed being at the Calverts' because among other things they were a family, they were complete. And she liked Rhiannon, who was vain and languid and funny and kind.

That Monday afternoon, while Dad was out at work, Ginny and Rhiannon went down to the beach and tried to swim in the chilly water, and then lay in the scorching sun before drifting back to the house and sitting in the garden.

Rhiannon lay in the hammock, her long dark hair drifting silkily over the edge. Ginny had often tried to draw

her, but she'd never succeeded in getting her sinuous le-
thargic grace onto the paper. You needed to be someone
like Burne-Jones for that, she thought, having just read a
book about the Pre-Raphaelites; for herself, she preferred
Picasso or Van Gogh. Only they'd have been able to draw
her too. Keep trying.

They lay under the trees talking idly, and then Rhiannon
said, "Oh! I know what I was going to tell you. My sister
rang up yesterday."

"Your sister? I never knew you had a sister!"

Ginny was amazed. She'd always thought of Rhiannon
as an only child like herself.

"Yeah, well, they don't talk about her much. She's a lot
older than me—she's twenty-six or something. She left
home; I mean, they threw her out, I think. There was
some kind of quarrel when I was young. A terrible row. I
don't know what it was about, but they've never spoken
about her since. . . ."

"Wow, that's incredible," said Ginny, trying to imagine
a quarrel as bitter as that. "What's her name? Why did
she ring up?"

"She's called Helen. She rang up to ask about you, actually."

Ginny sat up to see if Rhiannon was joking. She was
simply lying there languidly, trailing a hand through the
dry grass beneath the hammock, gazing up with half-closed
eyes through the sunny leaves above her. She turned to
look at Ginny.

"It's true," she said. "Mam answered the phone, okay,
and she didn't recognize Helen's voice. Well, she wouldn't,
probably. She came in the living room and said it was for
me, so I went out and shut the door 'cause I thought it
might be Peter; he said he'd ring. And this strange woman's voice said, 'Listen, don't sound surprised, I don't want

Mam and Dad to know, this is Helen, your sister.' Well, *Duw annwyl*, I didn't know what to say, you know—it was like a voice from the grave or something. I said, 'Where are you?' And she said, 'At home in Porthafon.' "

Porthafon was a town about twenty miles up the coast. Ginny was sitting upright now, watching Rhiannon bright-eyed.

"And you never knew she was living there?"

"I told you, we never speak about her. I didn't really know she was living at all. She gave me her address, Twelve Jubilee Terrace. She said she was married. Her husband's called Benny something—Meredith, I think. He sells thermal windows. And she works in an architect's office. They've got no children. She told me all that kind of thing; she sounded really nice, really friendly. I couldn't believe who I was listening to, you know. She kept saying, 'You're sure they're not listening? They can't hear me?' as if she was scared."

"Scared? I can't imagine anyone being scared of your mam and dad. But what did she say about me?"

"Oh, yes, right, I was coming to that. Well, she asked what class I was in at school, and I told her, and she said did I know a girl called Ginny Howard? I said yeah, and she said . . ." Rhiannon paused a moment and seemed to be adjusting her position, or avoiding Ginny's eye, before going on: "She said were you adopted?"

"*What?*"

"That's what she said. So I said no, of course not. I told her what, you know, what you've told me, about your mam and all that. . . ."

"But why did she want to know?" Ginny was bemused. "How did she know about me anyway?"

"Well, I asked her that, course I did. She just said she'd met your dad, see. And she was curious about you, I suppose. She probably fancies him. Hey, if she leaves her husband and marries your dad, you'll have to call me auntie."

Ginny smiled, but she wasn't sure how she felt about this stranger asking questions about her. She supposed it might be flattering, if you felt confident about yourself. You might assume that someone was asking about you because you were attractive or interesting; she was sure Rhiannon would feel like that. But Ginny didn't; she felt threatened.

Then she felt that Rhiannon had something else to say. She looked up and saw the other girl blushing.

"And then she said—" Rhiannon began. "This is crazy; you won't believe this. She said was it true that your dad had been in prison?"

Now Ginny felt really stupid. She knew she was gaping, she even felt her mouth open and thought: *So your jaw really does drop*, but she could find nothing whatever to say.

"I told her no, course not, what a stupid idea," Rhiannon went on, "and she said no, it didn't seem very likely. Something like that. So I asked her where she heard that from, and she said, 'Oh, someone in town.' Mam came out then, and I had to say good-bye."

"Prison?" said Ginny. "That's ridiculous. Why? What's he supposed to have done?"

"I don't know! 'Cause *she* didn't know. She only heard this rumor, and she wanted to find out more, I suppose. It must be a mistake. Oh! I knew there was something else. Dad says d'you want a job? Just in the morning, doing coffees, setting tables for lunch."

"Everyone's offering me jobs," said Ginny.

"Who else is, then?"

"The Yacht Club. You know Andy's back? Andy Evans?

He told me about it. I'm going to work there in the evenings."

"Well, don't tell Dad. He thinks Harry Lime's trying to pinch all our customers—you know how he gets obsessed. Mam thinks he's crazy, because they're different sorts of customers anyway, and everyone knows Angie Lime's a good cook. You going to come and work in the Dragon, then? Be a laugh anyway."

"Yeah. Tell him I will. And thanks. When do I start?"

"Tomorrow, if you want."

"Great . . . Rhiannon, is your sister going to ring up again?"

"I don't know. She might. I want to meet her, but I'm nervous, you know?"

"So do I want to meet her," said Ginny.

"Oh, hey, listen, I'm not supposed to've told you, okay? She said, 'Don't tell her.' So . . ."

"But I want to find out what it's about! And I can't ask him."

"No, course you can't. Forget it. It's nothing."

NOTHING?

Nothing of the sort. When Dad came home, after Rhiannon had gone, Ginny looked at him differently, trying to imagine him a criminal. She couldn't; there wasn't any crime she could think of that she could see him committing. Then, for the first time in a week, she remembered that social worker, Wendy Stevens, and what the visit had made her worry about. To hear of someone talking about prison in connection with her father wasn't nothing, by any means.

That Monday was her first evening at the Yacht Club, so she didn't eat with him. She'd have something when she came in later, she told him, and set off down the lane. At the parking area by the beach, she turned left and into a field full of tussocky lumps of gorse and marram grass and little sand-filled depressions, just like bunkers on a golf course, which led along beside the estuary as far as the little harbor next to the railway station, where the Yacht Club stood. It was a hot evening, and the sun shone full on the great round hills behind the main road, and the sky above them was a bright pearly blue. Sheep, lazy tattered fat things, moved slowly aside as she wandered past. This warm marine light, this silence . . . they were the emblems of her kingdom. She was at home.

Harry Lime was young and short and thickset, with long-lashed blue eyes. Both he and Angie were ambitious: they wanted to make a name for the restaurant. But that didn't stop them from laughing or being friendly. Angie was short too, and her laughter was of a different kind. She was wittier than Harry, more cynical and shrewd. She was in charge in the kitchen and Harry was in charge in front, and there were a couple of students who waited on the tables, and an elderly lady who worked the dishwasher, and a girl called Gwen, who helped Angie in the kitchen. Ginny's job was to set tables, fold napkins, make sure the biscuits and the cheese board were stocked up, trim spring onions and celery, top up the salt and pepper, and do any one of a dozen other jobs that Harry or Angie wanted doing. She soon found that she was going to love it. She loved the atmosphere in the kitchen, brisk and clean and hot and busy, full of temperamental cursing and sudden flurries of singing. And she loved the two dining rooms—the front one, cool and open, overlooking the yachts and the river and the little wooden railway bridge, and the smoky little back one where the bar was, with Harry darting this way and that, grinning gap-toothed and tossing olive after olive absentmindedly into his mouth and forever hitching up the trousers that kept slipping under his paunch.

Within half an hour Ginny felt so much at home that she was able to tell them she was going to work at the Dragon as well.

"That bugger Calvert, he's neurotic," said Harry. "Don't you think he's neurotic, love?"

"If he wasn't when you started going on about him, then he should be by now," said Angie, who was stirring some kind of sauce.

"Oh, come on," said Harry, "you should hear what he says about this place. It's slanderous, I swear it is. And what's that I saw on the wall there the other day? I was just looking through the window as I went past—has he got paintings hanging up there?"

Painting was Mr. Calvert's latest hobby. Ginny felt she ought to defend him, though privately she thought his pictures were terrible.

"He does them himself," she said. "They're—"

Harry was fascinated. "He did 'em himself? He does these paintings and hangs 'em up in his own café?"

"He sells them," Ginny told him. "They've all got prices on."

"What? He actually sells 'em? Are they any good?"

"Well . . ."

"Don't lie, girl," said Angie. "I can tell."

"How much does he ask for 'em?" said Harry.

"Forty pounds, fifty pounds, that sort of price."

Ginny was cutting up French-style loaves into chunks and putting them in little baskets. Harry picked up a piece and absentmindedly started tearing it apart, he was so interested in these paintings of Mr. Calvert's.

24

"And has anyone bought one?" he said, throwing a piece of bread into his mouth.

"I don't know. I'll ask tomorrow."

"Look at you, you messy pig," Angie said to him. "Crumbs all over you. Get out, go and do some work, go on."

Winking at Ginny and tossing up another piece of bread, Harry Lime went out without the lemon he'd come in for. Angie saw it on the table and asked Ginny to take it through to the bar.

"Silly bugger, he'd forget his trousers if they weren't sewn on," she said.

When Ginny got back, there was someone else in the kitchen, sitting at the table calmly slicing some carrots into matchstick-sized pieces with quick, accurate taps of a knife.

"Andy!" she said, delighted. "What're you doing here? Have you left the Castle?"

"I got the sack," he said. "It's all right, it's quite fair. I was next on the list. Pass me that dish."

"What list?" Ginny sat down to fill the salt and pepper mills.

"Carlos, the chef, right, he fires people in strict rotation—first in, first out. Every so often one of his rackets gets busted, and he has to have someone to blame. Someone to take the rap. *Duw annwyl*, you should have seen us last night. We were all in there and he was making *Glühwein*—"

"*Glühwein* in the summer?" said Angie, listening.

"What's *Glühwein*?" said Ginny.

"Oh, you know, mulled wine. You heat it up with spices and stuff and drink it with your après-ski kit. I know it's the wrong drink for the summer, but Carlos is insane, man, he's deranged. He sent me up to the bar for some port, to stiffen it a bit, he says. He had to send to the bar because the boss has put a new lock on the cellar and Carlos hasn't found the key yet, but he will. Anyway, Barry in the bar's drunk, see, so he gives me a bottle of brandy instead. 'Brandy for my friend Carlos,' he says, 'give him brandy.' 'Duw,' says Carlos, 'look at this, lads, Welsh port— this'll warm your cockles up.' There's us all sweating like pigs in there already. He pours it all in—beautiful stuff it was, Rémy Martin or something—and then he takes this poker thing he's been heating in the gas flame. It's red hot, and he bungs it in, and whoosh! The whole lot goes up. The flames hit the ceiling, Carlos's eyebrows are burnt off, all the waiters are squealing with terror, and then the boss walks in.

" 'What's going on? Good God! Good God! What's happened?' he says, and Carlos points the poker at me.

" 'This casual staff,' he says, 'entertainment is all they care about. Swallowing the knives is bad enough, but I will not have fire-eating in my kitchen.'

" 'Out!' says the boss. 'Out! Out!' "

"I don't know how that place is still standing," said Angie.

"So that was it, see," Andy went on. "Still, it was a good laugh. Carlos gave me a whole side of smoked salmon to take away. I had to stuff it down me leg to get it past the porter. Me and Dafydd, we're living on smoked salmon and baked beans now, in the trailer. We're taking it down the beach on Wednesday. You ought to come and pay a visit."

"I will," said Ginny.

The last of the sunlight through the open door soaked the whole kitchen in gold, and everything was wonderful. Andy was there, and everything was great.

26

NEXT MORNING, in the Dragon, she looked more closely at Mr. Calvert's pictures. He was a science fiction fan, and these were science fiction pictures—women in brass corsets fighting huge green lizards, or sunsets on Jupiter with smudgy purple shadows going the wrong way. The colors were so violent and applied so clumsily that Ginny felt uncomfortable looking at them. What was more, she knew from her own efforts that while drawing human beings wasn't easy, if you looked carefully enough and tried hard, you could usually see how bodies fit together. To look at Mr. Calvert's paintings, though, you'd have thought it was impossible. They had titles like *Interstellar Alchemy* or *Dragon Dawn*, and Ginny wouldn't have given 10p for the lot; but there they were with little stickers saying forty pounds or fifty pounds. She liked Mr. Calvert, so she had to pretend to be impressed.

She had something else on her mind, though, and she didn't want to tell Rhiannon about it. As soon as she finished, which was at twelve o'clock, she slipped away and went down the hill to the station. She was just in time to catch the midday train to Porthafon.

It got there at a quarter to one. The station was next to the harbor, which at one time had been a working place, full of ships taking on cargoes of slate, but now was cluttered with expensive yachts belonging to tourists. Ginny wandered around and sat on a bollard eating some chips and an apple, then she set off to look for Jubilee Terrace.

She didn't know what she was going to say to Rhiannon's sister. She didn't really know whether she was going to call on her at all; she felt nervous, and her heart was beating as if she had stage fright. When she found the house, in a little slaty terrace above the town, she walked past it and down to the end of the terrace before telling herself not to be so weak.

She turned back and rang the doorbell. The narrow garden was neatly kept, with bright geraniums edging the path, and unlike its neighbors, this house had no net curtains, so Ginny could see how tidy and clean the front room was.

When the door opened, the woman who stood there blinked in the sunlight, shading her eyes, and took a little step backward in surprise.

"Mrs. Meredith?" said Ginny. "Rhiannon's sister?"

Helen Meredith blew out her cheeks and ran a hand through her dark hair. She knew who Ginny was; she was utterly taken aback.

"Come in," she said, standing aside in the narrow hall. "She . . . You must be Ginny. Is that right? God, I'm sorry to be so . . . It's just a surprise, that's all. She must have told you."

"Well, she's my friend," said Ginny.

She stepped inside, and Helen Meredith shut the door. There was a pause, and they both spoke at once, and Ginny said, "Sorry. You go first."

"I was going to say would you like some coffee or something?"

"Oh, thanks. Yeah, I would. . . ."

She followed the woman into the little kitchen and sat on a stool while Helen filled a kettle and got out some mugs. Everything was so clean that it looked new. Ginny used to think that other people had newer things than she and Dad did, newer carpets, newer curtains and furniture; it took her some time to realize that it was just that she and Dad didn't clean things as often as everyone else. But then they both had better things to do, as he said when she pointed it out.

"I told her not to say anything," said Helen Meredith. "I'm embarrassed now."

She sat down on the other side of the little breakfast bar, and Ginny could see that she was blushing deep pink. She didn't look away or try to hide it, either.

"What did she tell you?" she said.

"She said you'd met my dad, and you wanted to know about me, whether I was adopted."

Helen Meredith nodded. "Just being nosy," she said. "I'm sorry."

"Didn't you ask Dad?"

"No. I don't know why. And . . . I thought it was time I got in touch with Rhiannon. . . . That seemed to be a way. I don't know. . . ."

The kettle boiled, and she got up to make the coffee.

"Oh, by the way, don't call me Mrs. Meredith. I'm Helen," she said, with her back to Ginny.

"Oh. Right."

She was quite different from Rhiannon, Ginny thought: clearer and more vivid; stronger, perhaps.

Quickly, while Helen's back was still turned, Ginny said, "Rhiannon said you asked if my father had been in prison."

"Oh, God," said Helen.

She brought the mugs over. Her face was screwed up with embarrassment, and deep red. Ginny had never seen a grownup look so ashamed.

"I didn't want her to," she said. "I knew I shouldn't, soon as I said it. Stupid of me. You haven't asked him, have you?"

"What?" Ginny said. "Course not! He doesn't know I'm here; he doesn't know anything about it."

"Good. I'm sorry. I shouldn't have listened. . . ."

"Listened? Who to?"

"Someone . . . my husband knows. He said that as far as he knew, your dad had . . . been in prison. That's all. It's probably a mistake."

"But . . . what was he supposed to've done, to get sent to prison?"

"I don't know," said Helen, looking really unhappy. "It's probably . . . like I said, it's probably a mistake."

Ginny sat watching her for a few moments. Helen was toying with a teaspoon, pushing it slowly around like the hand of a clock, not touching her coffee.

"Well, if you know Dad," Ginny said finally, "couldn't you ask him?"

"I couldn't. Not yet. I don't know him well enough. Maybe I wouldn't anyway. It's just . . . No."

"Does your husband know?"

"Benny? He's never here. He wouldn't know." She sipped her coffee. "Tell me about your mam," she said.

Ginny liked the Welsh *mam* better than the English *mum;* it was almost *maman.*

"She came from Haiti," she said. "She was an art student, and she met Dad and they fell in love and got married, and I was born, and then she got hepatitis and died. That's all, really. She was called Anielle. Anielle Baptiste, that was her maiden name."

"So you never really knew her?"

"No. I've got a picture of her."

"*Where* did you say she came from?"

"Haiti. Where the zombies come from. Zombies and voodoo. She spoke French and Creole. But I don't know any Creole; there was no one to teach me."

"You've never been there? Never seen her family?"

"My family too," Ginny said. "No, I never have. I don't think Dad would have anything in common with them, really."

"They'd have you in common," said Helen.

"Yeah, well . . . Anyway, I get the feeling Dad never

got on with them. They just . . . I don't know anything about them, to tell the truth."

She wished she did. But whenever she'd asked Dad, he'd told her they were a wealthy family from Port-au-Prince, the capital, but that was all he knew.

"We don't talk about her much," said Ginny. "It's just me and Dad, really."

They sat quietly for a while. It was easier now, much easier than Ginny had thought. Helen told her a little about her own background, how she had quarreled with her father over some boy and how it had got out of control, so that they'd all said more than they'd meant, and how difficult it was to make the first move back. Ginny came away thinking how nice Helen was, how lucky Rhiannon was to have such a sister. Families were strange, to quarrel so bitterly.

3

The Mobile
Home

GINNY SPENT Sunday waiting impatiently for Dad to go
out so that she could call Rhiannon and tell her about her
visit to Helen. He spent the morning slumped on the sofa
reading the paper, as usual, but finally in the afternoon
he decided to go and look at a boat he was thinking of
buying, and she rushed to the phone at once.

"Rhiannon—guess what? I've been to see your sister!"

"*What?* When?"

"Yesterday. She's great, honestly; she was so nice. . . .
Her husband wasn't there; she was on her own. The thing
about my dad, you know—it was just a rumor she'd heard
from someone who knows her husband. Probably a mistake. But I had to go; I couldn't help it. . . ."

She sensed that Rhiannon wasn't pleased. It was as if
Ginny had somehow stolen Helen for herself; or it might
simply have been that her parents were nearby and she
couldn't respond with more excitement. She'd have to be
tactful, Ginny thought.

In fact, next day in the Dragon, Rhiannon was able to
speak more easily, and they spent most of the morning

talking intently behind the coffee machine on the counter, analyzing everything Ginny could remember about what Helen had said, what the house looked like, what she looked like, what Ginny had said to her.

"You'll have to go and see her," she told Rhiannon. "She's really friendly. You'd love her, honest."

It would have to wait till next weekend, they realized. Maybe they could go together. But no, thought Ginny, be tactful: let Rhiannon meet her sister on her own first. She felt extremely virtuous about that and half wished she could tell Rhiannon and be admired, but that would have spoiled it. Then she realized that too, and laughed.

ON WEDNESDAY afternoon, Ginny went down to the beach to help Andy with his mobile home, as he'd taken to calling it.

It was hotter than ever. The parking lot was full, and there was a line of children waiting to buy ice cream from the two old ladies in the little shop. They sold postcards and cups of tea there as well. The postcards at the front of the rack were all faded, but the ladies left them like that on purpose, to keep the ones at the back nice and bright. Even the ones at the back were getting scratched and dog-eared, though, and they all had rust marks from where the salty air had corroded the rack. The old ladies looked like retired nuns. The tea they sold came not in plastic mugs but in proper cups on a tray. People didn't always bring the cups back, and the two ladies would comb the sand dunes in the evening sunlight, chattering musically, the very souls of sweetness and melancholy.

Ginny sat on the wall by the parking lot to watch out for Andy and Dafydd, the boy he was going to share the trailer with. She didn't know what Dafydd would be driving; he worked in the garage on the main road, and she'd seen him drive about in dozens of different old cars at one time or another. When at last a car did arrive towing a trailer, she didn't give it more than a glance, because she was sure Dafydd wouldn't be driving a BMW.

But it stopped beside her, and there was Andy in the passenger seat, grinning up at her. She jumped.

"What're you doing in that?" she said. "That's not Dafydd. . . ."

Andy got out. "This is Stuart," he said. "I got another driver. Always wise to have a spare."

Stuart was leaning across, holding out his hand to shake. Ginny was taken aback; he was about thirty years old and so handsome he was almost unreal, like a model or a film star. At once she felt shy and didn't know what to say, but Andy was completely at ease.

"Well, now, we'll have to back up, driver," he said. "Just about a couple of hundred feet, I reckon."

There were three cars already waiting behind them, unable to pass in the narrow road. Stuart put the BMW in reverse and started to move back, but the other drivers wouldn't budge. Andy went to speak to the first driver. Ginny wondered why Stuart didn't just go on the final hundred feet into the parking lot and turn around there, but she could see that he and Andy were playing some sort of game, and she settled back to watch it.

Andy was having trouble with the first driver, a brick-faced man with a carful of children.

"What d'you expect me to do? Bloody vertical takeoff?" the man was saying heatedly.

"No, no, you could go in the field. Look," Andy said helpfully, starting to open the gate in the stone wall beside him.

"Why don't *you* go in the field?" roared the driver. He

obviously couldn't see that Stuart could have driven straight into the parking lot. Andy scratched his head, looking doubtful.

"Well, I dunno," he said. "The old turning circle's not what it was. I'll have to consult the chauffeur. I say! Carruthers!"

Stuart got out. "Anything wrong, sir?" he said.

"If this gentleman's kind enough to move back a little way," Andy called back, "can we reverse up here and insert the mobile home through this gateway?"

The contrast between Stuart's gleaming BMW and uncanny good looks and the filthy battered old trailer and Andy's scruffiness, not to mention Andy's pretense of picking his nose innocently, was making Ginny giggle. By this time five cars were waiting to get past, and they all had to reverse about ninety feet to let the big BMW back to the gate, and when it got there it wouldn't go in, because no matter how skillfully Stuart reversed it, the trailer was too wide. Andy ran back and forth, pretending to be helpful. At one point he leapt inside the trailer and came out with a twelve-inch ruler, with which he started measuring the width of the gateway. A cry of anger rose from the first car. People started getting out of the vehicles farther back, their arms full of towels and beach balls and picnic boxes, leaving the drivers to sort out the mess; and meanwhile Stuart was happily doing whatever Andy told him to do, as Ginny sat on the wall and watched, laughing.

"Why don't you go in the bloody lot and turn round there?" shouted one of the drivers.

"There must be a catch in that," Andy said. "What d'you reckon, Gin? Sounds too easy to me."

"No; do that," she said.

Stuart nodded, and the BMW surged forward. The trailer

door flew wide open with a bang, and a plastic bucket fell out. Andy stood in the middle of the road, nodding wisely.

"See," he said. "I told you there was a way of doing it."

The first car hooted, and Andy jumped aside, taking the bucket with him. The cars in the line followed Stuart into the lot, the drivers scowling and frowning at Andy, who stood holding the bucket like someone collecting for charity. It took less than a minute for Stuart to turn the car around and come out again, facing up the lane. He stopped for Andy and Ginny to get in, and said, "Where do we go now?"

"Up to the railway bridge," said Andy. "We can't get into old Alston's field down here anyway."

"Well, why did you come all the way down?" Ginny asked.

"To pick you up," said Stuart.

She was sitting in the front, Andy in the back, and now as she looked at Stuart she felt overcome with shyness again. He must be a film star, she thought; no one could be that handsome and not be famous for it. He had dark curly hair and bright-blue eyes, and his clothes were like his car, expensive and luxurious: soft cream trousers and dark-blue polo shirt. His bare feet on the pedals looked tough and expert.

"What do you do, Ginny?" he said, maneuvering smoothly past another car.

"Oh, I'm at school," she said. "That's all. What about you?"

"I'm a playboy," he said.

"You know that house by the Yacht Club?" Andy said from the back. "The one on stilts? Stuart's renting it."

"Oh, I love that house!" Ginny said.

"You know it, then?" said Stuart.

"Only from the outside."

"You'll have to come and visit."

The one-story wooden house was built like a boat, with railings around a flat roof and portholes instead of windows. When the tide came in, the house stood above the water on its stilts, and a flight of steps led down to where a dinghy was usually tied up. Ginny had loved it from the moment she'd first seen it, but she'd never found out who lived there. Now that Stuart had come to enter her kingdom, though, the least she could do was pay it a state visit.

"Is this where we go?" he said.

He turned the car into the courtyard of the shop by the railway bridge, then waited while Andy opened a gate into the field next to it. They bumped over the tussocky grass to the far corner. There was a hedge that separated it from the trailer site, and in the very center of the field stood the half-built shell of Mr. Alston's house, with piles of bricks and a cement mixer beside it.

"Where d'you want it?" said Stuart.

"This'll do," said Andy.

They got out, and Andy began to screw down the legs of the trailer.

"Can I look inside?" said Ginny.

"Help yourself," he said. "Put the kettle on, that's what you can do. We'll have some coffee."

It was a shabby, battered old trailer, and worse inside than out, with holes in the hardboard paneling and yellowing tape over a crack in the window and a broken catch that wouldn't hold the cupboard door shut. There were two foam mattresses on the bunks and a couple of sleeping bags lying in a pile of dirty clothes on the floor.

She found a kettle and a plastic container of water and some matches, and lit the gas in the tiny stove, holding the kettle in place while the trailer rocked and shook as they settled it on its legs. When the water boiled, she found some more or less clean mugs and made the coffee. There was no milk, of course, and no sugar, either. When she opened the little kitchen cupboard, a powerful fishy smell came out, and she wrinkled her nose and took a step back before looking more closely. A vast pink slab was lying there sweating.

"What on earth is that thing in the cupboard?" she said, taking two mugs of black coffee outside. Andy and Stuart were sitting on the step, and they moved to make room for her between them.

"Oh, that's me smoked salmon," said Andy. "We better finish that off tonight; it's getting a bit vigorous. You fancy a slice now?"

She made a face.

"You not having any coffee?" Stuart said to her.

"I've seen the mugs," she said.

He looked at his doubtfully but sipped anyway.

"What do you really do?" she said. "You're not really a playboy, are you? I didn't think they were real."

"Oh, they are," he said. "They play polo, they gamble, they go skiing and motor racing and jet setting."

"Not here, though," she said.

"No; I'm on holiday," he said. "All that pleasure, it wears you out. No; really, I'm an anthropologist."

"A what? Do you go in jungles and things?"

"Not if I can help it. I study religion, magic, witchcraft. I was in Brazil earlier this year. Fascinating."

"Have you been to Haiti?"

"Yes, I have, actually."

"My mother came from there."

"Did she? Do you speak Creole?"

"No. She died when I was only little. I've never been there."

38

"It's an amazing place. I spent some time with a voodoo priest, learning all about it."

"Could you teach me about voodoo?"

"Sure."

"You ought to do voodoo on Joe Chicago," she said, turning to Andy.

She felt him tense. He didn't say anything for a moment or two, and Stuart turned to see why.

"Who's Joe Chicago?" he said.

"He's a thug," said Andy. "White trash."

"Why's he called Joe Chicago anyway?" said Ginny.

"That leather jacket he wears, it comes from Chicago," Andy explained.

"Is that all?"

"It's true!"

"But that's as if I called myself Ginny Korea because of my sneakers," she said.

"Why's he after Andy?" Stuart asked her.

"He won't tell me," she said.

"You want to stay away from him," said Andy shortly. "He's horrible, he's dangerous. Don't have nothing to do with him."

He wouldn't say any more. Presently Stuart said he had to go and see about renting a boat. "Come and visit my house," he said before he drove off. He'd left most of his coffee, Ginny noticed.

"Is he rich?" she said.

"His dad's a millionaire. But he's too busy to spend his money, so Stuart spends it for him."

"He's nice. I like him."

Andy had closed his eyes. They sat there in the sun, listening to the shouts of children on the beach or in the sand dunes and the sound of a distant aircraft taking off across the estuary.

"Andy," she said after a few minutes, "when you were a kid, did you feel different from everyone else because you were black?"

He didn't answer for such a long time that Ginny eventually prodded his foot with hers.

"I'm thinking," he said. Then he said, "I feel different for all sorts of reasons. Being black's one, of course it is. Being adopted's another. Being . . . well, everything else I am. Course I feel different."

"Do you know who your real parents are?" she asked.

"No, and I don't care, either."

Ginny couldn't believe that. She said, "But don't you want to know where they came from and who they were? They might be nice. They might be really glad. You can do that now; I read about it. If you're adopted, you can find out who your parents are."

"Nice," he said bitterly. "Hundred to one, you know what she is, my mother? She's a prostitute. And my father, he'd be one of her customers. Then when I was born she ditched me somewhere and the council shoved me off on them down there." He nodded toward the south, meaning the town where his adoptive parents lived. "Nice, you reckon? Bloody rubbish. You think I want to look it all up and find that out? I couldn't care less about her. She just left me, didn't she? To hell with her. I don't want to know. I am what I am. I'm free, see. I got no ties."

She leaned against the doorframe, watching him. He was gazing down at the grass; she couldn't see the expression in his eyes, but she felt it to be distant and cold.

"Different . . ." he said after another pause. "I can't go anywhere without being different. I'm not even the same as other black kids. When I was in Bristol, right, doing my catering course, I felt a bloody idiot because these other guys, black guys, they came up to me first day and

40

started talking dialect, patois, you know? Rasta kind a ting, maan? Well, *Duw*, I never felt such a fool in all me life. I couldn't understand a word. . . . And what could I say? Sorry, fellers, I can't understand you, I'm Welsh? Ridiculous. Okay, I sound Welsh, but I'm not Welsh. . . . Not African, either. I'm just a white kid with a black face, that's what I am. Don't belong anywhere."

"Right!" Ginny said. "That's just what I feel, exactly what I feel!"

"You're all right anyway. When you draw pictures, it doesn't matter what color you are."

"Ah, no," Ginny said. "That's not true. I think it *does* matter. I think there might be a difference between the way white people paint and the way black people do. Just as there's a difference between French paintings and Chinese paintings . . . You can see it."

"What is it, then? What's the difference between black art and white art?"

"That's what I don't know, you see! That's the point! That's why I said I feel like you, I don't know where I belong. . . ."

"Right. So you're free, then, ain't you?"

"Free?"

"Free to do anything. Like me. I don't know where I belong, so I'm free. No one's got a hold on me."

Except Joe Chicago, thought Ginny. But he wouldn't tell her anything about that. And it was more difficult than she'd said, more difficult than she could explain. After a while they went and bought some ice cream from the two old ladies and looked on the beach for crabs, but the crabs must have been hiding, because they didn't find a single one.

GINNY *was good at drawing; everybody said so. The teachers would soon find out how good her pictures were and put them on the display board. At one school she tried drawing badly on purpose, but they still praised her and still pinned up her pictures. Then she saw how stupid they were at that school, and hated them for it, and grew so unhappy she could hardly breathe.*

That was the place where they lived in a basement. Dad slept in the sitting room and she had the only bedroom. The stove and the fridge and the kitchen sink were all in the sitting room too. There was a little boy who lived upstairs. They used to play in the yard together, but he was always crying. He got scratched by a cat once and had to be taken upstairs to lie down. When they'd taken him up, Ginny stayed in the yard alone, making a town for her plastic rabbit to live in among the flowerpots behind the big coal bin, wondering if the little boy would die from the cat scratch.

In another school she had to wear a dark-green uniform with a straw hat held on by a tight elastic band under her chin. The playground was two streets away, and they walked there in pairs, each girl holding her neighbor's hand. Ginny had to walk with a girl called Jackie. Jackie kept letting go of her hand, until the teacher saw and told her off.

Ginny had a photograph of her mother in a leather frame, which always stood beside her bed. Everyone said how alike they looked. Her mother was called Maman, which was French. Ginny spoke to Maman every night, asking her to ask the Virgin Mary to send some angels to guard her against bad dreams. Once some girls wanted to tell her a secret, and so that she wouldn't give it away, they made her swear on her mother's deathbed. She was very frightened. She thought about it that night and couldn't get it out of her mind. She imagined a deathbed as a special sort of bed which was delivered to the house when it was time for you to die, and you'd know, everybody would know, and slowly it would get closer to bedtime and you wouldn't want to go to bed, but you must, you had to, it was time. What happened on the deathbed was too horrible to think of. She lay rigid that night, and when Dad came in to kiss her, as he always did before he went to bed, he found her pillow drenched with tears. She couldn't explain it at all.

4

A Phone Call

JUST AS Ginny was leaving next morning to go to the Dragon, the phone rang. She recognized the caller's voice at once and found her heart thumping, because it was Wendy Stevens.

"Hello, Ginny! Is your dad in?"

"No, he's at work. D'you want his number? He's probably in the office—"

"I've got his work number, thanks, love. I thought he'd be at home, for some reason."

"Oh. Well . . ."

"Don't go. Are you busy?"

"Well, I've got a job to go to, I've got to be there in half an hour, but . . ."

"A job? What're you doing, then?"

"In a café. Nothing special."

"Nice. Listen . . . Did your dad say anything the other day after I left?"

"What, about you?"

"Yes. About why I came."

44

Now her knees were trembling. Ginny sat down on the floor and steadied her elbow against the wall.

"No," she said.

"He didn't tell you about what's happening in Liverpool?"

"Liverpool . . . I don't know what you mean. What *is* happening?"

"Well . . . Oh, look, let me ring him now. He'll tell you himself; it's better."

"No! Wait! What is it? *Please* tell me! I asked him about you the other day, but he wouldn't say anything. I *knew* there was something wrong. But if you're thinking what I think you are, it's not true, it's a lie, I swear it."

There was a silence then for a second or two.

"What d'you mean, love?" said Wendy Stevens, in a different voice. "What do you think I'm thinking?"

"About . . . You're investigating him, aren't you? Isn't that it?"

"Investigating him? Whatever for?"

Now it was Ginny's turn to pause.

"I thought someone might've—you know—might have told you something that wasn't true. About him and me. You know, like you read in the papers, when they take kids into care. That's why I thought you'd come, you see. I was afraid . . ."

"Let me get this straight. You thought I was checking up on whether your father was abusing you? Is that what you mean?"

"Yeah." Ginny felt breathless. "Yeah, that's it. And if it wasn't that . . . well, us being different races. I know they don't like white parents having black kids. So I thought maybe it might be that. . . . I don't know."

"That's only a guideline, and it only applies to adoption

or fostering, and you're not adopted or fostered, you're his child, so forget that. As for the other thing—*is* he abusing you?"

"No! God, no! Course not!"

"I never thought he was. It wasn't that at all. But you mean you've been thinking this all the time? Didn't you ask him about it? Actually, no, it wouldn't be easy, would it?"

She was sounding far more straightforward and sensible than she had the other day. Maybe it was because Ginny couldn't see her smiling all the time; or maybe she wasn't smiling now.

"Well, what is it about, then?" Ginny said, worried differently but no less worried.

"That's why I need to talk to him. I don't think I ought to tell you like this, over the phone."

"But you can't leave it like this! I won't see him till nine o'clock, probably; he's working late. . . . You're not going to split us up? You're not going to take me away?"

She knew she sounded distressed, but she couldn't help it; she genuinely didn't know what powers they had.

"No," said Wendy Stevens. "No one could do that. No one wants to do that, even if they could."

"Then what's it about? Is it about my mother? Is she alive or something?"

That was a shot in the dark: about the wildest thing Ginny could think of. Wendy Stevens hesitated again.

"What do you know about your mother?" she said.

"Only what he's told me. She died soon after I was born."

"Ah," she said. "Right. Well, listen, Ginny. What's going on concerns your dad, but not in a bad way, not in any way that'll split your family up or anything of that sort. But *he's* going to have to tell you what it is; I can't. It wouldn't be right. What I'll do is I'll ring him now at work

46

and tell him what's going on, so he'll know, and I'll tell him what we've said this morning—"

"Don't tell him what I was worried about!"

"The abuse business?"

"Yeah. Don't tell him that, *please*. I don't want him thinking . . . Just tell him I was worried, okay?"

"I understand. And listen, Ginny . . . I'll be coming down again in a couple of days. We'll have a talk then, if you like."

"Oh . . . right. Why are you coming down?"

"That's what he'll have to tell you. You better get off to your job now; you'll be late."

"Yeah . . . Thanks."

"Ta-ra, Ginny."

The phone receiver buzzed in Ginny's hand. She stood up slowly and replaced it.

SHE HAD a lot to tell Rhiannon and no time to tell her in; the Dragon was busier than at any time she'd known it, and what with serving coffee, clearing dirty cups away, selling doughnuts and scones and pieces of Mrs. Calvert's homemade cake, and trying to get the tables clear and set up for lunch with their salt and pepper shakers and sugar packets and plastic ketchup bottles, she hadn't managed to exchange two words with her friend all morning.

And since Rhiannon was going shopping with her mother that afternoon, there wouldn't be time then, either. So Ginny came away frustrated and spent the afternoon drawing the neighbor's cat, which liked to sleep on their garden wall; and then she went to the Yacht Club and did her job and got more and more tense, waiting to hear what Dad would tell her.

He was in the garden when she came home, lying in the hammock with a can of lager, playing an old Paul Simon tape on his Walkman. Ginny could hear it: he had it far too loud.

He saw her coming and took it off. She sat down in the deck chair, facing him.

"Dad? Did Wendy Stevens phone you?"

"Yup. She told me you'd spoken."

He must have had a few lagers already, because he was speaking very carefully and more slowly than usual.

"She said you'd tell me what it was about," she said.

"Yes. She's right. I didn't like her at first, but I think she's okay, probably. It's very difficult."

She didn't know what he meant by that, because he said it in the same tone as the rest; he might have meant that it was difficult for her or difficult for him. She waited.

"Ginny, love, she said you were worried they were going to take you away or something. Is that right?"

"Yeah. 'Cause no one said what it was about. I thought they could do that if they wanted to. . . . 'Cause they do that, don't they? They take black kids away from white families?"

"Well, they can't. No way. There's no question of that. This is something else entirely. Ginny . . . you've got a brother."

A *brother?*

Silence. She had no idea, absolutely not the slightest notion, of what to say next. He was watching her with careful eyes.

"He's not a child of Maman," he said after a few moments. "He's your half-brother. I met . . . his mother before I met Maman, you see. Now what's happened, what this is all about, is that his mother has been ill, very ill. She's been looking after him on her own. Like me and you. But she's got cancer, and she's going to die any day. I didn't expect . . . I didn't . . . Anyway. She's in hos-

48

pital. She might die tonight, next week, next month, who knows. Robert—that's the boy—he's in care for the moment, but he's going to need a home. So the only place for him is here, you see. That's why Wendy Stevens came the other . . . whenever it was . . . last week. I didn't tell you then because his mother was going to have an operation. It might have been all right, and then everything would've gone back to normal, and nothing . . . no one would've . . . I don't know. But unfortunately it wasn't good news. She's very ill. And . . . obviously the poor kid, the boy, Robert, he's got to come here."

He tilted the can of lager back. It was nearly empty. Ginny looked down at her hands, her dark-brown hands, twisted in her lap.

"Is he black?" she asked. "Was she black?"

"No."

Perhaps it wasn't a good question. Too bad: too late.

"When's he coming?"

"In a week or so. There'll be a funeral. Well, good God . . . I mean, there could be a miracle; that's what God's supposed to do; she could get better. But I don't suppose she will. So after . . . Whenever she dies. Sometime . . . soon."

A brother, she thought. A white brother. This was the strangest news she'd ever had. Not even Rhiannon's sister was such strange news as this. Rhiannon would understand part of it but not the rest; only Andy would understand the rest. Because she'd be more isolated now. White brother, white father, black sister. Talk about a sore thumb!

"How old is he?" she said.

"He's a bit older than you."

"A bit? How much?"

"I can't remember. A few months."

"Is he the little boy that got scratched by the cat?"

"Scratched by the cat . . . I don't know, love; you must be thinking of someone else. You've never seen him, I do know that."

"Did you . . . When did you . . . I mean, when you married Maman, did you . . ."

"As soon as I met Maman, I forgot everyone else. She was the only one. Ginny, I've been stupid not telling you before. I'm sorry to do this to you. I'm not very good at . . . I'll never love anyone more than you, chick. I . . . What I'm trying to say is . . . things are going to change. I can't let the boy grow up in some home somewhere. I'm responsible. You're not responsible, but you're going to have to . . . share the burden. It's not going to be easy. I'm just apologizing. Not your responsibility, but you're stuck with it. It's not fair to you."

He stopped. His eyes were shut. Ginny felt all kinds of emotions—bewilderment, anger, jealousy, incredulity, excitement, apprehension, even glee—turning over and over inside her like clothes in the tumble dryer. She watched them, but she wasn't connected to them. Perhaps they were feelings she thought she ought to be experiencing rather than those she was; it was too puzzling to tell.

"Robert," she said.

"That's right. His mother's choice of name."

"What was she called?"

"Janet."

"Have you . . . What does he . . . Have you ever seen him?"

"Never. He'll be as new to me as he is to you. But I'm going to go up to Liverpool first, see him, maybe see Janet. Sort things out."

"Where's he going to sleep?"

There were only two bedrooms. It was a small house, but it had never felt small till now.

He sighed. "There's a lot of adjustments to be made. I don't know. Probably the office. I'll move all that stuff into my room. We'll manage."

The office, Ginny realized for the first time, was actually another bedroom. So it was really a three-bedroom house after all.

"Will he go to the school?"

"Yup. I suppose so. Well, yes, he will. I'll have to see the head—what's his name—Bill Evans."

"He'll have to learn Welsh."

"You'll have to help him."

Ginny said nothing. There was a long silence. He reached down from the hammock and squeezed her hand, and she nodded.

"Yeah," she said finally. "Right. Wow."

THE best time ever in her life was a bright sunny morning with the wind chasing fat white clouds through the blue sky, and there was a lady pinning out sheets on the line, and they billowed like the clouds, big fresh-smelling moist clouds that swelled and flapped and swung up high. The lady was singing, and the song thrilled through the clouds and the sheets and filled the immense beaming sky, and Ginny felt that she was so light that she, too, could swing up and be blown along in the wild blue splendor; and then there was Dad, and it came true, she was flying, up she went onto his shoulders, over the sheets, up with the wind in the song and the clouds and the endless dazzling sky, and she beat on his head for joy in a world of snowy-white sheets and billowing clouds and the immortal wide intensity of blue.

5

Gwynant

THE FIRST THING Ginny wanted to do was tell Rhiannon. They spent the morning talking closely together by the coffee machine; behind its steamy fragrant shelter they felt that secrets were safe. More than one customer had to cough loudly and tap on the counter to be noticed that morning.

In the afternoon they took their bikes and rode up the Gwynant valley. The river that entered the sea so widely and placidly in the Yacht Club estuary had a quite different character in the hills: it was narrow, sparkling bright, and icy cold, splashing and tumbling over ancient gray granite and falling in cascades through mossy oakwoods. Ginny and Rhiannon toiled up the twisting road with the sun beating off the rocks beside them until they reached a narrow bridge over the river, where there was a slow-swirling pool to swim in.

Cold as the water was, they plunged in at once. It didn't take long, in that icy brightness, to cool down; after five minutes they climbed out and lay dripping on the hot lichen-patterned rock. A great sloping shelf of it had split hundreds of years before into clumsy rectangular blocks as big as cars, and smaller blocks lay tumbled and confused in the river itself. The water rushed smoothly between them and splashed into whiteness below. You could get to the other side of the river in three jumps, or steps, if your legs were long enough.

They lay there saying nothing, feeling the cold on their skins gradually melt into heat and listening to the endless splash of the water and the scraping of the insects in the grass.

"So," Rhiannon said eventually. "Robert, eh?"

"Yeah. What'm I going to *do?*"

"I'm giving it the best of my attention," said Rhiannon lazily. "I shall come to a conclusion shortly. Be patient."

"You discover a sister, and I discover a brother. Isn't it crazy? At least your sister's all right."

"I can't say much for her husband, though."

"What? You've met him?"

"Aha. I went there last night. Didn't I tell you?"

Ginny propped herself up on her elbows. Rhiannon was smirking, but Ginny didn't mind; it relieved her of the guilt of having stolen the first visit.

"What happened?" she said.

"Oh, I told Mam I was going out with Peter, and she thought great, 'cause she likes Peter. But I just went on the train and rang the doorbell, and that was it. Her husband was there. He's a *creep.* My brother-in-law. *Ach y fi.* He was wearing a business suit and business shoes, and he had a neat little black business mustache. *Duw,* you'd think he was a young executive, and all he does is sell thermal windows. Wow, what a prune. I don't know why she married him, I really don't."

Ginny tried to imagine the warm, vivid person she'd

met the other day in love with a neat little man with a black mustache.

"So what did you talk about?" she said.

"Well, it was so strange, you can imagine: this grown-up woman looking like me and—d'you think she looks like me? Do I look like her?"

"Yeah . . . She's not as droopy as you."

"What d'you mean? I'm not droopy."

"Bendy, then."

"*Bendy*," repeated Rhiannon with utter contempt. "Graceful, that's what you're trying to say. So she's not as graceful as me. Well, fair enough."

"But what did you *say?*"

"I was coming to that. It was, oh, how's Mam and Dad, do they ever talk about me? She said that a couple of times. I couldn't say no, could I? So I said yeah, they did some-times. I told her about the Dragon. They didn't have that when she left; see, Dad was an engineer on the airfield."

"I didn't know that."

"Well, he was. She said she couldn't imagine him run-ning a café, and I said he doesn't, Mam and I do. And she wanted to know about me, you know, all school and dull stuff like that. And bloody Benny sitting there listening, suspicious, checking me out. I mentioned you, right, I said you'd told me you'd seen her, and her face went red all at once. She shook her head, just a tiny bit, so he couldn't see, and she went—"

Rhiannon mouthed *No* and looked frightened. She was a good actress; Ginny could see it exactly.

"Because of him?" she said.

"Yeah. She didn't want him to know. She *does* fancy your dad; I could tell. And later on, when I had to go, she came down into town with me, and then she could talk more easily. Benny's so jealous, he's jealous of everything. He knows that Helen knows your dad, but he thinks it's only because your dad was setting up some computer thing in the office she works in, this architect's place. That's all. If he thought there was anything else, I don't know what he'd do. I *think* she's seen your dad since, maybe they had lunch together, something like that, went for a drink or something. But I tell you—you know the thing about your dad being in prison? You know where that came from?"

"What? Where?"

"Benny told her, 'cause obviously he was jealous, he wanted to put her off. But *he* heard it from that Joe Chicago you told me about!"

Ginny blinked. "Get off," she said. "How would Benny know Joe Chicago? He comes from Aberystwyth. That's miles away."

"Ah, that's it; he doesn't. He lives in Porthafon, Helen said. And he knows Benny because . . . I can't remember. He just does. But he was the one it came from."

"Stupid!" said Ginny, rolling over on her back. "That's impossible. Joe Chicago has nothing to do with my dad."

"Well, Helen said Joe had been in jail, see, and he knew your dad because that was where they met."

Ginny scoffed. She'd never heard anything so hopeless in her life. High up in the profound blue above her, an aircraft like a little silver speck was leaving a condensation trail of pure white. The aircraft was too far away to hear, but up there somewhere was a lark, trilling and caroling like an angel. She could see the airplane but not hear it, hear the lark but not see it, and the two things came together in her mind, a plane that sang like a bird. Sleepy, warm, and moved to an incomprehensible happiness by the blue and the white and the singing, she dismissed the fantastic nonsense about jail and gangsters and window salesmen and gave herself up to the sun.

Rhiannon was saying something. Ginny murmured, "What?"

"I said it looked as if it was stuck on. His mustache. Part of a kit, probably. The young executive kit. He probably washes it overnight and leaves it on the edge of the bath. I bet he's got a pretend car phone too; they always have. He probably pretends to be speaking into it while he's waiting at traffic lights. What d'you reckon it's like, kissing a mustache?"

Ginny came a little more awake now. In all her life, she was certain, the only male kiss she'd ever received had been from her father. Here was that question again, awake in the darkness: Who would kiss her if she was a different color? But she had to answer.

She said, "Like nuzzling a carpet."

"You know what the Victorians said? I read it in the *Daily Mail*. They said kissing a man without a mustache is like eating an egg without salt!"

That seemed so funny that Ginny burst out laughing. "Eating an egg without . . . Oh, *Duw*, that's amazing! Eating a man without salt is like kissing an egg without a mustache!"

Rhiannon was giggling too. "Kissing a mustache without salt is like eating a man without an egg. . . ."

Now they were helpless, rolling about on the bumpy rock aching with laughter. On and on it went, getting crazier and crazier, and the dark question turned around and retreated back into the dimness it lived in. Still awake, though; not asleep.

Later on they jumped across the river and into the little grove of trees below the bridge. They were oak trees, gnarled and bent and hardly any higher than the stone wall that ran along the road above. Ginny felt that they were very ancient, these trees. Under their shade it was quiet and still, and the moss-covered rocks, flecked and dappled with sunlight, seemed like hassocks in a ruined church. She supposed that the Druids would have come to places like this to worship their gods.

Ginny said, "Did she know who you were when she came to the door?"

"Who, Helen? Not for a few seconds. After all, I was six or something when she left. I'm bound to look different. I've got bosoms, for a start. I keep trying to bring them to Peter's attention."

"Doesn't he notice?" said Ginny.

"He's too nice. He's kind. The trouble with kind people is they're not sexy. Maybe I'll ask Helen about it. She's bound to know the answer to life. Worldly wise, that's what she is. Bound to be."

"Maybe it's worth having a kind person, even if they're not sexy," Ginny said, plucking shreds of moss from the rock she was sitting on.

"No," said Rhiannon, sighing. "It's funny, isn't it. Sexy people couldn't care less if they're kind or not, but all the kind people'd love to be sexy. The trouble is, you're either one or the other."

"I bet some people are both."

"Impossible. It's tragic. Life's a tragedy, see."

"Oh, right," said Ginny.

She threw some moss at Rhiannon and hit her on the nose.

"Get off," said Rhiannon wearily.

"Why's this bridge newer than the rest of the road?" said Ginny.

"It's the broken bridge. Pont Doredig."

"Pont Doredig . . . *Le Pont Cassé*. Why's it broken?"

"Well, it's mended now, stupid. There was some accident here, some story about a car. I don't know . . . a long time back."

Ginny looked up at the bridge. It was narrow, with room for only one car to cross at a time, and the stonework was newer than the old dry-stone wall that bordered the road. She tried to imagine a car crashing through and into the river, but perhaps that wasn't what had happened. . . .

"What did your dad say about Robert?" said Rhiannon.

"I told you."

"Tell me again. I want to work it out exactly. *How* old did he say he was?"

So they went through it again, and crossed back to the rock where their towels were, and drank some of the cold pure water from the river by lying down like lions and dipping their faces into the flow; and then they gathered their things and freewheeled back down the valley, hardly having to pedal at all. They went over and over what Dad had said, but there was no more in it than there had been before, and Robert was still a mystery. Ginny knew what she felt now; she felt apprehensive. A sister living twenty miles away, a grown-up sister with a house and a job and worldly wisdom, was a piece of good fortune; but an unseen brother your own age who was going to invade your own home was a threat.

ONCE she visited her Grandma and Granddad. The house was very quiet, and Ginny had to tiptoe across the shiny wooden floor in her slippers. If she stood on the rug and slid one foot toward the other, the rug came up in a straight ridge between them, but she mustn't do that; the rug wasn't made for that.

She heard Granddad and Grandma whispering together once in the kitchen while she stood outside, and through the frosty glass door she saw Grandma hit Granddad and heard him say, "Hush, quiet, for God's sake," in a loud, shaky whisper, and then he turned away, holding his arm.

There were old books in the living room. She was allowed to read books if she sat on the sofa with them. Sitting on the floor wasn't allowed: we don't sit on floors in this house, we don't have dirty little girls who sit on floors in this house, we don't read books on the floor. Ginny sat with her book on the sofa in the endless cold silence that smelled of furniture polish, the silence that was sliced into regular little pieces by the tick of the tall clock behind the door.

Granddad kept licking his lips. His eyes were the same color as the blue in the curtains, and they didn't look at you, they looked sideways past you. When he turned the page of a magazine he licked his forefinger and pressed it on the page, squeezing up the corner between his thumb and his wet finger just the way Ginny had done with the rug in the hall.

6

The Ghost Train

AT BREAKFAST TIME on Saturday, Wendy Stevens phoned again, and Dad came back into the kitchen after taking the call and said, "Well, that's it, love. I've got to go to Liverpool, sort things out."

"Has she died?"

"Yes. Last night. Damn it, I should have gone yesterday, I knew I should. But she wouldn't have known. . . ."

He sat down and pushed his cereal away. Ginny watched him carefully. His mouth was tight, and his eyes weren't looking; they were focused on something a long way away.

"Did you love her?" Ginny said.

"Well, it's complicated; you can't tidy things up in a sentence or two. . . . Sorry, love, I'm just thinking about it—it's all rather mixed up. D'you want to come to Liverpool? I'll only be going to see the hospital and the undertaker, I suppose, that kind of thing. Wendy Stevens. See the boy too. Poor kid. It won't be very interesting, but come if you like."

"No! I can't! I'm working . . . I mean, they're expecting me, I can't let them down. . . . Anyway, I'd be in the way."

"Well, you wouldn't, but okay. I don't know when I'll be back. You'll be all right?"

"Will you be bringing him back?"

"No, no, not today. No, he'll stay there till the funeral . . . next week sometime."

"What about Granddad and Grandma? Couldn't they have him?"

She heard the urgency in her voice. She hadn't meant to sound like that, but everything was more urgent now that it was settled and there was no last-minute hope that she'd get better.

"No. Impossible."

"Why do we never see them, Dad? It's as if they're dead or something. They looked after me once, didn't they?"

"I can't stop and talk about it now, love. Sorry. But they're out of the question. I'll tell you more later—I've got to move."

He bent and gave her a scratchy kiss, and then he was gone. A couple of minutes later, she heard the throaty rasp of the car starting and driving away up the lane toward the main road.

RHIANNON was full of sympathy, but it wasn't for her; it was for the mysterious Robert.

"Imagine it," she said, her beautiful eyes practically melting with tears. "He's lived all his life with his mam and he doesn't know anyone else, and she gets cancer and dies. Then he has to leave his home and go and live with strangers. It must be terrible for him."

Ginny was silent and a little ashamed. In fact, she

thought, she was a lot ashamed, because she simply hadn't considered that aspect of it at all.

"Yeah," she said. "I wish I knew what he was like. I wish I knew more about this woman—I mean, his mother. And my grandparents too. It's weird, you know. I remember staying with them once when I was a kid, but I never saw them again. They never write or anything. And he never talks about them."

"Probably like Helen and my parents: they probably had a steaming row, and they're both too proud to make up," said Rhiannon. "I bet you."

"But how could he *do* that? I mean, how could he have a child with one woman and then go off and marry another one and never mention the first one? All this time I thought I was the only child, and then suddenly, bang, there's another one. . . . How could he *do* it?"

"Ah, well, your dad's just sexy."

"You reckon?"

"Take my word for it."

"I'll tell him—"

"I'll kill you. Don't you dare."

Ginny wondered if that meant, according to Rhiannon's theory, that Dad couldn't be kind as well. But she knew it was too simple; things were more complicated than that.

THAT AFTERNOON, she went to see Andy. When she arrived at the trailer, she found him spraying himself with aftershave lotion so pungent that it defeated even the reek of baked beans and smoked salmon.

"What're you putting that on for?" she said.

"You like it?"

"It's *horrible!* I'd rather smell sweat; I'd rather smell dirty socks, even!"

"Ah, well, they'll know I'm there anyway. You coming to the fair?"

"Is it on? Today? Brilliant!"

"Dafydd's got the car working. You're just in time—how about that. Who's a lucky little Ginny, then?"

He patted her cheeks with his aftershave-laden hands.

"*Ach,*" she said, slapping at him but secretly delighted.

Dafydd was a big, slow, sweet-natured boy of twenty or so. He had long black hair, like a heavy-metal freak, and strong, oil-stained hands that could do anything with machinery. When Ginny was much younger she'd fallen off her bike and twisted the handlebars. She'd hauled it tearfully to the garage on the main road, hoping they could mend it before Dad came home, and it was Dafydd who'd gently listened to her and taken the battered little bike and set the front wheel between his knees and twisted the handlebars till they were straight again. Better still, he'd shown her how to do it too. She'd fallen in love with him on the spot, but he was thirteen and she was nine, and so he was all but grown up and out of reach.

Later he'd passed on to her the comics he loved to read, and they'd shared such delights as *Tank Girl* and *Halo Jones* and *Watchmen* and *Raw* and, best of all, *Love and Rockets*. When she looked at comics she felt a strange knowledge growing inside her, a mixture of excitement and certainty, and she copied the artwork until she could draw Batman and Superman and El Borbah and Maggie and Hopey and Tonantzín, all the classics, almost as well as the originals. Dafydd admired that as much as she admired his skill with engines, but he was still four years older; sixteen and twenty were almost as far apart as nine and thirteen. Besides, she thought now, with Rhiannon's worldly wisdom, he was a kind person; Andy was the sexy one.

"You coming to the fair, then?" Dafydd said, emerging from the hood of his ancient MG, parked out of sight behind the trailer.

"Yeah! Great! I didn't know it was on," she said. "Is there room for me?"

"You're skinny," said Andy, patting her bottom. "Fold your little drumsticks up and get in the back. Go on."

She did, and with Andy sitting like a lord in front of her, Dafydd got the engine going at the third attempt and they bumped off over the grass and through the gate.

The road along the coast was busy. There wasn't much of a bus service, which was why people used the train, but there was talk of the train service being cut; in which case everyone would have to have a car, Ginny thought, and pump more carbon dioxide into the ozone layer, or whatever it was.

In the meantime, she loved sitting in the back of Dafydd's fume-belching MG and listening to the boys talk. The wind rushed past her face, and the engine roared, and everything was fun.

As they went below the Castle Hotel, Andy said, "Duck, lads, this is Carlos's day for practicing his golf."

"Does he still have putting competitions on the roof?" said Dafydd.

"No, he's taken up driving now. He uses hard-boiled eggs," Andy said quite seriously.

"I don't believe in Carlos! I think you're making him up," said Ginny.

"No, it's true!" said Andy. "There's this little lad from Wrexham, on some training scheme—Carlos calls him Polka Dot cause of all his spots, right. Anyway, he says to him one day, Boil me up fifty eggs, Polka Dot, give 'em ten minutes, not a second less. So Polka Dot thinks he's going to be let into some Cordon Bleu secret, and he counts out the eggs, one two three four fifty, boils 'em all for ten minutes. Now go up on the roof, says Carlos, taking a practice swing with a ladle, set 'em all up on the edge a foot apart, facing out to sea. Well, Polka Dot's mystified, but Carlos is The Man, you don't argue with The Man, and up goes little Polka Dot with this plastic bowl full of eggs, and taps 'em all on the end and sets 'em all up along the edge. Carlos goes up with his clubs and flies into a passion. You fool! he says. Whoever heard of pointed golf balls, you've got 'em on the wrong end, turn 'em over, turn 'em over! So Polka Dot has to crawl along, turning 'em all the other way up, only he's so nervous he drops half of 'em into the flowerbed below, and Carlos makes him go and pick 'em up and make a salad out of 'em. Mustn't waste food, he says, first duty of a good chef."

"Oh, go on, it's not true," said Ginny, but she felt as happy as if it had been.

Dafydd parked the car in a side street, and they swaggered into the harbor parking lot, where the fair had set up. The smell of hot dogs, the crash of amplified rock and roll, the hum of electricity filled the air. The best time to come was after dark, but any time was good. They went on the Flying Jets and the Dodgem Cars, and Andy put his arm around her shoulders while she drove and crashed and spun; they climbed the rickety old Helter-Skelter and stood at the top, making it sway from side to side, till the owner yelled up to quit it and get on down; they shied at coconuts and got none, they shot at Ping-Pong balls on jets of water and Dafydd won a teddy bear, they played the arcade games in the tent; and there they came face-to-face with Joe Chicago.

Ginny was playing a pinball game, with Andy banging

the table for her, when suddenly he fell silent. Ginny felt a rush of fear and looked up, and there was Joe Chicago not two feet away, staring at Andy with bleak hot eyes.

He was big, but his bulk looked like muscle, not fat. Lank strands of sandy hair seemed pasted to his greasy head. The famous leather jacket was open, and she saw a thick fur lining and thought how hot he must be, but he seemed as cold as ice.

She felt a hand on her arm: Dafydd, tugging her gently away. She went with him and left Andy there, seemingly at his ease, talking expansively to Joe Chicago as if they were the best of friends.

"What's he want?" said Ginny. "Why's he after Andy?"

" 'Cause Andy's a bloody fool," said Dafydd. "He gets mixed up in things and he doesn't know how to get out of it. You keep away from that guy; let Andy sort it out."

She stood by Dafydd while he played a machine that picked up candies with a crane and dropped them into a tray. He managed to get two, his deft oil-stained hands working their usual charm over machinery, but Ginny kept her eyes on Andy, and she saw Joe Chicago suddenly, without warning, punch Andy hard on the upper arm, a vicious blow that knocked him sideways a couple of feet. She gasped, but Andy didn't seem at all worried, and no one else appeared to have noticed. Ginny was breathless. Without showing the least sign of surprise or alarm, Andy took a couple of ten-pound notes from his pocket and handed them to Joe Chicago, who nodded and strolled away without looking back.

The whole scene lasted hardly more than a few seconds, but the strange atmosphere between Joe and Andy left Ginny weak. She suddenly seemed to have looked into a pit of dark and strange behavior of which that punch was only a symbol, a pit that had opened for a moment and then closed again, leaving the sunny surface of the world shadowy and insubstantial.

"Here, have it," said Dafydd, pushing a toffee into her hand.

"But did you see—"

"Let Andy sort it out," he said again. "Don't worry about him. He's got more lives than a cat. Talking of cats, let's have a hot dog. . . ."

Two minutes later they were all eating soggy hot dogs dripping with grease and ketchup.

"Boiled onions," said Andy in disgust. "I ask you. I should've brought Gertie along—we could have had a slice off her."

"Who's Gertie?"

"That bloody smoked salmon," said Dafydd. "Honest, I'm going to sling it out. I'm fed up with it."

"She's just getting ripe," said Andy.

"It lies there singing in the dark," said Dafydd. "It's going to climb out the cupboard and kiss me one of these nights. Aye, aye, look, here's a Ghost Train. . . ."

They'd missed it the first time round. Of all the fairground rides, Ginny loved the Ghost Train best of all, and this looked like a good one, the ghosts howling and clanking away inside and Freddy Krueger brandishing his iron fingernails on the front.

Andy wouldn't go on it; he said he was too highly strung. Ginny scoffed and got into the nearest carriage with Dafydd, who paid, and then the siren howled and off they went, bashing through the double doors into the raucous darkness.

Skeletons leapt out, phantoms gibbered, ghouls gnawed corpses, and evil banshees wailed; it was the best Ghost Train Ginny had ever been on. But suddenly everything stopped. The carriage lurched to a halt, the light on the nearest coffin went out, and the distant thud of the generator faltered and died.

They sat in the darkness and silence.

"What's going on?" said Ginny.

"The generator's packed up," said Dafydd. "We'll be here forever. What it is, they need some more ghosts, probably. Just our luck."

Someone called from outside. "Don't move! We'll get the power back on in a minute!"

From somewhere ahead in the darkness, a muffled voice said, "Can't we walk out?"

"No! Stay there! Stay in the carriage!"

Then it was silent again. Outside there was all the noise of the rest of the fair, but it only made the silence in the Ghost Train deeper. Dafydd lit a cigarette, and the glow of light and the smoke around his face made him look like a god in a mysterious temple, surrounded by incense.

"Dafydd?" said Ginny after a while.

"Yeah?"

They were speaking quietly, almost whispering.

"Is Andy in trouble?"

"No more than usual. Just let him be, I would."

"Has Joe Chicago been in jail?"

"Well, that's what they say. I wouldn't know, myself."

They sat in silence for a few moments. Then she thought of something else.

"Dafydd, you know Pont Doredig?"

"Oh, the broken bridge, aye. Up Gwynant. I used to go swimming up there."

"What happened to the bridge? Why's it broken?"

"Oh, that was years ago. This bloke was driving up there one night with his kid in the car, only a baby, and it was a winter night with snow all over the place. I don't know exactly what happened, whether he skidded or went

70

through the wall or something, but anyway he had to leave the car there and go for help. He left the kid there, in the car, wrapped up in this fur-lined jacket, sheepskin, I suppose, to keep it warm. When he got back from the nearest farmhouse or the phone box or whatever, the jacket was gone, stolen, and the kid was dead. Frozen stiff. That's it, really. I don't know who the bloke was or if they ever found out who nicked the jacket or what."

Ginny sat there in the dark, her mind spinning. She could see it: the white desolation, the car abandoned on the bridge, a dark figure making off with the warm fur-lined jacket. . . .

"It is true?" she managed to say.

"True? Well, as far as I know. It happened a long time back, mind. Ten, fifteen years, maybe more. Why d'you want to know?"

"I don't know. I just went up there the other day, and I heard it was called the broken bridge. I just wondered. . . ."

They were trying to start the generator outside. Ginny was glad of the noise, because it helped to cover up the shaking of her voice, and glad of the dark, because there were tears in her eyes. Suddenly the generator caught, and the power came on again. A siren howled beside them, the carriage lurched forward, one final skeleton sat up in its coffin, and then they were outside, blinking and shielding their eyes from the bright day.

"Sorry about that," said the boy in charge, hauling the carriages forward.

Andy was trying to get him to refund the fares.

"They could be severely psychologically damaged," he said, rubbing his hands together. "Exposing them to spiritual dangers and phantom anxieties, it's a case for the law courts."

The boy looked down at him. "Piss off," he sneered.

"Ah, yes," said Andy. "I see your point. Very well argued case. Sounds watertight to me . . ."

They left the Ghost Train and wandered out of the fair. It was nearly time to go home. Ginny wondered what Dad was doing now, whether he'd seen Robert yet, when the funeral would be, a dozen other questions; but more than that, she found herself gripped by the story of the broken bridge. Deep inside her, something had been changed, and she knew that the story was part of her now, part of what made her what she was. But as for what it meant . . .

"It was nice in there," said Dafydd, getting into the car. "I liked it."

"What?" said Andy.

"The Ghost Train. You could have a nice nap in there if it wasn't haunted, like. Ah, well. Let's go home, see if Gertie's got into my sleeping bag."

SOMEONE had been murdered in the woods. Ginny knew what "murdered" meant, because Maeve had told her: it meant someone cutting you with a knife so that all your blood ran out, and in a few seconds you were dead. When Ginny looked out the trailer window she saw dark water dripping off the leaves, running down each surface, and pouring off the point like a little spout. And there was water inside the trailer too, because the window was misty with tiny little drops of it. When you drew on it with your finger, you squashed them together and made a little river, and it ran in a jerk to the bottom.

The gaslight made a hissing noise. Maeve told her that another little girl had touched it and her skin had stuck to the bright part and come right away, so she had one finger that was only bones, no skin, no fingernail, just like a skeleton.

One day it stopped raining, and Ginny and Dawn played outside with two sheets of hardboard. They stood on one and put the other one down on the wet grass ahead of them, and then stepped onto that and put the first one down in front, and so on. They mustn't touch the wet grass or they'd be poisoned and die, but there at the side of the field the grass was long and bent over the boards, so they were both poisoned and dead many times. Then they reached the tree at the edge of the woods where the person had been cut with the knife, and Ginny whispered all about it in Dawn's ear. Her hair smelled funny. Dawn began to cry. She told Maeve when they went in for their dinner, and Maeve hit Ginny, crack, on the leg. Ginny was so surprised she could hardly breathe.

Another time she climbed onto Maeve's bunk when Maeve wasn't there, and found a little door. Ginny thought it would open onto the roof, but when she unclicked it she found a little cupboard there, hanging above the bunk like a tiny room. There was a bottle and a glass, and some cigarettes, and Maeve's makeup, and two books. She and Dawn put on some lipstick and pretended to smoke. They didn't light the cigarettes, but Maeve found out anyway and smacked them both. Cigarettes had a nice smell, but they made Dawn cough, so she had to breathe very carefully. Ginny lay in her top bunk and held her breath for Dawn as long as she could, listening to the thin beat of Maeve's cassette recorder through the folding partition, and the hissing of the gaslight, and the steady drip of rain from the dark leaves bleeding onto the roof.

7

The White Cuckoo

DAD CAME HOME at half-past ten that night. Ginny was waiting for him, and as soon as she heard the car turn into the lane she went to the fridge, intending to get out a can of lager for him; but there were none left. When he came in, looking exhausted, he dropped the car keys on the table, kissed her, and kicked off his shoes. She felt tender and protective. What could she do to look after him?

"Make us both a cup of cocoa," he said. "I'm worn out."

She took it through to the living room, where he was sprawled in his armchair, eyes closed. There was a Mozart piano sonata playing on the stereo.

"Here you are, Dad," she said. "Don't go to sleep."

He sat up and took the mug from her. She sat on the sofa with hers. The windows were open because of the heat, and behind the music she could hear the wide silence of the night, different from the narrow silence of the house. The floor lamp lit the side of his head, throwing his eyes into shadow and emphasizing the line from his nose to the corner of his mouth, so that he looked older and almost haggard. He sipped his cocoa, a child's drink, an old person's drink, and she wondered what it would be like when he was an old man and whether he'd have someone to look after him if she wasn't there. She loved him a lot, she thought.

"How was it?" she said.

"Grim. Difficult. The hospital, the undertaker business, that was straightforward enough. Seeing the boy . . . I hadn't realized what a mess everything was in. . . ."

Not knowing what he meant, Ginny couldn't say very much. And just now, seeing him as tired as he was, needing her help, she couldn't ask all the questions she was aching to ask. The mess he'd referred to: who'd left things in a mess? The boy's mother? And surely she must have a family—someone to organize funerals and things without Dad having to do it? No; she couldn't ask. She sat there keeping him company, finishing her cocoa, looking after him, reinforcing him. He was all she had.

BUT she didn't sleep. Next morning being Sunday, she wasn't needed at the Dragon, so she lay in bed till late, half dozing, half thinking back to when she was very young, trying to remember, trying to catch the little scraps of life before they vanished back into the darkness.

There was a trailer; she was certain of that. They must have had a vacation in a trailer, she and Dad, but it can't have been much of a vacation, because all she remembered was rain, an incessant drumming on the roof, moisture everywhere, damp sheets . . . and some delicious shiver of fear, she had no idea why: secrets, and murder, and horror. But it wasn't real. It was safe, it was a story, she could enjoy it.

Her grandparents—Dad's mother and father—she couldn't enjoy them. No murder there, but the atmosphere of their house, that strange time she spent with them . . . How she'd watched through the glass panel of the kitchen door as Grandma hit Granddad, and seen him turn away in pain, begging her to be quiet, and how she, Ginny, had felt sick and faint with unhappiness.

How strange, though, that they'd never been in touch again. Perhaps Rhiannon was right and they'd quarreled with Dad; perhaps that was what families did. But they were the only relatives she had. No cousins, no aunts or uncles, and her mother's side of the family were as good as mythical: a wealthy family in Port-au-Prince. She and Dad hadn't needed anyone else, though. They were self-contained. They shared jokes and housework and vacations, and he told her about his work and she told him about her drawing, and even though he'd shared his bed with the breakfast ladies, she knew that they were temporary and she was permanent. . . . No, the two of them were self-contained, a perfect relationship, father and daughter: nothing could be better.

And now she had to share it with a brother.

And there were only a few days left before all that world of sharing, all that grownup friendliness and intimacy, vanished forever.

How could he? How could he not tell her all these years—let her think she was the only one? How could he do it?

Stupidly, she began to cry. Hating herself for the selfishness that paid no heed to this lost brother, Robert, this bereaved boy coming among strangers, she sobbed into her pillow like a child.

DAD was out when she got up. Avoiding me, she thought. She had some cornflakes, looked in the Arts section of the Sunday paper to see if there were any interesting exhibitions coming up (not that she could get to them, but reading about them was something), and then went down to the harbor.

It was another still, sunny day, the best summer for years, perhaps forever. It might have been a blessing, Ginny thought; on the other hand, it might have been the greenhouse effect. It might mean that everyone was going to die. In the short time they probably had left, however, it was good to wander along by the estuary looking at the old wreck whose ribs stuck out of the mud at low tide and at the trim little yachts at anchor, to wave at the old porter in the station feeding the cat, to hear Angie singing from the kitchen of the Yacht Club and wave at her through the open door; and to go on down to the edge of the water and, just out of curiosity, take the path that led to the house on stilts by the little railway bridge, where Stuart was staying.

He'd said to come and see him, so she felt no inhibitions about climbing the ladder onto the veranda that ran all the way round the house, and knocking at the door, despite the fact that the porthole windows were still curtained.

After a minute or so the door opened, and Stuart stood there, wearing black boxer shorts and nothing else, fit and lean and silky-skinned, dazzling, glamorous, and sleepy. She handed him the Sunday paper the delivery boy had left at the top of the ladder.

"Ginny!" he said. "What's the time?"

"It's coffee time," she said. "Sorry if I woke you."

"It's all right," he said. "Come in."

The door opened directly into the living room. The atmosphere was close and warm and smelled of something she could only think of as maleness. But there was nothing here to threaten her or make her shy; even nearly naked, Stuart didn't do that. He was beyond being sexy, in Rhiannon's terms, probably because he was so impossibly grown up and handsome, and yet at the same time he wasn't kind, either, if kind meant safe and dull. Ginny felt teased and challenged by something not quite human, something between a frank, innocent animal and a powerful, mocking god.

"Open the curtains," he said. "If it's coffee time, I'd better make some. It'll taste better than Andy's."

The room was shipshape, just like the cabin of a yacht. The portholes were edged with brass, and a ship's clock and a barometer hung side by side on the white-painted wooden wall, and altogether they might have been at sea.

"Can I go on the roof?" she said.

"Help yourself."

There was a wooden ladder up from the veranda, and the roof itself was decked with planking. Ginny stood at the railing and looked out across the estuary and the Yacht Club from this unfamiliar viewpoint. *I've always wanted to see this house,* she thought, *and now here I am. I must be lucky. I can make things happen by wanting them. . . .*

She smelled coffee and climbed down the ladder.

"I love this place," she said. "I'll buy it when I'm grown up. And live here."

"What'll you do for a living?"

They were sitting on the edge of the veranda, the planks already warm under their thighs, the oily water nosing about below them among the reeds, around the little red dinghy, between the wooden piles.

"I'm going to be a painter."

"Why?"

"Because I'm good at it. Because when I look at things, I think automatically about how I'd draw them, how I'd paint them. And . . . also my mother was a painter. Was going to be a painter. So I'm carrying on for her."

"The lady from Haiti? They have a lot of painters there."

"Yeah," Ginny said, "primitives. Peasants. I know about them. But she wasn't like that. I can't be, either. See, once you know about Picasso and stuff, Matisse, all the modern painters, well, you can't pretend to be a peasant who's never seen them. . . . You're stuck, really. You can't go back; you've got to go forward. My mother, she was studying art properly, like I'm going to do."

"European art," said Stuart.

Ginny was silent for a minute or so. There was a question in what he said, and he didn't need to make it any plainer than that; it was exactly what she'd been trying to describe to Andy, and it was his problem with the black kids in Bristol: looking black, sounding white.

"Stuart," she said, "d'you think there's a difference between European art and, like, African art?" But that wasn't what she wanted to ask. Before he could reply, she went on: "I mean, I know of course there is. The subject matter's so different. I mean, in European art all the faces are white ones, all the landscapes are places in England or France or Germany or somewhere, but it's not just what the painting's *about*. . . ."

"I remember seeing a painting once," said Stuart, "a picture by a Chinese artist who came to England. It's a landscape in the Lake District. And it doesn't look like England at all, it looks completely Chinese, with the mountains sticking up out of the mist, just like they do in classical Chinese paintings."

"Ah, right," she said. "But that's different again. He was seeing it in a Chinese way, that's all. He had a tradition that he belonged to."

"And you haven't."

"That's right! It's not as simple as making pictures of

80

black people in a sort of fine-art way. Anybody could do that. A white painter could. I need to find a way that's different. . . ."

"African?"

"I'm not African, either. I've seen African sculptures, you know, ritual masks, that kind of thing. They're really strong, really powerful, but I can't . . . relate to them. I don't know what they mean. All that ancestor stuff . . . I mean, I've got English ancestors too, haven't I? It's no good saying like my ancestors were African, so I've got to go back to my *roots*. . . . It was my English ancestors who sold my African ancestors into slavery. Where does that leave me? Am I innocent or guilty or what?"

"You can't go back," Stuart said. "You can only go forward. You can't forget, either. You have to use everything you know."

"That's right! That's just what I mean. I can't pretend to be a Haitian primitive."

"You've never been to Haiti?"

"No. What's it like?"

"It's in a bad way at the moment. It's been in a bad way for years. Poverty and corruption and violence . . . It's pitiful."

Ginny said nothing. Words like "poverty" and "corruption" sounded like white people condemning black people for being uncivilized and savage, and she was uncomfortable about that. On the other hand, he'd been there, he'd seen it.

"What's voodoo like?" she said.

"It's a real religion. It's not just drums and zombies. There's a whole family of gods, and they come to life. I've seen them."

"They come to life?"

"They take possession of the worshippers. They enter your head, and you behave like them, speak like them, walk like them. You can recognize them at once."

He told Ginny about the gods and goddesses, the *loa:* about Agwé, the lord of the sea, and Ogoun, the fiery war god and politician, and Damballah, the serpent god. He told her about Erzulie, the goddess of love, who loved luxury and music and perfume and who wore three wedding rings, one for Agwé, one for Damballah, one for Ogoun; Erzulie, who gave and received love, and whose visitations ended in tragic boundless weeping for the shortness of life, the faithlessness of men.

But the *loa* who caught Ginny's attention most was Ghede, the god of the underworld. He was a joker, a trickster, and as she listened, Ginny imagined him with the face of Andy. Stuart told her that once in the 1920s Ghede had taken possession of dozens and dozens of men at once, and they'd all marched to the National Palace dressed in top hats, tail coats, and dark glasses, demanding money. The president had had no choice but to give it to them: what was a president beside the god of the underworld, especially when he appeared in dozens of copies at once? That's a story for Andy, she thought delightedly. But there was another side to Ghede the joker. He was also known as Baron Samedi, the lord of death, of skulls and bones and tombs; he haunted cemeteries and cross-roads; it was through Baron Samedi that zombies were brought up from the grave. . . .

Ginny listened, transfixed. Africa was too far back, but Haiti came closer as he spoke; the gods began to stir into life. Seeing how interested she was, Stuart drew some elaborate curly designs, including a heart surrounded by lacy swirls and spiky ornamentation.

"These are *vevers,*" he said. "The priest draws them in

flour on the ground before the *loa* come. This is Erzulie's.
. . . Sometimes it has a sword through it, like this."

He drew another version. Ginny was enchanted by the
prettiness of them, their mysterious delicacy.

"Thanks a lot," she said. "I'm going to go there one day.
Find the rest of my family. I'm good at French already;
that's about my best subject apart from art. I don't know
about Creole, though."

"I should think you'll manage. I'd like to see your paintings sometime."

"Right! Okay . . ."

I'll have to bring my brother too, she thought. *Can't
leave him out. Nothing'll be the same from now on.*

"What was your mother's name?" Stuart asked.

"Anielle. Her family name was Baptiste. Why?"

"Just in case I see any of her paintings."

"Well, she was only a student, more or less. . . ."

"Have you got anything of hers? Any drawings or anything?"

"No . . . No. Nothing. There's nothing left. I don't know
why, actually. Dad might have kept something and not
told me about it. . . . I don't know."

"There must be something still about. Things don't just
vanish; they stand around for years, and then people find
them in the attic and sell them for a million pounds. There'll
be some of her work around somewhere, I guarantee."

Ginny looked up at him in surprise. He was right, and
she'd never thought about it.

"Yeah," she said rather breathlessly. "Right! There must
be. *She* wouldn't have thrown it away, and he
wouldn't. . . ."

"We'll keep our eyes open," he said.

She finished her coffee and left him to his Sunday paper.

GINNY and Dad agreed that since lamb was likely to make you radioactive, and beef to give you mad cow disease, pork was the only safe meat to have for Sunday lunch—until creeping pig fever was discovered anyway. So it was pork she found Dad taking out of the oven when she got home.

"Hungry?" he said.

"Yeah. Sort of."

"Who's the man in the boat house?" he said as they sat down.

"He's called Stuart. Did you see me there, then?" She was surprised, as if he'd been spying on her.

"I was looking at someone's boat."

"Stuart's a friend of Andy's," she explained.

"Oh, that's all right, then."

"Why were you looking at a boat?"

"I thought we might get one. Just a dinghy to start with. To learn to sail, so that we can all, I don't know, start something together. Instead of Robert having to fit into a lot of things that grew up without him."

She was silent, smothering a piece of meat with applesauce. It was probably a good idea.

"Dad," she said, "when Maman died, were there any paintings of hers left? Or drawings, or anything?"

"No," he said. "Very little, unfortunately. I suppose it went back to her family."

"What d'you mean, you suppose? Didn't you have all her things in the house with you? Didn't she leave them to you in her will or something? Or to me?"

He said nothing, finishing his mouthful, going to the fridge, opening a new six-pack of lager, fetching a glass, pouring it, sitting down again; and something in his manner made her put down her knife and fork and watch him, apprehensive.

"Ginny," he said, "I was going to put this off for a while, till you were older, but there's no point anymore. It's too late, what with Robert coming. . . . The thing is . . ."

He took a deep breath. Ginny could see a pulse beating in his temple. He went on:

"Part of the reason I didn't tell you about Janet and Robert was that I'd have to tell you something else as well, the thing I was going to keep. Something about Maman. I should have told you years ago, but I never thought this other business would come up. . . . The thing is that we were never married, me and Maman. I was married to Janet. That's why I couldn't . . . Anyway. I was married to Janet, and there was the child, Robert, and then I met Maman, Anielle. The one I should have married. Janet and I . . . well, it wasn't working, it never worked. I was stupid, I was young. And then you were born. And then there was no Maman. So obviously I was . . . I had to look after you. There was no one else. I didn't want anyone else to do it, I wanted you. And here we are, the two of us. If . . . Eventually . . . If she hadn't fallen ill, then one day I'd have told you. I'm so sorry it was forced on us. There's hardly time to take it in before he comes. Can you understand? So to answer your question about paintings and stuff . . . if there were any left, they were packed up and sent back to Haiti, back to her family. There was very little I had, except that photograph. Ginny, I'm sorry."

There was no end to these surprises, she thought numbly. First I have a long-lost brother, and then he turns out to be the legal son. No—what was the word? Legitimate. So that made her illegitimate. Born out of wedlock. A bastard. That's what they'd have said in the old days.

Not that anyone cared about that now, except that because of it she felt herself being pushed further and further to the edge of things. All the sympathy she'd been

85

carefully educating herself to feel for Robert was blown away in a moment, so it couldn't have been very real, she told herself. She was being shoved aside by this invisible cuckoo, this white son and heir of a proper marriage, while she was the result of something like an affair with a breakfast lady. . . .

The food was getting cold on her plate. He wasn't touching his, either.

"When's he coming, this Robert?" she said. Her voice sounded shaky.

"The funeral's on Wednesday. I'll go up for that and bring him back. Ginny, he's a nice boy. None of it's his fault—"

"Oh, sure," she said savagely. "It's probably nobody's *fault*. It's probably just something you get, like measles or something. Nobody could have guessed, could they? Absolutely unpredictable . . ."

She'd never felt so angry, never been so surprised at herself, at him, at everything. She shoved her plate away and stood up.

"You don't understand—"

"How can I understand when you don't bloody well tell me things?" she stormed at him, feeling lightning in her eyes.

"Ginny, wait—"

"What's the point? What else are you going to tell me? You found me in a ditch or something?"

"Listen . . . I know I should have told you before; I've already said I'm sorry about that. I realize now—"

"It's a bit late for that, isn't it? What else is there? What else is he going to do me out of?"

"He's not going to do you out of anything, Ginny, for God's sake—"

"He already has!"

"No, he hasn't. Come on, this doesn't change anything as far as we're concerned. We're the family, you and me; we'll always be okay. He's the one who's lost, he's the one who's hurt."

"Okay! Okay! D'you think I don't realize that? I just don't know what else you're keeping from me—I mean, what else *is* there? All that stuff about Haiti—is that not true, either? Did she come from Jamaica or something? Or was she real in the first place? Did you just get me from a children's home? Or maybe she wasn't an artist— is that it? Maybe she was just a shop assistant or something, maybe you just fancied her when you went in to buy a pair of socks, and then you were stuck with *me* as a result—"

"Ginny, this isn't getting us anywhere. If you knew how much I wish—"

"I don't care what you wish, Dad, I really don't."

"At least let me—"

"And you couldn't even keep her paintings! Couldn't even keep *one* of them!"

She flung her chair aside and rushed out, slamming the door, and ran down toward the beach, away from the house, away from home, away from him.

8

Robert

So GINNY still had no answer to the question at the front of her mind: what was he like, this brother? She'd wanted to ask when Dad came home the night before but, feeling sorry for him, hadn't brought it up; she'd been going to ask that morning, but he'd gone out; and now they wouldn't speak till one of them made the first move toward friendliness again. They so seldom had rows that this state was uncomfortable, unfamiliar, and Ginny found herself wondering what exactly she had said, and whether any of it was unforgivable.

But it was his fault, she told herself savagely, as she sat in the dunes and trickled hot sand over her bare feet. He had no right to keep that secret. I should have known . . .

Finding out something about yourself that other people have known and haven't told you makes you feel stupid, as if they were laughing at you for being so naive. Dad had known, this Janet had known, even Robert had known—they'd all known Dad wasn't married to Maman; it was only she who hadn't. She felt angry, and foolish, and sorry for herself.

She stayed out till five o'clock, dozing in the dunes, wandering among the rock pools, gazing for half an hour or more at one particular sea anemone; and she went home at half-past five only because it was nearly time for the Yacht Club.

The restaurant was never very busy on Sundays, so there might have been time to sit and chat with Andy, except that he was in a surly, scratchy mood for once; or it might have been that the whole world was irritated and ill at ease with itself. On the way home again, she found herself wandering, more and more slowly, wishing time itself would stop.

Dad was watching television with half his attention, the rest being paid to some papers spread out on a board across his lap.

"There's some salad in the kitchen," he said shortly.

"I had something to eat at the Yacht Club," she said, pausing inside the door.

The silence between them trembled for a moment. If he'd looked up at her it might have broken, but he didn't.

She pretended to look at the TV for a moment and then went out and shut the door.

Actually, she hadn't eaten at the Yacht Club, and as she had hardly started her lunch before the row began, she was hungry. Ignoring the salad, she cut some bread and spread it thickly with peanut butter and took it, with her sketch pad and charcoal, up to the main road.

There she sat on the wall in the golden light and tried to capture the precise way the road dipped and curved, flowing like a gray river between its grassy banks. Charcoal was better than pencil for that—you could rub it on thickly, push it around with your fingers, express the flow of it. This was still her kingdom, after all; she hadn't been disinherited of that. And she claimed it not through birth but through love and talent, and she thought sometimes, when she looked at her work as objectively as she could, that she *was* talented. This sketch was alive. It showed not only the road but her feelings about the road; it expressed movement and restlessness and energy.

Working, she decided, was the best thing in the world. Even better than knowing who you were was knowing what you had to do.

As she drifted down to the house again in the dusk, she wondered if her mother had felt like that. Those lost paintings . . . If only she could find them! They might show her the answer to that unspoken question of Stuart's, the problem of how to paint, the problem of finding a tradition for herself.

But she felt strong, as she let herself in, strong and in control. She pinned up the drawing beside her bedroom door and looked at it as she got undressed for bed. It was good. She was going to find a language, even if she had to invent one.

And as she went to sleep, she thought: Suppose the pictures *are* still around somewhere? They might not have wanted them, this Haitian family. They might just be in storage, or even in a gallery. Anything might have happened; Dad might not have told all the truth still.

WEDNESDAY, when it came, was an anticlimax. Dad phoned from Liverpool, after the funeral, to say that he'd be coming home alone after all: Wendy Stevens would be bringing Robert down the next day.

It felt like being reprieved, but it left her frustrated. What could she do with this freedom? She spent most of it, in fact, with Rhiannon, staying overnight at her house and leaving a message on the kitchen table for Dad to see when he got home Wednesday night.

They'd come to a sort of truce by that time. They'd had to; neither of them wanted anger in the air when Robert arrived. So they'd talked a little more, but Dad still hadn't told her much about Robert. Her brother was quiet, reserved, polite, with dark hair, and that was all she learned. So for Ginny, he was still little more than a blank, which she filled in alternatively with a cold, evil, triumphant usurper and with a bewildered, lost, unhappy semi-orphan. The latter idea was largely Rhiannon's, and Rhiannon had a different idea about Ginny's own background too. It was much better like this, she said; it was really romantic to have your parents unmarried; it showed she was a child of passion, Robert merely one of duty. Ginny wasn't convinced.

Thursday passed in a jumpy, nervous blur. Wendy Stevens and Robert were due at half-past five, and Dad said he'd be back from work in time to greet them. Ginny had got the evening off from the Yacht Club, and she spent the afternoon with Rhiannon, getting a lavish tea together: finding the one tablecloth they had, ironing it, setting the tea out on the lawn with currant bread and butter, scones, jam, ginger cake, and the bone-china tea set they'd bought for some reason years before and never used. The tea was her idea: her contribution. She hadn't told Dad.

"We're going to leave decorating his bedroom till he comes," she said. "Let him choose. I suppose that's best, really."

"Suppose you fall in love with him?" Rhiannon said. She was lying in the hammock watching Ginny fussing with cups and saucers. "Apparently it often happens."

"What d'you mean?"

"When long-lost brothers and sisters meet. They fall in love," Rhiannon said complacently. "With what they've got in common, it's just too much to control. There's an irresistible sexual current. . . ."

"Oh, don't be stupid. I never heard anything so bloody cracked, even from you."

"Well, don't say I didn't warn you. God, I better go. They'll be here soon."

She scrambled up, but Ginny shoved her back. "No! Listen! I just remembered something. You know the broken bridge? Pont Doredig?"

"Yeah? What of it?"

"Dafydd Lewis told me the story. Did you know what happened?"

Rhiannon shook her head. "Something about a car crash . . . I don't know. What was it, then?"

Ginny told her what Dafydd had said. As she recounted the story of the abandoned baby in its fur-lined coat, and the coat's disappearance and the baby's death, she found her eyes pricking embarrassingly with tears. Luckily, Rhiannon was just as affected. But Ginny had something else to add.

"Listen," she said. "I saw Joe Chicago at the fair. Close up. And I saw his jacket, and *that* had a fur lining. . . ."

"Oh, don't be stupid! It couldn't be him."

"It *could* be."

"Oh, go on. That's mad. . . ."

"But listen . . . He was in jail, wasn't he?"

"Yeah, but—"

"And it was about fifteen years ago, Dafydd reckons, and Joe Chicago must be thirty at least, so he could have been fifteen or more then. . . . He could easily have done it."

Rhiannon watched her, pretending a skeptical look.

"The thing is . . ."

"What? I bet I'm right. I bet that's what he went to jail for."

"The thing is I don't reckon that story's necessarily true. I mean . . . who'd go off and leave their child alone in a car like that?"

"Plenty of people," Ginny said firmly. "It happens all the time. Anyway, I *know* it's true. I bet if we looked through the paper we'd find it, eventually, in the files in the library. . . . Hey, could your sister ask her husband about it?"

Rhiannon's face was too mobile and expressive to hide her interest. She wasn't convinced, but Ginny, seeing she was intrigued, felt a shiver of pleasure: here was something other than Robert to occupy herself with. A private mystery.

"Well, she might," said Rhiannon.

"Let's go and ask her!"

"What, now?"

"No; course not. Later on sometime. I'd like to see her again anyway."

"Okay," said Rhiannon, nodding. Then she rolled over and got out of the hammock. "I'm going to go. I'm getting nervous—they'll be here in a minute."

"Don't tell her about it before we go," Ginny said. "I want to ask her myself."

"All right. But I bet you're wrong."

"I'm right," said Ginny. "No question."

AT HALF-PAST FIVE, Ginny heard Dad's car turn into the lane. She shut the comic she'd been reading and swung one leg over the side of the hammock. She'd been afraid Wendy Stevens would arrive first, leaving Ginny to meet Robert on her own.

She looked down at the tablecloth spread out, the milk jug, the sugar bowl, the teaspoons, and suddenly thought how pretentious, how fake, what a condescending gesture it was. Was it too late to put it all away? Hide it, pretend it had never crossed her mind?

She heard Dad opening the front door and then heard another car turning into the lane and stopping, and Dad calling to someone, "Hi! You made it, then," in a false, hearty voice; and she lay back, thinking: *Well, it's not such a big thing. He might be really nice, and I don't have to spend all the time with him anyway. Brothers and sisters don't necessarily, do they?*

"Where's Ginny? Ah! Lazing in the hammock!" Cringe-making jolliness, she thought. *Please* be natural, Dad. . . .

She sat up. Wendy Stevens was just coming out the kitchen door, dressed in a suit again, looking too hot, too strained.

"Hi," she said, and Ginny smiled and stood up.

Behind her was Dad, and behind him was Robert.

They looked at each other with instant, savage, and mutual hatred.

She saw a thin, stoop-shouldered boy with pale skin and lank brown hair. His face was narrow, foxy, and sullen. Everything about him, every line of his body—and she prided herself on reading appearances—spoke of suspicion, reserve, a sort of mistrustful contempt. He was taller than she was by a couple of inches, and she found herself standing up straight and holding her chin high to face him. There was a moment's silence while they measured each other like that, and then Wendy said, "Hey! What's all this? Been making tea for us, then?"

"Ginny, why don't you show Robert the bathroom?" said Dad.

He was nervous. He hadn't said a thing about all the

work she'd put into getting this bloody tea ready. She just nodded.

"It's this way," she said to Robert, coldly, and went past him into the kitchen.

She saw a shabby suitcase in the hall, standing next to a dusty cardboard box containing cassettes. Was that all he had to bring with him? Now she was confused again, as if she felt pity.

"I'm sorry about your mum," she said, not looking at him.

He said nothing. She thought he was just being rude, until she caught a glimpse of his expression: it was one of utter misery.

"Your bedroom's here," she said, opening the door on the landing, "and the bathroom's over there. There's a loo downstairs as well."

He nodded. He hadn't spoken yet.

On her way back, she glanced into the box of cassettes and saw names she'd never heard of. No clue there, then.

"Ginny, this is a smashing tea," said Wendy Stevens, buttering a scone.

"Yeah, well, I thought . . ."

"Great, love," said Dad.

Dad was sitting on the grass, Wendy in the deck chair. She exchanged a look with Ginny; Dad wasn't looking at either of them.

"Your dad tells me you've got an evening job," she said. "Are you working tonight?"

"No. I've got the time off. It's not much anyway. I'm just helping in the kitchen of this restaurant."

"Because I thought we might have a chat, maybe, before I go."

"Oh, right. Okay. Are you going back to Liverpool tonight?"

"I've got to. Busy morning tomorrow. Ah, Robert, love . . ."

He came and sat awkwardly on the grass, as far away from Ginny as he could get while still being approximately part of the group.

"Tuck in," said Dad. "Ginny's done a good job here."

Oh, these scalp-crawling pleasantries, how they made Ginny cringe, and how she wished she'd just spent the afternoon hanging about with Andy or Stuart and rolled in later, casual, indifferent. When you try to be friendly you expose yourself to so many embarrassments, she thought. It's probably better to be selfish and say to hell with it, let him sink, we never asked him to come here.

She wasn't aware of how rebellious and angry her expression was becoming, nor of how she was shredding a paper napkin between her fingers, folding and tearing, folding and tearing, her eyes down, staring at nothing.

Wendy Stevens saw, though, and put her plate down. "Ginny," she said, "come and show me where your restaurant is."

Ginny blinked and nodded. "Right," she said, standing up.

Robert watched them go from the corner of his eyes. He still hadn't said a word.

"I don't really want to see the restaurant," said Wendy as they walked out into the lane. "Anywhere'll do."

"We could go down to the beach, if you want."

"Okay. Anywhere."

As they walked, Ginny trailed her hand along the warm stones of the wall. "You know what this feels like?" she said after a minute or so.

"What? Tell me."

"It feels like being invaded. He doesn't belong here.

He obviously doesn't want to be here. He obviously hates me."

"Stop feeling sorry for yourself."

"I'm not; it's a fact. Couldn't you see how he looked at me? I'm not bothered by what he thinks anyway; it makes no difference."

"No difference to what?"

"To what I feel. I hate him."

"Well, that's honest."

"I'd hate him if he was invading this place or not, brother or not, whoever he was. There's people you just instinctively hate, whoever they are, and there's nothing you can do about it."

She looked at Wendy defiantly, almost as if she was expecting her to do just that, to do something about Ginny's hating him. But Wendy just walked slowly along, her eyes half-closed against the sun.

"What did your dad tell you?" she said.

"Bloody liar he is too," Ginny said. "See, I can't trust anyone anymore. He told me after all these years, all this time, he told me on Sunday that he wasn't married to my mother after all. He was married to Robert's mum."

"That's right. They never divorced, you see. Never even legally separated. Did he not tell you that?"

"No."

"Did he tell you anything about your mother?"

"Nothing new, except that he wasn't married to her. I'm beginning to wonder if she was true anyway, whether he just made her up. He's always told me she was an art student, see. . . . And that's very important to me, because I want to be a painter too—that's the most important thing in my life."

"The most important thing?"

"Yeah. Absolutely the only thing. Because I think I'm like her, see, my mother, I'm kind of doing it for her, doing the things she couldn't do. I'm going to grow up and live and be a painter in the way she couldn't. And if it turns out that . . . This is going to sound really snobbish, really *horrible*, right, but . . . if it turns out that she wasn't an artist at all but a shop assistant or something, then I'm going to feel really *cheated*. Because her being an artist, that's something proud, something to live up to. That's something to inherit. Especially now . . . Especially now he's come. Robert. Now he's the . . . the sort of real one. I've got nothing, except her. So . . . That's why it's important."

They walked on slowly. Insects were chirping in the grass at the foot of the wall; the sun beat up at them from the bronze-colored sea beyond the dunes.

"I told him he had to tell you," said Wendy. "It wasn't fair. But *he* feels terrible about the whole business. Robert's sixteen; he could have stayed in care for a couple of years, till he finishes at school, but your dad felt it was right to do this—"

"Did anyone ask Robert what he wanted?" Ginny asked.

"Yes. I did. Naturally. He wasn't in a state to make that sort of decision. He was very close to his mum."

"There aren't any more, are there? No more brothers or sisters hidden away? No, I suppose not. How can I get on with him? What can I do?"

"Just be yourself. You don't have to put on an act."

"To be myself, I *have* to put on an act," Ginny said bitterly.

"What's that mean?"

"It means I don't know who I am."

"I thought you said you were an artist. Just be that."

They walked on for a minute or two.

"Wendy," Ginny said, "suppose someone's adopted, right, and they don't know they are, or they think they are and no one'll tell them . . . Can they find out?"

"That's not the usual question I get," Wendy said, stopping to lean over a gate. "The usual one is: I know I'm adopted, and can I find my mother?"

"And can they?"

"When they're eighteen, yes. But as for your problem—why d'you think you're adopted?"

"Well . . . The thing is, after this . . . I mean, now I'm finding out a load of things I never knew, and it's got me thinking. There's things I can't sort out in my mind, things I remember from way way back, and I ask Dad about them and he doesn't know. Or just pretends. Like there was this trailer, I was staying in it, near some woods, and it was raining and raining, and I wasn't with Dad. . . . I used to think I remembered him there, but now I know I didn't. There was me and this other little girl, and there was a woman in charge of us. She had red hair and she smoked all the time. And she drank gin. I know that because the other night, in the restaurant, I smelled the smell of gin and it all came back. . . . Dad never has gin in the house, he doesn't like it, so I hadn't smelled it for a long time. But it brought it all back. And that's not the only thing. . . ."

She told Wendy about the time she'd stayed with her grandparents, that unhappy, inexplicable few days in the middle of nothing.

"So where was Dad? There's a whole stack of memories without him, and they're all kind of scattered, and then he starts coming into them and they're all joined up and I know where I am, then: it's kind of connected to me. But all those early ones he's not in."

She looked carefully at Wendy and saw she was listening. Ginny went on:

"Because I heard something about Dad the other day that I could never ask him. Someone said they'd heard he'd been in prison, only they didn't know what for. And . . ."

She shrugged.

Wendy said, "If that's true, then it would explain why you can't remember him early on. But that doesn't mean you're adopted as well. You ought to ask him."

"I can't. But say I *was* adopted: how could I find out for certain?"

Wendy looked doubtful. "There's the adoption register: you could write and ask if your name's on that. Or you could write and ask for your birth certificate. But they both take time and cost money. And if you'd been born abroad, there might not be a birth certificate in your name anyway, or your real name might be different. . . . I'm not sure what you'd learn from the adoption register, either; I've never had to answer this question before."

"Can you tell me the address?"

"Not now; I don't know it offhand. I'll send it to you. What was your mother's name?"

"Baptiste. Anielle Baptiste."

"You might be registered under her name, that's all."

"You mean Howard might not be my name?"

"It depends how it was registered. D'you remember anything else about this trailer?"

Ginny closed her eyes, trying to catch the flickering memories as they darted through her mind like little fish in a rock pool.

"The woman was Catholic. There was a crucifix on the wall, I remember that. She was called . . . Maeve? I don't know how you'd spell it. And the other little girl was called

Dawn. Oh, yeah, and someone had been murdered in the woods."

She opened her eyes to see Wendy looking at her sharply.

"I just remember someone telling me," Ginny explained. "These woods by the trailer, all dripping wet and cold, someone had been killed there. We were dead scared . . . I think. I *think* that was it. That's all I remember."

"You must have been very young."

"Well, that's the point: too young to remember. Anyway." She shrugged.

"I'd better be getting back," Wendy said. "I'll send you that address."

"Can I ask you something? Something personal?"

Wendy looked surprised, but nodded.

"Why do you wear a suit?" Ginny asked. "It must be ever so hot. And you'd look much nicer without it. More natural."

"If you don't wear a suit these days, people think you're not working hard," Wendy said. "They want value for money."

"I'm never going to wear a suit."

"You get used to it. You get used to anything. Even having a brother."

Ginny made a face. "Yeah, well," she said.

They walked slowly back to the house.

ONE DAY Ginny and Dad got in the car and just drove away for miles and miles, and then Dad drove the car onto a ship and when he drove it off they were in another country, where even the chocolate tasted different.

And they drove on and on until it was nearly night, and there was no house to sleep in, no bed to lie on, no food to eat. Ginny thought they'd have to sleep in the wilds.

Then Dad stopped and opened the back of the car and took out a tent, and there were big soft bags to sleep in, and a little stove that he cooked some sausages and beans on. Everything they needed, and it was all so neat! She'd never dreamed anyone could be so clever.

That was their first vacation, and every year they went off like that, heading for anywhere else. They'd drive off the ferry, and he'd say, "Left or right?" and she'd choose, on the spur of the moment, and whenever they came to a crossroads she'd decide which way to go. They never knew where they'd end up. One year they went as far north as they could get, along the coast of Norway and into the Arctic Circle, where the sun never set. They sat out in the open at midnight, playing cards, eating strange meals: fried fish and chocolate sauce, cherry pie and chutney, as if it were the most natural thing in the world.

They went everywhere. One day in Milan he took her to a fashionable shop and bought her the most beautiful dress in the world, and that evening they went to the opera. In his tuxedo and his black bow tie he looked like a king, and she felt like not his daughter but his queen; and the audience clapped and cheered, not for the singers or the orchestra but for Ginny's dress, and for her handsome father, and for the elegant, mysterious way they looked together, stars, a king and a queen, beyond the reach of envy or despair.

9

The Barbecue

DURING THE next couple of days Ginny and Robert spoke about five times. Their longest conversation took place on Friday, late in the afternoon. Dad had taken some time off to be at home for a while, and after lunch he and Robert had gone down to the harbor to look at boats; and now he'd gone into town for some shopping, leaving Ginny and Robert alone together for the first time.

Robert was in the hammock, and Ginny, seeing him from the kitchen, didn't know whether to ignore him and go to her room or make the effort and talk. She didn't want to stay indoors, she wanted to go into the garden; and whether it was that or the feeling that she ought to be nice to Robert, in the end she went out, sat in the shade of the tree, and said, "Hi."

He'd been pretending to be asleep. He opened his eyes, frowning.

"Hello," he said.

"Did you see any good boats?"

"Dunno. I dunno anything about boats."

"Dad thought maybe we could all learn to sail."

He sniffed.

104

"Robert . . . Did you know about Dad and me before this happened?"

"I knew about him. Obviously. She might have mentioned you, I don't know."

"What did she tell you about him?"

"She told me who he was, that's all."

"Did she say why they weren't living together?"

"I never asked."

He seemed to be on the verge of adding something, and she waited, but nothing came. She thought that if she told him that Dad had never mentioned him, it might sound as if he didn't care. It was so difficult to find anything to say.

Finally she said, "Did you ever visit his parents? Granddad and Grandma?"

"We didn't have anything to do with them."

"What, nothing? Why?"

"Because my mum—my mother didn't get on with them. I dunno. She never said."

His voice was cold with scorn, and it kept breaking; she could tell he was self-conscious about it. She tried again.

"Did you actually live in Liverpool?"

"No. Outside."

"I've only been there a couple of times. . . ."

Silence.

"Did your mum have any other relations?" she said.

He swung himself out of the hammock and faced her furiously.

"Can't you bloody well shut up about her? Leave her alone! Just bloody shut up!"

His pale face was blotched with anger. He was quivering all over. Before she could even think what to say, before she could even feel shocked, he was gone, slamming the kitchen door after him.

She looked down at her fingers, twined in her lap. Maybe

she had asked too many questions about his mother, but there wasn't much else to talk about. *Narrow self-righteous prim stuck-up superior constipated pig,* she thought. *Okay, if he doesn't want to talk, that's fine; suits me.*

She'd been going to offer to make them some coffee. Instead she left the house and set off for the Yacht Club early, calling in at the trailer first to say hello to Dafydd. She found him sprawled on the step, reading *Love and Rockets.*

"Is that the new one?" she said. "Has Hopey come back yet?"

"No, she's having a bad time, Hopey is. Get off! You can have it when I've finished. How's your brother, then?"

She'd told him and Andy about it all, hesitantly at first, but finding them as fascinated as Rhiannon. She'd thought boys weren't as interested in relationships as girls were; this would teach her to be sexist, she'd thought.

"I've just had a row with him," she said, and told him about it. "I don't know what I did wrong. I can't just say nothing about his mother, can I? And there's not much else I can ask him about."

"Well, he's probably feeling bad," Dafydd said. "Bound to be. Just leave him alone for a bit; he'll be all right."

Looking at Dafydd's strong oil-stained hands, his big slow kind face, she felt like kissing him. Why hadn't he a girl-friend? There was a story that he'd gone out with Carol Barnes once upon a time and didn't kiss her till the fourth date, and then only because she made him. Ginny couldn't remember who'd told her that. It was probably Rhiannon, and she'd probably made it up.

"You ought to fetch him down here," Dafydd said. "He can go a couple of rounds with Gertie."

"Isn't she finished yet?"

"I'm going to take her out and bury her tonight, I tell you. But then she'd probably dig herself out and lie there howling. Hey, if we hid her in old man Alston's house, they might think it was haunted."

"Dafydd . . . You know what you told me about Pont Doredig?"

"Aye."

"Well, I've been thinking. . . . It might have been Joe Chicago who did it. Who took the jacket. Because *his* jacket's fur-lined; I saw it at the pinball table."

"Yeah, but . . . *Duw*, there's lots of jackets like that. Anyway, it's just a story. It's probably not true. He wouldn't still have it, would he? The police would have got it off him and given it back to the bloke in the car."

"He might have hidden it," she said. "I bet I'm right. And it *is* true, I know it."

She could see it in her mind's eye as clearly as her father's face or her mother's photograph: the snow-covered road, the moonlight, the car, the broken parapet, the dark figure, the jacket, the baby crying on the empty seat. She found herself laying it out like a comic strip: a wide panel here to show the emptiness, the wide white desolation, with the little car at the center crumpled darkly on the bridge; and a close-up there to show the face of the killer, the thief, Joe Chicago's face, blurred as if through the misted glass of the car window. . . . It would be almost entirely in black and white, but with subtle grays and browns and ghost-colored shadows.

She could do that. She could paint it. A painting laid out like a comic strip; or a tragic strip.

The idea gave her a little thrill of pleasure. She realized that Dafydd was saying something and came back to the present.

"What?" she said.

"I says take no notice of your brother; leave him. He'll be all right. I remember when Gwilym's mum died, he hardly spoke for a year."

He went back to *Love and Rockets.*

"See you, then," Ginny said, and drifted off toward the Yacht Club.

As she turned into the field that led along beside the estuary, she heard someone call her name, and turned to see Glyn Williams coming toward her. She stopped to wait for him.

Glyn was about her own age. He lived in the village, where his parents kept the greengrocery, and although she hadn't had much to do with him, she liked him well enough. She was probably going to see more of him next year, because like her he was one of the few who'd opted to do French at A Level.

"Hi," he said. "I've been looking all over for you. Who's that at your house?"

"Oh, that's Robert. My brother. My half-brother, really."

"Well, well. I didn't know. Anyway, listen . . . We're going to have a barbecue tomorrow night. Eryl, Siân, all the rest, the usual thing. Bring your brother, why not?"

"Oh, great. Well, I don't know if he'll come, but *I* will. Thanks."

"See you, then. . . ."

He gave a grin and turned away. He was a strange boy, she thought, abrupt and quirky and not bad-looking, with his dark-red curly hair and his lean, muscular body. For some reason she thought of what she'd said to Wendy Stevens, about not wanting to discover that her mother had been a shop assistant, and alone as she was, she blushed; because Glyn's father earned his living in a shop, but he was a bard too, a Welsh poet well known in the *eisteddfodau,* the Welsh language conventions where poets and musicians competed for prizes, and he had two published collections to his name. He was at least as much of an artist as Ginny's mother, in fact. Nothing was as simple as it seemed.

WHEN she told Robert the next morning about the barbecue and made it clear he was invited too, he nodded and said, "Yeah. Okay, I don't mind."

She was so surprised by his mildness that she didn't know what to say next.

That was at breakfast. He and Dad were going into Porthafon—to get Robert some decent clothes, Dad had told her when Robert had gone to the bathroom; he only had what was in that tatty suitcase.

"I don't know what she thought she was doing," he said. "Maybe she'd been ill for longer than I thought. Are you getting on with him all right?"

Ginny thought: Why don't you look, and then you'd see? But she said, "Yeah, fine . . . Dad? You know your parents? Granddad and Grandma? Where did they live? Was that Liverpool too?"

"Not far away. Chester, as a matter of fact."

"Robert said his mother didn't get on with them."

"Oh, really?" He was trying to fold back the newspaper and making heavy weather of it, flapping it back and forth to get the crease straight.

"Was his name the same as yours?"

"Whose name?"

"Granddad's, of course."

"What d'you want to know that for, for goodness' sake?"

"I just want to know about myself," she said, looking at him openly. "About my family."

He didn't look at her. "His name's Ken. Kenneth Henry Howard. Her name's Dorothy. Now, is there anything you want in Porthafon?"

"No, thanks," she said demurely.

The reason she'd given for wanting to know her grandfather's name was true, but not the whole truth. As soon as Dad and Robert had gone, she phoned Directory Enquiries and asked for the number of Mr. K. H. Howard of Chester.

The operator found it at once.

"Can you give me his address?" Ginny asked.

"Sixteen Grove Road," said the operator.

So now she had her grandparents' name and address and telephone number. Feeling pleased with this secret knowledge, she went off to the Dragon and told Rhiannon, who hadn't been there to hear it the day before, everything she knew about Robert.

ON SATURDAY EVENING, the Yacht Club was busy. Ginny sensed the atmosphere as soon as she walked in.

"Ah, here's my little girlfriend," Andy said, whisking something creamy in a bowl.

"You haven't got a girlfriend, you pillock," said Angie Lime wearily. "Hurry up with that sauce. I need it chop-chop."

There were six chickens ready instead of the usual four, and Angie was cursing about the vegetables, because the supplier hadn't delivered any zucchini. Ginny, caught up in the busyness, swung into the routine at once; this was somewhere she felt at home. She cut the bread, filled the baskets, took them into the restaurant, picked up the salt and pepper shakers for filling. Harry was fiddling with the beer tap.

"How's old Picasso? Has old Calvert sold any pictures yet?"

"Yes, he has, actually," Ginny told him. "He sold one today for forty pounds."

"Get away!" said Harry. "He never!"

"He did; I was there. There was a young couple having

coffee, and the man was really keen on them, but she wasn't, I could tell. Mr. Calvert was telling them all about the pictures, what they meant, and finally the man said, 'I'll buy one.' I could see her expression. He's probably regretting it now."

Harry chortled, slapping his hands together like a performing seal. "What sort of picture was it?" he said.

"He does all these sort of science-fantasy ideas. . . . This one was called *Alchemical Harmony*. There were three glass jar things floating in space, with a nude woman in one of them."

"And that was it? A naked woman in a jar, and he gets forty quid for it?"

"And two other jars," she said, laughing too.

"Fantastic . . . Have you told Angie? *Duw*, that's a good one. Have an olive, go on."

He threw one in the air, tried to catch it in his mouth, missed, and laughed again. She took one for herself and went back to the kitchen, where she found Andy on his own.

"Harry reckons we'll do the ton tonight," he told her.

"What's that mean?"

"Do a hundred dinners. We had ninety-two last Saturday. That's why Angie's in a panic."

"Are you coming to the barbecue?"

"Oh, yeah, I'll be along later. Is your brother coming?"

"Yeah. I think so."

"What's it like, having a white brother?"

He couldn't have asked that with Angie Lime there, and she knew it.

"He doesn't seem like anything to do with me," she said. "We've got nothing in common at all. . . ."

He looked up from the onions he was chopping. His eyes were bright, his face shiny with heat and brimful of vivid life and mockery. She felt her heart beat faster, felt as if the world was full of possibilities, that anything might happen; but Angie Lime came back into the kitchen, and the moment passed. The first customers were arriving. It was time to work.

When she went home she had a shower and washed and oiled her hair, and then spent a long time deciding what to wear. It was only the beach, but it wasn't only the beach, because Andy would be there, and she wanted to look as good as she would if she felt good, which, she found rather surprisingly, she did. No jeans tonight, no cycling shorts, nothing clinging and Lycra tight. She wanted to look Haitian, or at least Caribbean. A wide flowered skirt, a white top that left her arms bare, a pink silk scarf twisting into a roll and tied around her hair; and then, hesitantly, a drop of perfume on her throat—sandalwood, which she liked for its heavy tropical richness.

So she was ready, and she went to the living room to find Robert.

His eyes widened in brief surprise when he saw her, and she was surprised too, because he'd combed his hair back and shaved, or washed, or something; and he was wearing a new cream-colored shirt and black jeans, and altogether, she thought, Rhiannon would approve.

"Okay, then?"

He got up. Dad was watching, half anxious, half relieved that they seemed to be getting on.

"Back by midnight," he said.

"Oh, go on, Dad! We'll have hardly any time there!" she said.

"All right. Just this once. When do *you* suggest?"

"One o'clock? Since it's summer?"

"One o'clock. If you're not back then, I'll come down there with a torch."

"Thanks. And can I take some lager?"

"You're supposed to be making money. Buy your own."

"Not allowed to. *Please* . . ."

"Two cans, then. And pay me back."

She kissed him, and they left. Both she and Dad knew that this was a performance for Robert: wheedling sister, indulgent father. What Robert made of it she couldn't tell, because he was looking sullen again, and he obviously wasn't going to speak unless she spoke first.

God, I wish I'd asked Rhiannon to come to the house first, she thought.

"I got some bratwurst," she said in desperation after a couple of minutes. "You know, German sausages. For the barbecue. I saw them in the deli in town this morning. Dad and me, when we went to Germany last year on vacation, we had them all the time."

"I haven't brought anything," he said.

"It's all right; this is for both of us. We usually have a couple of barbecues like this every summer. Last year it was raining too much. But it's not special or anything; it's just some kids from the village, that's all. I'm sorry if I went on about your mum yesterday. It was different when my mum died, 'cause I never knew her, obviously."

"She dead, then?"

"Didn't Dad say? She died when I was born. But I won't ask about your mum anymore. I was just interested. You know . . ."

He sniffed. "Yeah," he said.

The walk down toward the sunset-colored beach seemed to take much longer than usual. Whether or not he was conscious of her, she was unceasingly conscious of him, and of the current of suspicion that came from him like a cold wind.

"Have you been to the beach yet?" she said.

"No. I've not had time."

"I suppose not. . . . Is Dad really going to buy a boat?"

"He said so. I don't know."

Silence again. They were walking some way apart, and when they heard a car coming up the lane, they separated, each going to a different side. She wanted to find a way of asking him about the idea that Dad had been in prison, but not yet; she couldn't guess how he'd take it. If only he'd say something on his own instead of letting her start every conversation. If only . . . She could think of a dozen *if onlys* without even trying.

At the parking area, almost empty now that the visitors had gone to their bed-and-breakfasts, their rented cottages, their mobile homes, Ginny stopped. Robert drifted to a halt a little way off.

"I'm just trying to work out which way to go," she said. "Sometimes they have it off to the right, in the high dunes; sometimes they go the other way. Let's go left."

She climbed the gate into the field behind the dunes, the field that on its far side bordered the estuary. He joined her hesitantly, as if he wasn't sure it was allowed.

"It's all right," she said. "Everyone goes through here. As long as we don't let the sheep out . . ."

"What's that?" he said, pointing to a lichen-crusted slate roof among the dunes.

"That's the church. It's half buried. In the Dark Ages, right, when they had Viking raids and such, there was a monastery on an island out at sea somewhere, and whenever a monk or a priest died here on the mainland, they'd take his body over there to be buried. And the night before they sailed, they'd leave it in this church, all night long. It's called Saint Cynog's. That's why the village is called Llangynog, see. They open up the church in the holidays and have a service for the people on the beach. Otherwise it just sits here in the sand."

"Are those graves in there?" he said, looking through the tumbledown lych-gate.

"Yeah. The sand drifts around and covers them up and uncovers them again. It's really really old."

They clambered up past the tiny church and some way into the dunes, and then Ginny heard music and saw the fire, built in a wide hollow in the sand hills facing the sea. The whole scene was varnished with gold like an old picture of gods and nymphs. And if the ancient gods had barbecues, this was what they'd have looked like: healthy, happy figures drinking, or hauling a log up from the beach, or preparing food for the fire.

But then she looked again and thought, No, they're not gods and nymphs, these are human beings. Gods never changed. It would take someone like Watteau to paint this, with that strange air he had of delicate melancholy under the enjoyment: the sense in the shadows and the color of the sky that time was passing, that the happy maids and courtiers would change, part, grow old. . . . How could she show that here? If Watteau had painted a barbecue . . . Couldn't draw it; need color. Oil? Tempera? With an underglaze of gold . . . It would all be in the color, precious, fading . . .

The tide was high; it would be fully in by midnight. Rhiannon's kind Peter was there, thrusting a stick into the fire, and suddenly there was Rhiannon herself beside them, bright-eyed, pretty, curious.

"Hi!" she said. "You must be Robert. . . ."

And so they arrived at the barbecue.

GINNY'S experience of parties and discos and barbecues was of other people having a good time and of herself watching. When she was younger, she'd thought that that was what a good time was and she was having it, but in the last couple of years, seeing other girls dancing with

115

boys and holding their hands and being kissed, she'd come to realize that having a good time involved some so far imaginary boy, one who, if not sexy, was at least kind. At the same time she despised her timidity: why didn't *she* take charge? Why didn't she go up to a boy she fancied and . . . And what? was the question she hadn't worked out the answer to.

But tonight was different. Andy was coming, and the tide was high and the air was warm and the good smell of cooking food came drifting from the fire, and music was playing, and she felt pretty and light and tingling with expectation. So when he did arrive, slipping into the circle round the fire to shouts of "Andy! Great! Have a drink!" she felt everything was going to come right. And there was Dafydd, his heavy eyes smiling at her, and—she checked—there was Robert, sitting silent on one side of Rhiannon while Peter, looking kind, sat on the other.

"Did you do the ton?" she asked Andy.

"No. Ninety-eight. Harry wanted to get the last two to go round twice, but *Duw*, we'd had enough. *Iesu Grist*, it's bloody hot. Give us a bite to eat. Look, I've got a bottle of wine, lads . . ." He dragged a bottle of Lambrusco out of some capacious pocket and screwed off the top. "Have a swig."

Ginny tilted the bottle back. It was sweet and fizzy and cold, and some of it went up her nose and made her sneeze and laugh.

"Don't stick it up your nose," he said. "*Dreadful* manners. Hey, I was going to bring Gertie, give her a good time, but I thought the excitement would be too much for her. Where's that sausage? Give us a bite."

"Who's Gertie?" said Eryl. "You changing your spots, Andy?"

"No spots on me. I'm an Ethiopian."

"First time I've heard it called that," said Eryl, but Andy was off on the story of how he came by the smoked salmon. It was quite different from the first version. Dafydd winked and rolled his eyes up at Ginny with a vast secret enjoyment, and she sat clasping her knees beside Andy, the dazzling quicksilver trickster, as he spun one fantastic lie after another. She knew they were lies, knew that the incredible Carlos had probably never existed, but it didn't matter a bit. Listening to Andy was like sitting under a fountain of champagne.

When the bottle of wine was half-finished, she felt dizzy and confident, both at once, and she tugged at his hand and made him get up and dance. It was a slow, romantic soul tune, and several couples were swaying in each other's arms, feet dragging in the soft sand. She faced him for a moment, looked at his dark face directly, and then stepped close and put her arms around his waist.

His body was warm and slender, his arms light around her, and she rested her head on his shoulder and breathed in the complex intoxicating smell of him: the faint remains of cooking and cigarette smoke, the wine, some distant hint of aftershave, and clean sweat. She marveled at the tension of the smooth muscles of his back, the hollow between them where his spine lay, the way his hips swayed. . . . He had no sense of rhythm whatsoever, and such was her state of mind that his lack of it seemed only one more perfection.

She was no longer aware of the other kids, of the fire, the sea, the music, Robert. Everything was Andy; she was obsessed, she was drunk with him, she was in love. . . . This was it, love, she was there, it was hers. She moved her head slightly and brushed his neck with her lips, once, twice, and then kissed it gently, lost.

Then someone spoke nearby. There was a muffled laugh.

117

Andy's body tensed at once; she could feel it like electricity. She looked up at his face, dismayed, and saw it grim and cynical.

"Take no notice," he whispered. "They're not worth it. They're just a bunch of stupid kids."

"But what did they *say?*" she whispered back, though she knew. Someone had joked about them, about their being black, some crude racist crap. . . . Her *friends*. Andy, sensing her anger, held her tight and didn't let her whirl around to confront them.

"They don't understand," was all he said.

"But we have to *fight* this, Andy! Not just for us but for everyone! We can't just *give in*. . . ."

There was something disconcerting about his response. She couldn't see his face clearly enough, because he had his back to the fire, but she sensed a sadness in him she'd never known before. The music stopped, and they stopped moving, and someone put another tape in. The moment had gone.

They sat down. She was puzzled. There he was, talking to Glyn and Siân and Eryl, making them laugh, accepting a cigarette, offering the wine; and Ginny found herself next to Robert. Something had happened, but she didn't know what it was.

Robert was saying something. She had to ask him to repeat it.

"Who's the gay pair?" he said quietly.

"Gay pair? What're you talking about?"

"Those lads. The one you were dancing with and his mate. What's their names?"

She was bewildered. "Gay?"

"You know. Homosexual."

"What d'you *mean*, gay? How can they be—you don't

118

mean Andy and Dafydd? Whatever gave you that stupid idea?"

"Rhiannon told me. Anyway, it's obvious."

And suddenly it was.

A hundred little meaningless things—comments, looks, jokes—acquired a meaning all at once. And she knew what the whispered voice had said that had made Andy at first tense in her arms and then sad—it was all as clear as water, and she'd been duped again. Everyone else had known, and she hadn't. Rhiannon had known; her best friend. Even Robert had known. It was too much to bear.

With a choking sob, she flung herself up and away from the fire, into the darkness of the dunes. She plunged over the top of the nearest one and fell down into the cool feathery sand on the far side, stumbling and sprawling, and then scrambled up again and struggled through the yielding sand, the pricking marram grass, till she was out of earshot of the group by the fire and their mocking voices, their knowing eyes; and then she sank to her knees and beat her fists into the white unresistant softness all around, the hot tears scalding her hot cheeks.

She'd never felt so humiliated in her life. The worst of it was that she'd made her infatuation for Andy so obvious; she'd flaunted it. . . . And *Rhiannon* had known. And Angie had known: *You haven't got a girlfriend, you pillock.* And Eryl, just now: *First time I've heard it called that.* And Stuart: suddenly everything about Stuart became clear. God! Even her father—seeing her with Stuart, and hearing that Stuart was a friend of Andy's, he'd known what that had meant, and said, *Oh, that's all right, then,* meaning *You'll be safe with him. . . .*

And she hadn't seen it. Stupid, naive Ginny, the only person in the world who didn't know. She knelt there, her head bowed, the tears soaking into the sand as they fell from her eyes.

Minutes went by, and little by little the crying stopped. She sat up slowly and mopped her face with the skirt. She was alone, and that was how she wanted it.

Very dimly, in the faint starlight, the roof of the old church was visible over the marram-fringed rise in front of her. She sighed a long shaky sigh, stood up and brushed the sand off her skirt, and slowly climbed the slope.

There was a single strand of wire marking the boundary of the churchyard, but the posts were sunk so low in the sand that it was easy to step over it. She slid down among the graves, the leaning tombstones, and made her way to the corner of the church.

In front of her the wide field spread out to the estuary, and beyond it the water, high now the tide was in, gleamed like steel. A cluster of little lights marked the Yacht Club and the railway station, the only sign of human life; and beyond everything else lay the great round hills, dark against the dark sky, immeasurably ancient.

Gradually, as she stood with her right hand on the corner of the tiny church, the shame and the anger cooled down. In the presence of those vast hills, it seemed petty. Maybe the old monks had felt the same about their sorrows, gazing up at that skyline. This church was a thousand years old; such a long time. . . . At some time in those thousand years, Ginny thought, someone else must have stood in the same spot, hand on the wall, and looked up at the hills and felt better for it.

At her left hand there was a slate-covered tomb the size and height of a table, a big dark box half covered in sand. The light grains against the black surface reminded her of something. She brushed the top clear and, taking a handful of sand, let it trickle through her fingers onto the slate.

After a little practice she found she could draw a strong clear line.

She was thinking of what Stuart had told her about the *vevers*, those magic figures the voodoo priest would trace in flour on the ground to evoke the *loa*, the gods. Carefully she drew the outline of a heart, pierced by a sword, with lacy fronds and tendrils extending from the top and bottom. In the ghostly starlight she could see it clearly. It was the *vever* of Erzulie, the tragic goddess of love, whose visitations were brief and ended in weeping, but who brought beauty with her, and grace, and laughter—tragic things, because they lasted so short a time and then died.

When it was nearly finished she stood back and looked at it. The handle of the sword was too large; she brushed it away and corrected it. She did the same for one of the tendrils at the foot, which didn't balance the one on the other side. Then it was done.

She straightened her back stiffly, conscious that she'd made a decision of some kind. She felt very tired and oddly happy, and her mind was filled with a tangle of thoughts: *I can see in the dark. I can't see so well in the daylight, can't see the obvious things like Andy being gay, but that doesn't matter because I can see in the dark. I can understand mysteries. Like the broken bridge. I know the truth of that, because I'm the baby, I'm the father, I'm the thief. And I understand the old monks who built this church, and Erzulie, I understand her, and the hills too, I can hear what they're saying to me. And African-ness. I'm beginning to understand being black. And my mother. Something happened when I was born, I know it did. I'm going to find out. I'm going to find her paintings. . . . They're not going to hide things from me. They're so stupid! They hide them in the dark! If they hid them in the light I'd never see them, but the dark is where I live, like*

Maman. I'm an artist, I'm a sorceress, I'm at home there. . . . So whatever it is you concealed, Dad, you made a mistake. I'm going to find it. And then I'll paint the truth. . . .

She found herself wandering through the field, her feet wet in the dew, her head ringing.

There was a figure sitting on the gate by the parking lot.

"Robert?" she said.

He got down on the other side.

"Thought I'd better wait for you," he said.

"No need. But thanks."

She climbed the gate, and they began to walk up the lane. She was immensely tired. For the first time she thought what it all must mean to him: His mother had died only a week ago, and this stranger, his unknown sister, takes him to a barbecue and involves him in her own little emotional dramas. She wanted to apologize, but it was more comfortable being silent; at least they weren't hostile anymore.

Almost the last thing she realized that night came to her as she was getting into bed. Holding Andy in her arms, the voice, her anger, his sadness . . . He was sad for her, because he'd seen her mistake and known he could do nothing about it. She felt very fond of him, fond of Daf-ydd. It wasn't their fault, after all. That things could be like that . . . How strange. How *strange*. It was like losing a twenty-pound note but then seeing a new color.

Her very last thought concerned Joe Chicago, as she realized the meaning of his connection with Andy. Things were fitting into place. Maman, the broken bridge . . . It was beginning to make sense. But there was a lot more to find out yet. She went to sleep almost at once.

10

The Only Thing
to Do

GINNY WASN'T SURE what she was going to say to Rhiannon, so it was a good thing the next day was Sunday, when she didn't go to the Dragon. Instead, after lunch (difficult, with Dad trying to be cheerful and fatherly and Robert being grim and silent), she went off on her own and caught the train to Porthafon.

At the corner of Jubilee Terrace she almost turned back, because outside Rhiannon's sister's house there was a man washing a car—obviously Helen's husband. Washing cars was discouraged if not actually forbidden because of the water shortage, so getting it clean was clearly very important to him. He was a neat, trim little man with hairy arms and the famous neat mustache, and he looked at her with open curiosity as she went past him and rang the doorbell.

Helen answered it seconds before her husband got there, chamois cloth dripping in his hand.

"Ginny . . . Come in."

A quick, hostile glance at him, and she closed the door behind them, shutting him out.

"Come on through. I'm in the garden," she said.

Ginny had forgotten how definite she was, how clear and decisive and un-Rhiannon-like. They sat down on the little patch of grass, with children playing on a swing next door and a man on the opposite side of the fence dozing under a newspaper. It felt very open compared to her back garden; she imagined everyone would be listening.

"I've heard about your brother," Helen said.

"From Rhiannon? Or from Dad?"

Helen hesitated. "Both," she said.

"Do you see Dad a lot, then?"

"Well . . . quite often."

She looked frankly at Ginny, as if inviting her to ask more. But Ginny didn't want to, yet.

"So. What's this brother like?" Helen said.

"Difficult. I have to keep telling myself he's my brother, or I wouldn't believe it. Half-brother. And that his mum only died last week. It's no wonder he's unhappy. And what he thinks of us, God knows. I try and ask about his mother. . . . Actually I don't anymore, 'cause he got angry, but I was just so curious, I wanted to *know*. And Dad won't tell me. . . ."

"Why won't he?"

"He just clams up. He won't say anything except stupid vague answers that don't mean anything. I want to know about my mother, for instance. I thought they were married, but they weren't; he was married to Robert's mother. Did you know that?"

Helen nodded, looking careful.

"What else has he told you, then?"

Helen blew out her cheeks and ran a hand through her hair. "It's not easy. . . ."

Ginny felt a flash of anger. "What d'you mean, it's not easy? What d'you think it's like for me? There's everyone knowing more about me than I do myself—what d'you think that's like?"

Helen looked down. Ginny pressed on recklessly:

"Are you having an affair with Dad?"

"*What?* Ginny, I can't answer—"

"Is that what it is? You can tell me, for God's sake! I don't *mind* or anything! I mean, *are* you?"

"Have you asked him?"

"Yes," said Ginny, staring at her flatly.

"And? What did he say?"

"He said no, of course not, what a stupid idea."

"Well, then . . ."

"But he's a liar, isn't he? He lied about my mother. He might be lying about this. That's why I'm asking you."

Helen's eyes were closed. Ginny was hating herself for this, but now she'd started, she couldn't stop.

"Ginny," said Helen, "I like your father very much, but I can't answer questions like that. Let me talk to him—"

She stopped, and Ginny looked around. Benny was watching from the kitchen doorway.

"All right?" he said, as if Ginny had been starting a fight.

"Yes, thank you," said Helen coldly.

"Who's this, then?" he said, smiling at Ginny.

"Ginny. She's a friend of Rhiannon's."

"I better go," said Ginny, thinking that they'd never be able to talk with him there.

"No, don't. Wait a minute, I'll come with you," said Helen, getting up.

Ginny pushed past Benny in the kitchen doorway, not looking at him, smelling his pungent aftershave.

"Let's go down to the Locker," said Helen. "Have a coffee and a doughnut or something."

Davy Jones's Locker was a café on the harborfront, all hung about with lobster pots and fishing nets and glass floats, and someone had painted mermaids and pirate wrecks on the walls. The owner was a big careless cheerful man with one leg, who sometimes wore a pirate-style striped jersey and stumped about on a wooden peg like Long John Silver. The whole thing was tacky, but Ginny liked the wooden booths and the smell of fresh coffee, which came in chunky earthenware mugs that didn't balance properly on the saucers.

"Have some carrot cake," said Helen. "Help you see in the dark."

Ginny decided that she liked her a lot.

"I'm sorry I said that about Dad," she said. "I didn't really ask him at all. I couldn't, even if I wanted to. But I'm just so confused, what with Robert and all, I don't know anything. And last night . . . There was this boy, right. . . ."

She told Helen about Andy, about how she'd felt, about what had happened. Helen listened with all Rhiannon's intense interest but with a lot more sympathy.

"It's funny, though," Ginny said. "I don't feel cross or anything. It's just embarrassing, really. The real thing about it is Joe Chicago, how it links up with him. You know the story of the broken bridge?"

"No. What's that?"

"You *don't?* I thought that was just one more of the things everyone knew but me. A long time ago there was a man with his daughter, a baby, driving up Gwynant way, and it was a winter night, and the car crashed into the bridge. They weren't hurt or anything. The man had a warm kind of fur-lined leather jacket, and he wrapped me up in it and went for help. But while he was gone someone stole the jacket and the baby died, just froze to death. And *I* reckon that the person who did it was Joe Chicago, and that's the same jacket, the one he wears. Now, if he knew my dad was in prison, okay, then Dad's connected with that story in the same way. So I really need to find out all I can."

"Why did you say *me?*"

"Me?"

"You said *he wrapped me up in it.* Instead of *the baby.*"

"I didn't, did I? Did I really?"

Helen nodded and sipped her coffee. "It's a Freudian slip," she said.

"What's that?"

"It means it's what you really think. Your unconscious mind speaking for you."

"But I don't think . . . It wouldn't make sense anyway, 'cause I'm not dead, am I?"

"No. Probably just a slip of the tongue."

Ginny slid further into the corner of the booth, pulled her feet up on the wooden seat, and hugged her knees, staring unseeingly at the fishing net spread out on the opposite wall.

"Rhiannon said that Joe Chicago knows your husband," she said.

"Yeah," said Helen after a second or two.

"Do *you* know him?"

"He's been to the house a few times."

"He's involved with that boy I told you about. Andy. I think he's blackmailing him or something. And I think I know why now, after last night. D'you think he really knows my dad?"

"I don't know . . . I don't know. The thing is that Benny's so bloody jealous of everything, everyone, and he knows I've seen your dad once or twice. . . . He might have made that up. To try and put me off, see. I never heard it from Joe himself, only from Benny."

"So it might not be true?"

"Or it might."

They were silent. Helen pushed the plate of cake toward Ginny, who shook her head.

"I can already see in the dark," she said.

They sat there a little while longer and then went out to the harbor and sat looking at the cottages, the old slate warehouse that was now an Industrial Heritage Museum, the amusement arcade. It was another hot day. Helen was fanning herself with her straw hat.

"Helen, does he ever talk about my mother?" Ginny asked. "Because I want to find her paintings, you see. I can't understand why he didn't keep them."

"Well . . . I couldn't say, really. Listen, now. This is going to sound stupid, but did you ever think that maybe your mam was still alive?"

Ginny blinked with astonishment. How ridiculous!

"Of course she's not," she said scornfully. "I'd know if she was alive, wouldn't I?"

"How, though?"

"I'd have heard of her. She'd be a famous painter. Anyway, I *know* she's not alive. She'd never have left me if she was. It's out of the question."

She was a little angry that Helen could even consider it possible. They sat in silence for a while, and Ginny began to wonder why she'd come, what this woman had to do with her, why she'd wasted her time. Well, she'd leave in a minute, as soon as she found a way of saying good-bye.

But Helen said, "Why are you so interested in Joe Chicago?"

"I told you. Because of the broken bridge."

"Suppose you found out it *was* him: what would you do?"

"What would I do? Well, I'd be able to make him leave Andy alone, for a start. And . . . make him tell me about Dad."

128

Before she said the words the idea hadn't existed, but now that it did, she knew it was absolutely right. She felt a little thrill of certainty.

"Does he come to your house often?" she said.

"Whenever Benny brings him, I suppose. I don't take much notice. I'm not very close to Benny these days. I don't know what they've got in common anyway. I think Benny's afraid of him. He's just trying to show he's tough, going around with a thug."

"Helen, could you help me?"

"Help you talk to Joe Chicago?"

"Yeah. Could you?" She was sitting forward on the wooden bench, twisted to look Helen in the face, and Helen, her straw hat low over her eyes, was leaning back languidly in the heat, looking tired.

"*Please?*" Ginny said.

"I think you're crazy. He's a horrible swine, he's hateful, you don't want to talk to him. . . . What makes you think he'll tell you the truth anyway?"

"I'll make him," said Ginny. "I will. Me and Baron Samedi, we'll make him."

"You and who?"

"My voodoo friend. No; no one—I don't mean it. Just me."

"But what are you . . . ?"

"I just need to be alone with him for a few minutes, Helen. I just want to ask him. *Please* . . . When he comes to your house next time, can you let me know? I'll get someone to bring me."

Helen pursed her lips. Then she shrugged.

"Well, can't do much harm, I suppose. . . . Are you going to tell your dad?"

"No! Course not."

"And . . . are you going to tell him you've been to see me?"

She'd put her sunglasses on; Ginny couldn't read her expression.

"No," she said. "If he's got secrets from me, I can have secrets from him. I can't talk to him anymore, not now Robert's here. We're never alone. Anyway, I don't trust him."

"You should."

"I can't. I'm on my own now."

"No, you're not," said Helen unconvincingly.

"I am."

"BUT HOW was I supposed to know?" said Rhiannon the following afternoon. "Know you didn't know, I mean, stupid. Everyone's always known. That's why he left home, 'cause his parents chucked him out for it. I mean, it was such an *obvious* thing. That's why you've got nothing to worry about."

"Explain," said Ginny coldly.

"No one'll think you didn't know. They'll think you were dancing with him just as a friend, kind of thing."

"Oh, yeah?"

"Oh bloody yeah."

"And what about when I ran off into the dunes? I thought they were all laughing at me."

"You don't suppose anyone noticed anything by that stage, girl? I certainly didn't. I was in the second degree of bliss," she said with a comic smugness. "That's a technical term."

"The second degree of bliss . . ." Ginny said scornfully, but she couldn't help smiling. "I suppose Peter took you there, did he? And how many degrees of bliss are there?"

"Judging by that one, I reckon about seven hundred. Still, it's a start. Hey, someone's waving at you."

They were sitting on the old wooden jetty outside the Yacht Club. Ginny looked where Rhiannon was pointing.

"That's Stuart," she said, waving back.

"Who he?"

"A friend of Andy's. Yes," she said, answering the question in Rhiannon's raised eyebrows. "And I didn't know before, no. But he's nice. Let's go and say hello."

They stood up, bare feet on the hot planks, and took the path along by the railway bridge to the ladder that led to Stuart's house. He was sitting on the roof, sunbathing. Rhiannon drew in her breath as she saw him.

"What a *waste*," she said quietly, climbing the ladder just behind Ginny.

"I'll tell him," Ginny said.

When she came face-to-face with Stuart again, Ginny felt herself wondering what did it *mean*, being gay? What did they *do*? Had he kissed Andy, for instance?

"Hi," he said. "I've got something for you. Hello," he added to Rhiannon.

"This is Rhiannon," Ginny said. "My social secretary."

"I'm Stuart," he said. "I haven't got one of those, I'm afraid; you have to deal with me directly. How's things?"

"Mixed," said Ginny, sitting down beside him on the decking of the roof. Rhiannon sat down too, and Ginny saw with pleasure that her friend, for once, was shy. Stuart was wearing the smallest possible swimming costume, and his body, as far as she could judge male bodies, could probably take you to the five hundredth degree of bliss merely by being looked at. "Did I have a brother when I saw you last? I can't remember."

"You didn't mention him. Has he just appeared?"

"That's him down there, in the boat with my dad. Dad's the one with the beard."

Stuart looked across the water to the edge of the jetty,

two hundred yards away, where the apparent owner of the boat was demonstrating how to do something nautical with the sail. Dad was looking brisk and keen, and Robert was sitting in the stern, staring down into the water.

"He doesn't look very happy," said Stuart.

"No. Well, he's probably not. . . . How are you, then?"

"Roasting. I thought it was supposed to rain all the time here."

"Well, it's the end of the world. Everything's going strange. What's this thing you've got for me?"

"A magazine. It's downstairs on the table."

"What is it? What magazine?"

"Well, you're interested in art; I thought you'd like it. Read it carefully. Oh, and I want to see some of your pictures. Is she any good?" he asked Rhiannon.

"Yeah, brilliant," said Rhiannon. She *was* shy, Ginny thought gleefully.

"D'you ever go to the Yacht Club?" she asked.

"Yes. I've been several times. Why?"

"Well, next Saturday, you've got to go three times. They want to do the ton—that's a hundred dinners. They got up to ninety-eight last Saturday, so if you have three meals, they might make it next time."

"Or bring two friends," said Stuart.

"Yeah, that'd do. . . ."

They stayed on his roof for half an hour, watching Dad and Robert in the little boat, gossiping, joking. Rhiannon hardly spoke, but Ginny was completely at her ease, laughing and flirting in a way she knew she could never have done with a boy her own age, or someone who wasn't gay. She found herself thinking that it would be an ideal relationship, all easy, all happy, all surface. All sun, all skin. But that wasn't enough now.

"Don't forget that magazine," Stuart called as they left. "Come and see me again."

"Yeah, we will," said Ginny.

The magazine on the table was thick and glossy and called *Modern Painters*. Well, that's nice, she thought. I'll read it tonight.

AND SO she did; but it wasn't until some days later that she saw why he'd given it to her. There was just so much of it—articles on painters she'd never heard of, articles on painters she had heard of, an article by an English painter explaining why an American painter wasn't as good as everyone had thought, an article by a Scottish painter explaining why a Spanish painter was better than anyone had thought, articles by critics attacking other critics—pages and pages of it, and Ginny read it all avidly, because this was her world now, these were her people. And the illustrations were beautiful.

But she hadn't seen Andy since the barbecue, and something was weighing on her mind. Should she pretend nothing had happened? Should they talk about it? In the end, it was easy. She was sitting moodily on the beach on Tuesday afternoon, and suddenly there he was, beside her, holding out an ice cream.

"What's the matter? You wanted chocolate? Tough. You got this."

She took it, and he stroked the back of her neck for an awkward second. It was the only awkward action she'd ever known him to perform, and she knew exactly what it meant: it was an acknowledgment, and a consolation, and an apology, and she realized with a little rush of relief that the ideal relationship she'd imagined while talking to Stuart already existed between her and Andy.

"Listen," she said, "you know Joe Chicago?"

"What about him?"

"Where did he get that jacket from? His leather jacket."

"Oh, you heard that story, have you?"

Her skin prickled. "What story?"

"He nicked it. That's what I heard. There was a plane that crashed in the hills, and he went up and took it off the dead pilot. That's what he likes to tell people. Wants to make himself sound really hard. Big pillock."

"A plane . . . Wow. How things change. You know he's friendly with Rhiannon's sister's husband?"

"Has she got a sister? God, the whole world's coming out in siblings. Tell me more. . . ."

It felt good to have him back. No, it felt better, because now both of them knew what their relationship was, and if she had to put a name to it, it would have been the one he'd just used: they were siblings, kindred, blood relatives.

She felt far more his sister than Robert's. It wasn't getting any easier at home; Dad tried to get them to talk at mealtimes, but since the things they had in common were the things that neither Dad nor Robert wanted to talk about, conversation faltered. They couldn't even talk about school. Robert had just finished his GCSEs, as she'd done, but she had no idea what he was intending to study next. She didn't even know if he was smart. What he seemed mostly was grim and angry.

And Ginny understood, or tried to, but she could find nothing to say to him; and so while she hung around with Rhiannon or with Andy and Dafydd, and worked in the Dragon and the Yacht Club, Robert drifted about alone on long walks in the hills; and while he sat silently with Dad in front of the TV, she spent the evenings at her drawing table, penciling the story picture of the broken bridge.

On Thursday night she'd got it laid out as she wanted it, ready to be inked. It was midnight when she finished, and she was tempted to go on, to ink just the first frame, to lay the pure Indian black on the crisp white bristol board; but she knew that her eyes were tired and her hand was cramped, and she didn't want to risk spoiling it. Instead she had a shower and went to bed. The window was open; it was too hot for pajamas, and even her bedside lamp, shining on *Modern Painters,* was uncomfortably warm. Eyelids drooping, she lay flicking through the magazine before falling asleep.

And suddenly she found herself frozen. A shiver, a chill, made her skin crawl, and she realized her heart was racing as she tried to work out what had caused it: someone prowling outside? a ghost? what?

It was the magazine. She sat up and looked.

A gallery in Liverpool was advertising an exhibition called "Les Mystères: Haitian Painting of the Past Twenty Years," and one of the painters was Anielle Baptiste.

She clenched her fists, alive with triumph. So the pictures *had* survived! And that was why Stuart had given her the magazine! When was it opening, this exhibition? On Tuesday next, for a month, at L'Ouverture Gallery in Sandeman Street . . .

She couldn't lie still; she was far too excited to sleep now. Wide awake, grinning helplessly, she switched on the work light over her drawing table, uncapped the ink, and choosing her finest brush, began to work on *The Broken Bridge.*

11

Baron Samedi

By this time, Ginny was in a strange state of mind, with three things pressing equally on her attention: her painting of the broken bridge; her mother's pictures, and wondering what they'd be like, and keeping the news of them secret; and the crazy quest to get the truth out of Joe Chicago. She looked haunted, absentminded, obsessed, anything but happy—though if anyone had asked her whether she was unhappy, she wouldn't have known what they were talking about. She was only aware that she was busy. And this, she dimly realized, was a state of mind as much hers as art, as seeing in the dark. It was the place where she was at home.

On Saturday at the Dragon, Rhiannon said (quietly, because Mr. Calvert was just outside the door), "Helen rang this morning with a message for you. She said she couldn't ring your house in case your dad found out. Hey, is she having an affair with him? I bet she is. I would, if I was married to Benny. But she won't say—"

"What's the *message*?" Ginny said.

"Oh. Right. Yeah. She said Joe Chicago will be there tonight. Ginny, what's going *on?* Why's she telling you that?"

"It's a secret code. It means something different."

"Oh, all right then, don't tell me. I just won't tell you about Robert."

"What about Robert?" said Ginny, though she didn't care. It wouldn't have surprised her at all if Rhiannon was interested in him. In fact, the only person who would have been surprised was Peter.

But to satisfy Rhiannon's curiosity, she said, "I'm having a bet with Andy, that's all. I want to find out something from Joe Chicago. And I told Helen, and she's going to help me."

"He'll kill you," said Rhiannon pleasurably. "With his bare hands. He's a sadist, you know. He indulges in unspeakable atrocities. You're taking your life in your hands, girl. . . ."

THE biggest problem was how to get back. If she left the Yacht Club exactly on time, she'd just catch the one bus that went that way on Saturdays, but there was no bus back, and no trains, either.

Well, ask, she told herself, and went down to the trailer to look for Dafydd.

He groaned. "I'm not getting involved with Joe Chicago," he said. "Nor should you. Is this Andy's idea?"

"No. It's all mine. You wouldn't have to get involved anyway, just be somewhere I can find you. And then drive me home. I'll pay for the gas."

"Forget the gas. I can fill the tank anytime. Well, I suppose so. All right. I reckon you're going round the bend, I really do. What time d'you reckon you'll want to come home?"

DAD suggested optimistically at teatime that maybe they could all go out and see a film and have a pizza that evening. Ginny wasn't aware of the look of contempt that passed over her face and would have been horrified if she realized he'd noticed; but they were communicating so little these days that she'd lost the habit of looking for his response to things. She told him that she was going out, and that she'd be back at eleven, and then forgot about him.

The Yacht Club was gearing up to do the ton. Angie Lime had made sure the suppliers had delivered all the vegetables they were likely to need; the bar was freshly stocked; all the staff were concentrating, flexing their muscles, thinking ahead. It was a heady atmosphere, and Ginny half wished she could stay and be part of it.

But she hurried away, wishing them luck, and then ran up to the main road so as not to miss the bus. When it came, she sat in the front seat, the evening sun full in her face, and felt an agreeable tension prickling its way along her nerves, like stage fright. In her jeans and sneakers and dark T-shirt, she felt light, athletic, ready to run and fight.

At Porthafon she got out by the harbor and wandered along past Davy Jones's Locker, wondering whether to go in and have some coffee, but the place was full of vacationers eating hamburgers. She moved on. The harbor was lively, with its cafés and pubs and the amusement arcade, but the rest of the town was very quiet. It was beginning to get dark as she turned into Jubilee Terrace. The light was on in the front room of Helen's house, but Ginny couldn't see anyone. Helen opened the door at once when she rang the bell.

"Come in, quick," she said, "before they see you. . . ."

Ginny hastened into the hall, and Helen shut the door quickly.

"They've gone to the pub to get some beer," she said. "Him and Benny. They're going to play cards or something. You haven't seen him close to, have you. He's frightening. You can't imagine."

"I have seen him," Ginny said. "You don't have to do anything. Just leave it to me."

"But what are *you* going to do?"

"I don't know! I'll think of something. I just want to talk to him on his own. . . ."

They were standing in the tidy little hall, talking urgently, the light shining directly down on them. Suddenly Helen seized Ginny's arm.

"They're here!" she whispered, and Ginny heard voices outside. "Get upstairs! Go on—quick!"

Ginny ran up the narrow stairs as a key turned in the lock. She hesitated on the landing, crouching low in the dark to peer down at Benny and Joe and two other men, all crowding in. They were speaking Welsh; Helen said something sharp to Benny, and Joe said something back that made the other men laugh. Ginny could see Benny's face, and saw that it was more important to him to seem good to these men than to stick up for Helen, and then she understood all Helen's contempt.

The men shoved their way into the front room. Ginny heard the snapping of aluminum can pulls, the sudden blare of the TV, quickly turned down. Then Helen was on her way upstairs.

"Come in here," she whispered to Ginny, pushing open a door at the top of the stairs that led into a stuffy little spare bedroom overlooking the garden. She didn't turn the light on. They sat on the bed and spoke quietly.

"What are they doing?" Ginny asked.

"Drinking. They'll play cards till they think I've gone to bed, and then they'll watch a dirty video. Benny gets them from someone downtown—I saw it in his shopping bag. God, he thinks I'm a fool."

"What does Joe do? Does he sleep here?"

"I wouldn't dare sleep with him in the house. No, he's got a council house somewhere; he always goes home. Listen, why don't you give up the idea, for God's sake? You don't know what he might do. . . ."

"I'll just wait here. Sooner or later he'll come up to the bathroom or something. Is the front door locked?"

"Well, it's on the latch—a Yale lock. What d'you mean?"

"Can you fix the latch so I just have to pull it open? You know, instead of having to turn the handle, if I want to run out in a hurry?"

"I could, but listen, I'm frightened now. I'm worried what he'll do to me if—"

She stopped. Heavy footsteps came up the stairs; a man pissed loudly into the lavatory bowl and didn't flush it or wash his hands before going down again. Fastidious Helen made a face.

"Was that him, d'you think?" Ginny said.

"Might have been. They're all horrible, *ach y fi*, and the worst is Benny. . . ."

"I saw him when Joe said that to you."

"I can't stay with him, Ginny; there's no reason to. He treats me like shit; he spends all his time sucking up to thugs like Joe . . ."

She was crying, silently but passionately, and then she turned to throw herself on the pillow, her sobs heaving her shoulders. Ginny felt helpless. She put her hand on Helen's back, but Helen didn't seem to feel it. Ginny had never seen a grown woman cry before; it was like a force of nature, Erzulie again: here on this narrow bed in this dark and stuffy room, the goddess was weeping. Ginny was awed by the power and intensity of it, and simultaneously she imagined painting the scene: the two of them in the light coming from the crack under the door, the dim room, Helen's cloud of dark hair, her own face baffled and anxious, her tentative hand. She found herself sketching it in her mind and moved her right leg to improve the balance of the composition—and then cursed her own selfishness. Art was a *disease,* to make you more concerned about pictorial values than about someone else's unhappiness.

Presently Helen sat up slowly and dried her eyes. She wouldn't look at Ginny.

"I'll go and put the door on the latch," she said. "Then I'm going to bed."

With a deep, trembling sigh, she stood up and went out. Ginny heard her descend the stairs, heard the kitchen door open and close, heard laughter from the front room, heard Helen coming up the stairs again, heard her bedroom door close.

Then, for the first time, with part of her mind she wondered what she was doing. If she had any sense she'd go quietly downstairs and leave the house, and wait for Dafydd, and forget all about the broken bridge.

But another part of her mind said: *Stick to it, I'm right, this is desperately important, I've got to find out the truth. . . .*

And the second voice won.

She opened the bedroom door a crack, so that she could just see the top of the stairs, and sat down on the floor to wait.

The sound of voices and the music from some TV show came from the front room. Occasionally a car drove past, its headlights sweeping across the ceiling of the landing. There was nothing from Helen's room but silence. Ginny had the feeling that she'd locked her door.

She sat back more comfortably, so that her legs wouldn't get cramped. A long time went by. Benny came up and went to the bathroom, tried Helen's door, made a face, and went down again. A little later, another man came up to visit the bathroom. Ginny could smell the beer as he went past the door. *Drink more*, she thought. *Go on, drink lots.*

And finally Joe Chicago himself came up the stairs. She heard his voice in the downstairs hall and kept pressed against the wall in the dark as the heavy steps came up the staircase and along the landing, as the thunderous splashing came from the bathroom.

Ginny stood up slowly. Her heart was thumping so hard it hurt. She heard him come out of the bathroom and pulled open the bedroom door to face him.

He stopped in surprise.

He was only a yard or so away. She'd forgotten how big he was, that monstrous bull-like mass, that bloated head. His red-rimmed eyes glared at her hotly.

Before he could speak she put a finger to her lips and stood aside, beckoning him into the dark bedroom. Slowly, like a wary animal, he walked in, and then she shut the door, committing herself to the dark with him.

"What d'you want?" he said after a second.

She could sense him beside her. She could smell him, the gross bulk of him, and into her mind came a picture of the broken bridge, the car, the abandoned baby.

Then something happened to Ginny.

She felt a blow inside her head, and then *she* was thrust aside, and there was someone in there with her. She struggled briefly against it, feeling dizzy and terrified, but it was no good: he was stronger by far. He was deadly and powerful and godlike: dark glasses, a top hat, a ragged coat: skeletons, corpses: Baron Samedi . . . She'd boasted that he'd help her, and here he was, and the room was drenched with fear, terrible panic fear.

She felt Joe Chicago take a step backward: he was afraid too.

She whispered, "Give me your jacket."

And it wasn't her voice. It was nasal, mocking, horrible; it spoke out of graves and cemeteries, out of the land of death.

"Give me your jacket," it said again.

The jacket? Ginny was helpless. What did Baron Samedi want the jacket for? There was nothing she could do except hold on faintly and watch; he was out of control. She'd never been so frightened in her life.

Joe was cowering against the wall. "What for? Who are you? What the bloody hell d'you want with me?"

In the dim light through the window, she could see the glitter of his red-rimmed eyes in a bulk of shadow.

"You've got to give it to me," she found herself saying. "You know why? You know what'll happen if you don't?" The fear was constricting her throat. She was losing altogether any sense of who she was. Ginny, that little identity so permanent and important a minute ago, was fading and vanishing, and there was the god in her place, the *loa*, Baron Samedi, mighty and terrible. "You know what'll happen if you don't?" said his voice, a singsong of death. "The spirits will get you, Joe. The ghosts will get you. The baby's ghost. The baby in the car. You remember that, Joe? The little baby freezing in the car? She wants the jacket back. She's been waiting long enough. Her ghost is here in the room with us. She's only an arm's length away from your heart, she's going to reach for it with her icy hands and take hold of it and squeeze hard, and you'll feel a pain in all your limbs, you'll feel the ice crushing your heart, you'll feel everything freezing inside you—"

"Shut up!" he bellowed. "Shut your bloody mouth, bitch!" and then she was Ginny again and she thought: *Oh, thank God he's broken the spell. What was I doing, what was happening?*

And then he tore off the jacket and flung it at her feet and turned away. "Go on! Go on! Take it! You want it, take the bloody thing! Leave me alone!"

And in the stale darkness of the little room she stooped and picked it up, and then she was out of the room and down the stairs and away, breathing the clean air of the night, tears running down her cheeks.

SHE didn't stop till she reached the parking lot by the harbor, where she was going to meet Dafydd. The lights in Davy Jones's Locker, the voices from the pub, music from one of the boats in the harbor where they were having a party—it was all real, and she didn't believe any of it.

Clutching the bulky jacket to her chest, she sat on the low wall and tried to work out what had happened, trembling in the mist of fear that still clung around her. Out of nowhere a god had come into her head. It was what happened in voodoo, Stuart had said; the gods came down and possessed the worshippers. It was her fault: she'd asked for it. *I'll make him. Me and Baron Samedi, we'll make him. . . .* He'd heard, and he'd come.

And she was still half in his world, half in a moonlit cemetery, shivering as the ragged top-hatted figure in the dark glasses grinned and jested with her. He'd come to help her. But did she want help like that? What price would she have to pay?

144

And the jacket—that had been the *loa's* idea. She hadn't had the slightest notion about that; she'd been as surprised as Joe. What on earth was she going to do with it?

She heard the familiar rattle of Dafydd's car and saw it stopping on the far side. She stood up and waved, and then stepped over the wall and made her way across.

"Okay?" he said. "What you got there? You nicked his jacket?"

She nodded and got in beside him. He had the top down, and his greasy hair was all swept back by the wind. He moved off quickly; a left turn, another left, a traffic circle, and then there was nothing but the railroad crossing and the toll bridge and then the long flat road home under the bright moon.

"You happy now?" said Dafydd after a mile.

"What?" She hadn't heard him. It was cold in the open-topped car, with only her T-shirt on and the sweat drying on her arms and breast. She pulled the jacket around her shoulders and shrugged herself into its warmth.

12

A Journey

THE JACKET was dark brown, cracked and stained, with a heavy zipper and a high collar and a thick sheepskin lining. A greasy, barely legible label over the inside breast pocket said that it had been made by Schwartz Brothers of Chicago. It could have been a flying jacket, as Andy's version of the story said; it would certainly have been the ideal thing to wrap a baby in to keep it warm on a winter's night.

On Sunday morning, Ginny pored over it for hours. She wrapped it around her pillow and drew it from every angle; she turned the pockets inside out, finding nothing but a couple of old bus tickets; and she wondered what on earth she was going to do with it. What did Baron Samedi want it for? The idea came to her of burning it, taking it up to Gwynant on a winter's night and setting fire to it, as a sacrifice to propitiate the spirit of the lost dead child.

It was all confused in her mind with the slip she'd made when she was talking to Helen: *He wrapped me up in it.* If she was the baby, what did that make the jacket? Her mother?

And in the meantime, she must keep away from Joe

Chicago. She still wasn't entirely sure what had happened in the spare room at Jubilee Terrace; it had been terrifying to feel her own personality shrinking and disappearing, brushed aside so easily by something stronger and far more ancient. Now she couldn't think which would be worse: to face Joe Chicago on her own, or to face him with that god in her head. Either way would be horrible. Like Andy, she'd just have to keep away from him.

LATER that day, she quarreled with Robert.

It was Dad who was the cause of it, because Ginny and Robert would never have spoken to each other if he hadn't suggested that they all go out in the boat he'd just bought. The two of them had reached a silent accommodation by this time; half-unconsciously they'd maneuvered themselves into a position where the first one to make a friendly approach would have admitted being the weaker, so now they ignored each other as much as possible, which was at least a way of getting by.

But when, after lunch, Dad, sounding a little desperate, suggested a trip in the boat, Robert rolled his eyes and groaned. Ginny noticed, and a savage instinct made her want to attack him at once; but she held back, and said, "No, thanks, Dad. I was going to see Rhiannon this afternoon. She'll be expecting me."

"Bring her too," he said.

"Not this time. She'll be seasick or something stupid. Next time, I promise."

So he went off alone, leaving Ginny and Robert together. As soon as Dad had left, she turned on Robert like a tiger.

"You don't have to be so bloody rude, rolling your eyes like that. He's only doing it for you—don't you realize that?"

They were in the garden, he in the hammock as usual,

she standing tensely nearby. He looked up from his book—
a cold look, direct, fully awake, charged.

"What about you last night?"

"What about me?" Ginny didn't know what he could
mean. "We're not talking about me. We're talking about
him and what he's trying to do."

"Oh, he's a saint, is he? He's like you, is he? He's perfect?"

"What's that supposed to mean?"

"It means stop bloody patronizing me and telling me
how to behave."

"Someone needs to."

"Why? You think I've got worse manners than you, you
snooty bitch? You've been looking down your nose at me
ever since I came."

"I have not!"

"You don't think you have, no, probably not. It's unconscious. You're so sure of how superior you are, it comes
off you like a stink, you know that?"

If she hadn't been holding herself in, tense and quivering, she'd have gasped. Instead she flared back, "So lying
about in the hammock expecting people to wait on you
hand and foot, so never lifting a finger to help get the food
or wash the dishes, that makes you a *democrat* or something, does it? And as for being superior, you're so bloody
superior we're not even allowed to know about your mother;
she's hidden in mystery; we're all supposed to *bow* or
something—"

"My mother?" He was sitting up now, his feet on the
ground on either side keeping the hammock still. "You
want to know something about my mother? All right, I'll
tell you this: she was *clean,* she was *proud,* you could
come into our house and never find dirty cups and plates
lying about, dust all over everything, dirty windows, a filthy

kitchen—God, I hate eating what comes out of the oven in there, it's so thick with filth and grease. She was strong, my mother, she had principles, that's why she wouldn't have anything to do with *him* after he went sniffing round *your* mother. I bet she was a—"

"Don't you *dare* say anything about her! You don't know *anything!* Cleaning the oven? Washing the windows? Christ, is that all you think women are for? You do, don't you! She probably brought you up like that! She probably waited on you like a servant, just because you were a *boy*; she probably had nothing else in her head but running round after you, picking up your dirty socks, being a *slave.* . . . Pathetic. At least my mother was an artist. At least she *thought* about things. She had a talent, she had a gift—"

"That's just what I mean, isn't it? There you go again, looking down on people! Your mum the great artist—so bloody what? Does that make anyone a better person, being a pissy *artist?* Does it? If you go about thinking that . . . well, Christ, it's no wonder everyone thinks you're such a snob, talking down to them—"

"What? *What?* Who thinks I'm a snob?"

"All your friends. Can't you tell? No, you probably can't; you're too high and mighty. Everyone else just looks small to you, probably, they're *amusing* in their little way, or *picturesque,* or *pitiful,* so you patronize them or give them a little bit of your attention, as if you've got something else more important to do but you're so wonderful you manage to fit them in anyway and give them the benefit of your wonderfulness—"

"What the hell are you talking about, Robert? Are you mad or something? This is just—I don't know *what* you're talking about. It's not *me* you're thinking about at all. I just don't recognize—"

"Well, bad luck, you better learn to. Probably no one's told you; they probably feel sorry for you for being so pathetic," he spat.

Ginny felt as if she were going to break in half.

"I don't know why he took you in," she said. "I'll never know why. You're just poison. You've got nothing to do with me, you don't want anything to do with him, and you don't *know* him—God, you don't *know* the effort he's making because he feels responsible to you. Okay, so you're not interested in the bloody boat, but you ought to *pretend.* . . . You know what you are? You're—"

"I don't need you to tell me who I am! At least he married my mother!"

"And *left* her, and I'm not surprised, if she spent all her time cleaning and polishing. God, how stupid! You know what you are? I'm going to tell you even if you don't want to hear—you're *nothing*. You're negative. You're a blank space full of hate, that's all you are. You don't do *anything*. So really I don't care a *shit* what you say about me, because at the end of the day at least I . . . at least I . . . At least I'm *trying*, I'm not just negative—"

"How do you know what I do, what I don't do?" he flared at her. "You just assume that no one else but you's got any talent for anything. You know what? You've got a total contempt for anyone who isn't like you, d'you know that?"

"*Contempt?* What are you *talking* about, for God's sake?"

"You. I'm telling you what you're like. Everything's got to be on your terms. You're the most arrogant person I've ever met. You never show the slightest interest—"

"Yeah, and what happens when I do? You remember when I tried to talk to you, when you first came? All you did was lose your temper. I tried to make conversation, and you just got angry. Turning on me like a bloody pit bull or something. How long is a person supposed to go on trying? Or maybe I'm supposed to know all about you by *telepathy*, is that it? You give out *waves* or something—we're all supposed to pick them up without you having to soil yourself by talking? You make me sick, Robert. You and your mother, you both . . ."

She stopped. They were only a yard or so apart, she with her fists clenched, he still straddling the hammock. His face was tight with misery, his eyes glittering, and the tension in his shoulders was making his whole body shake. Suddenly she found, to her consternation and embarrassment, that her eyes were full of tears and that all the fury that had welled up from nowhere had drained away.

"This is stupid," she muttered.

"You started it."

"You did, actually. If you hadn't . . ."

The words ran out. She shrugged.

He looked down, ran his fingers through his hair. Then he wiped his eyes with the back of his hand.

"I don't understand you," she said.

"Nothing to understand. You said it."

"Yeah, but I didn't mean that. I meant . . . Oh, I just meant . . ." She sighed, terribly weary suddenly, and speaking the next words with a great effort: "I just meant I can't understand you. Because . . . I don't *know* anything about you or your mother; I didn't even know you existed. It's no good asking Dad. If he's kept you secret from me all this time, and me from you . . . well, I can't trust him anymore. Can't you see?"

He was still looking down. He bit savagely at a thumbnail and spat it out.

"She didn't tell me, either," he said. "I don't know any more than you do. I don't reckon there's any point in talking. It's a waste of breath. We've got nothing in common, we never will have. I'm not sure I want anything in common with you anyway."

He swung his leg over the hammock and walked away. She watched him go, stifling the words that came to mind, words of appeal. She hadn't meant this to happen, she thought, but then she shook her head angrily at her own dishonesty: she'd meant something to happen, hadn't she? She'd wanted a fight, and she'd got one, and been hurt. Tough. Put up with it.

SHE brooded all the rest of the day over what he'd said, worrying at it like a dog for the scraps of truth that clung to it; because it couldn't all be true, she thought, surely. The idea of herself as a smug, patronizing snob was too painful to be borne. And it didn't *matter* that the house wasn't brilliantly clean, did it? Only to people with tiny minds who thought housework was important; or was that an example of her snobbery?

She was horribly confused and horribly unhappy, and the only thing that made it slightly better than it might have been was the realization that both she and Robert had held back from the final words that would have meant death, war, destruction, eternal hatred. The fact that she was black and he was white had no bearing on what they'd been quarreling about, but it might have come up, and it hadn't.

As she went to bed she found another disagreeable feeling slink in and join all the others, and that was fear. If the *loa*—the gods of voodoo—could come so abruptly and fiercely as Baron Samedi had done the night before, what was to stop them from coming again? Had she opened some channel for them to use whenever they felt like it? What had she done? Was she entirely crazy?

EARLY next morning, just after Dad had gone to work, Ginny was in the kitchen fixing breakfast when the phone rang. She jumped with fright. Eventually, reluctantly, she picked it up.

"Hello?"

"Ginny. Hello. It's Wendy Stevens. Are you alone? Can we talk?"

"Yeah . . . Yeah! Fine! Dad's at work, and . . . Yeah."

"How's Robert?"

Ginny paused. Robert was still in bed; they hadn't spoken since the quarrel. "All right," she said.

"I see. Well, listen, I've got some news for you. I'm not sure if I should be doing this—actually, I am sure, and I shouldn't. Did you know you'd been fostered?"

"What? Fostered? When? D'you mean I'm not—d'you mean that Dad's—"

"No, no, you're not fostered now. It was a long time ago—twelve, fourteen years or so. You don't remember?"

"No! God, no!"

"Well, never mind. You might remember, and that's my excuse. You know you told me about a trailer? And a woman called Maeve? And some woods where someone had been murdered?"

"Yes . . . go on. . . ."

"Well, that reminded me of something, and I looked it up. There's a place not far from here called Staunton Chase, a wild sort of wood, and there was a big murder hunt there, oh, fifteen years ago. I thought it might have been there. So I asked a friend who works in the Social Services Department there. He's been there for a long time, knows everyone. . . . Anyway, I told him about Maeve, and he recognized her at once. Her name's Mrs. Sullivan. Apparently she does a lot of short-term fostering, especially for a Catholic home in the area; she's done it for years. He gave me her phone number, and I rang her up."

"And . . . what did she say?"

"Well, she must've looked after hundreds of kids over the years. She didn't remember you at first, but then it came back. She said you were a difficult child."

"Me? Why?"

"She said you used to scribble over everything. And there was something about makeup; I couldn't understand it. . . ."

"I know what she means! I found it in the trailer and . . . But where was Dad? Why was I being fostered in the first place?"

"She didn't remember. She might not have known. There'd be no reason for her to."

"Fostered . . . I don't believe it. Well, I do believe it, but why hasn't he told me?"

"I don't know, love. There's no way you're going to find out unless you ask him."

Ginny said nothing. There was another way, and she'd just thought of it, but she didn't want to tell Wendy.

"Well," she said. "Thanks."

"You've got my number if you want to get in touch?"

"Yeah. You gave me a card."

"Okay, then. I'll keep looking, see if I can find out anything else. But you're going to have to talk to him in the end."

Ginny put the phone down, and hesitated, and then ran up to bang on Robert's door.

"What?" His voice was angry, wide awake.

She opened the door. He was lying fully clothed on the bed, hands behind his head.

"D'you want to find out the truth?" she demanded.

"The truth about what?"

"Us, of course. What you were saying yesterday. D'you want to find out or not?"

He sat up. "How?"

"We've got to go *now* if you do. There's a train in ten minutes. You coming or not?"

"Where?"

"Chester."

He shrugged. He was watching her carefully. "All right."

"Hurry, then. See you downstairs."

She ran to her room, grabbed her rucksack, shoved a few things in it, stuffed the jacket on top, and took all the money she'd earned. She scribbled a note: *Gone out with Robert—back sometime*, and left it on the kitchen table; then she locked the back door and ran to the front, where Robert was waiting.

He looked at her rucksack. "How long is this going to take?"

"As long as it takes. Come *on*—there's no time to hang about."

AT PORTHAFON they ran to the bus station, where there was a departure for Liverpool and Chester at eleven o'clock. They caught the bus with a minute to spare. Ginny, who had been shaking with nerves as they ran through the town in case she saw Joe Chicago, found herself relaxing as the bus pulled out and began to climb into the hills. She and Robert hadn't spoken on the train, but now they had three and a half hours to get through before the bus stopped in Chester. Ginny was sitting next to the window on the left, with her rucksack on the empty seat beside her, Robert across the aisle on the right. She was glad they weren't forced to sit any closer.

"What's in Chester, then?" he said finally.

"Dad's parents. Our grandparents."

He frowned, puzzled.

"They'll know what happened, won't they?" she said impatiently. "They know about me anyway, because I stayed with them once when I was a tiny kid. God knows why. But they'll know all about your mum and everything; they're bound to. So we'll go and ask them."

"He's never mentioned them," he said.

"No; he doesn't talk about them. There's too bloody much he doesn't talk about, and I'm sick of it. I just heard this morning . . . that phone call was Wendy Stevens, the social worker. She told me that I'd been fostered when I was younger. I never knew. I mean, I don't mind or anything, but I ought to bloody know, I reckon."

She was watching him closely, and she saw an honest bewilderment slowly growing. *All right*, she thought. *I don't like him, I'll never like him, but we're both in the same boat, Dad's messed us both up.*

And, briefly, a flicker of understanding passed between them, and what they understood was that this journey was a time out of battle, a time of truce.

She hesitated, and moved the rucksack onto her lap. He hesitated, and moved across to sit next to her. She began to tell him everything: Maeve and the trailer, Helen's first query about whether their father had been in prison, *Modern Painters* and the exhibition of her mother's paintings, Joe Chicago's jacket, Wendy's phone call.

At the end of it she said, "Whatever it is he's done, I don't care, I can forgive him for it, but I can't forgive him for not telling me. Telling us."

"This prison business," he said. "I can't believe it. You don't think it's got something to do with the murder in the woods—what's it called—Staunton Chase? You don't think he . . ."

"Course I've thought that. Of course I have. He's not a

156

violent person, but who knows, Joe Chicago is, and if they knew each other and he got mixed up in something . . . I just don't know."

"You think these grandparents will know who we are?"

"Course they will. You'll see."

"They might not want to tell us anything, though."

"They will. They'll have to."

A LONG, hot journey, and then they had to buy a street map from a newsstand in order to look up their way to Grove Road. They found a bus that took them to the nearest shop, next to a row of shops in neat 1930s brick, a wool shop and a florist's and a dress shop, all looking as if nothing had changed for fifty years. Grove Road, leading off the row of shops, was just as well preserved. Semidetached houses, tidy gardens, net curtains; and stillness, on that blazing afternoon, without even the sound of sprinklers on lawns now that water was scarce, the very insects stunned into silence by the heat.

Number 16 was as obsessively neat and trim as all the rest. Two rosebushes stood inside the white-painted fence, and the paving stones that surrounded them had been swept and dusted. Ginny found herself thinking: *I remember those rosebushes,* but she knew she didn't; she could remember very little. She looked at Robert, whose eyes were screwed up against the glare off the road.

"Ready?" she said.

"They can only tell us to get lost," he said. "They can't kill us or anything. . . ."

It sounded as if he was reassuring himself rather than her.

"That's right," she said, and went up the little path and rang the bell.

Footsteps, a shadow behind the opaque glass; they caught each other's eye and exchanged a faint smile. Then their grandmother opened the door.

157

13

Golden Years

SHE WAS in her sixties, stooped, gray-haired, with a closed, unhappy expression. She frowned at the two of them suspiciously.

"Mrs. Howard?" Ginny said.

The woman nodded. "Yes?" she said.

"Er . . . could we come in for a minute? It's a bit hard to explain. . . ."

She looked over her shoulder doubtfully. "Well, what's it about?" she said, looking at Robert with no more friendliness than she'd shown Ginny.

"It's a family matter," he said.

Then her eyes flicked back to Ginny, and slowly at first and then suddenly, the realization flooded through her, changing her expression like a blush. One second she was closed up and dour, the next alert, and animated, and frightened.

"It's Virginia," she whispered.

Ginny nodded. Her grandmother was holding the door tight as if to stop herself from falling. She looked at Robert again, and Ginny said, "And my brother. Robert."

"Janet's boy?"

"Yes," he said. "Can we come in?"

She looked overwhelmed, unable to move. There was a sound from behind her, and they looked past, down the hall and through the kitchen, and saw a man standing there, looking at them from outside the back door.

"Who is it?" he called.

"It's—" she began, then hastened back to speak to him from the kitchen door: "It's Virginia! And Janet's boy!"

"Shut the door, then," they heard him say urgently, as if the most important thing was to keep the neighbors from seeing. Ginny looked at Robert: did that mean they were going to be asked in, or not?

But their grandmother was back almost at once and urging them in. She shut the door hastily behind them. In the kitchen, their grandfather was standing on a sheet of newspaper and taking off his shoes before putting slippers on.

"Have you come from . . . ? Where's . . . ? Is your father . . . ?" She was nearly whispering in her confusion and emotion.

"No; he's at home," Ginny said, finding her own voice weaker than she'd expected. "He doesn't know we're here."

"And Janet . . . My God, I don't know what to say. Is she . . . ?"

"She's dead," said Robert. "She died last month."

"Oh, my dear . . . Ken? Did you hear? Janet's . . ."

He'd arrived in the hall by then, a heavy, quiet-looking man, with something of Dad's good looks but with a constant gnawing weakness about the mouth. Like his wife, he was utterly bewildered, quite unable to decide how to behave, what was the appropriate social form to adopt. Ginny felt that any naturalness had withered and died in them long before, and that if there was no established ritual to follow, they were lost, like children.

"Shall we—" she said, and he said simultaneously, "Why

159

don't we—" and she was opening the door of the front room, and Ginny and Robert went through.

Now Ginny began to remember things. The smell: wax polish, potpourri; the little carriage clock on the mantelpiece; the faded pink of the loose covers on the furniture. There was one picture on the wall—a woodland scene in a pretentious gilt frame, of the sort sold by the thousand in the furniture departments of large stores. No other pictures, no books, no records; just a hideous china cart horse with leather reins standing on the windowsill, and the TV set in the corner, with a lace doily on top of it and a little brass pot of artificial flowers.

She looked around, Robert close beside her, and heard whispering outside the door. A moment later their grandfather came in.

"Well . . . Sit down, sit down," he said. "Make yourselves at home, come on. . . . How old are you now, Virginia? Eh?"

"Sixteen," she said, sitting on the sofa. Robert sat next to her.

"And you . . . er . . ."

"Robert. I'm sixteen too."

"Ah. Yes . . . Getting on all right at school?"

She nodded. He shrugged. "All right, I suppose," he said.

"Good. That's the style."

He sat down heavily in the armchair by the fireplace.

"Have you had some tea?" he said.

"No," said Ginny. "We came straight here from the bus station."

"Grandma's getting some now. Soon be ready. Have you . . . come a long way?"

"Yeah. From home."

"And . . . where's . . . ?"

"You don't know where we live?"

He shook his head.

"Llangynog," Robert said. "In Wales."

"Oh, Wales? And your father, has he . . . he's not coming with you?"

"He doesn't know we're here. This was our idea," said Ginny, looking at Robert. "We thought we'd just like to find out about things. We didn't tell him. So . . . I found out your address and we just came. That's it, really."

"Ah. Yes. Right. Well, it's a big surprise, naturally; we're not prepared or anything. . . . You're a big girl now, Virginia; I'd never have recognized you. And your mother? How's she getting on these days?"

He wouldn't look either of them in the eye, or if he did, he'd look away after a second and direct his gaze over their shoulders or above their heads, so it wasn't clear whom this last question was directed to. Ginny and Robert looked at each other, and then Robert looked back at him and said, "Mum's dead. She died a short while ago. That's why I'm living with Dad and Ginny, you see."

"Oh! I'm sorry. I didn't grasp what she was saying out there, what she was going to say. . . . My dear boy, I— I'm very sorry to hear about that. She'd been ill, had she? Or . . . ?"

"Yes," Robert said. "She'd been ill for a few months."

"Ah," he said. "And what about your grandmother? Kitty? I heard that Janet's father had, er, passed away a few years back, but . . ."

"She lives in Spain now," Robert said. "She married someone with a lot of money. She sort of lost touch with us, I think."

Hearing him talk like this was a revelation to Ginny, and to hear him refer to her by name and call her Ginny and not Virginia, as their grandparents were doing, made it almost worth coming all this way.

"What should we call you?" she said into the little silence.

"Oh, I should think it would have to be Granddad, don't you? And Grandma."

"Because, you see, there're a lot of things we don't know. And we really came here to see if you could tell us. . . ." Ginny trailed off as the door opened.

"I expect you'd like to wash your hands," said their grandmother. "D'you remember where it is, Virginia?"

"No. Sorry. I was only four or something. . . ."

"Oh, less than that, I think," said Grandma, showing her the way.

Well, Robert should like this house, Ginny thought in the bathroom. Every corner of it was obsessively clean, the windows sparkled, the water in the lavatory was blue and foaming, two neatly folded towels hung side by side on the rack. Despite the cleanliness, there was a closed-up, unused feeling in the air, as if no one had visited the house for years, no one had trodden the carpets or drawn the curtains or looked out the windows but that silent, awkward, broken couple downstairs. And everything was so *ugly*. Didn't they have any idea how ugly it was? Or was that just her snobbery again?

She passed Robert on the stairs, and he blew out his cheeks and rolled his eyes, obviously finding it as difficult as she was.

Grandma was standing by another door, which Ginny vaguely remembered led into the dining room. The layout of the house was coming back to her, but it all seemed so small, so cramped. Grandma smiled, and Ginny smiled back, nervous formal smiles both of them, and then to her surprise her grandmother gave her a brief tight hug and then stepped away quickly. Ginny had no time to respond.

In the few minutes since they'd arrived, Grandma had laid the dining room table with a tablecloth, a silver teapot, cups and saucers, a plate of bread and butter, a cake, biscuits. . . . It was as if it had been ready and waiting for years.

Ginny, fighting her shyness, said, "I can hardly remember what it was like, being here before."

"Well, you weren't here for long; just a few days. And then your daddy came and took you away, and . . . that was that," she said with an attempt at brightness. "How is he? Is he all right?"

"Yeah, he's fine. He's—you know—working and things. He bought a boat last week. We haven't actually been out in it yet."

"Oh, a boat, eh?" said Granddad, who'd come in quietly.

"Is he . . . did he ever marry again?" said Grandma.

"Oh, no. No. See, he was never divorced from Robert's mum," Ginny said.

They both nodded wisely, as if they'd expected something of the sort, but Ginny could tell they were surprised.

Granddad turned to the door. "Here's the boy," he said, with a fragile heartiness. "Come and sit down. We'll have some tea, eh?"

"Expect you're hungry," said Grandma as they all sat down. "Come a long way."

"How did you get here?" said Granddad. "On the train?"

"No. There aren't any trains. On a bus," Ginny said.

"Oh, so you said, yes, the bus station . . ."

Polite, empty words, formal teatime courtesy: have a biscuit, let me cut you some cake, would you like some

163

more tea. It seemed to go on forever. Ginny knew that Robert felt as she did, that he wanted to bang the table and shake their stupid old tortoise heads and shout, *Tell us the truth, for God's sake!* And, like her, he was reining it in for Dad's sake—being polite to Dad's parents out of consideration for him.

Finally she'd had enough.

"Look, *please*," she said, "we want to ask you about Dad and everything, that's why we've come. Because Robert and I, we don't know anything about the family.
. . . I mean, I didn't know anything about Robert till a few weeks ago, I'd never heard of him, even, and I thought my mother was married to Dad. I never dreamed any of it would be like it is, and then I remembered being here when I was little, and I thought you'd probably know. . . ."

Her voice trailed off. They were sitting like sculptures: Robert looking down at his plate, Granddad gazing fixedly at the wall, Grandma with her eyes closed altogether. It was as if they'd all lost the use of sight but Ginny, and she was looking from one to the other, her eyes doing the asking that her voice had given up, and feeling herself hot-cheeked with embarrassment. Why did they have to behave like this? Was she different again, inwardly as well as visibly?

But then Robert helped her.

He looked up and said, "Yeah. That's right. See, Mum—my mother—she never told me anything. About you or about Dad. Nothing. It was just as if you—he'd—never existed. And I didn't know about Ginny, either. So I never knew Dad, and I don't know him now, really, not to ask about things. And Ginny can't ask him because he never told her about me, so we're both in the dark."

"And you're the only people we can ask," Ginny added.

"That's why we came. We won't tell him about it, if you don't want us to."

After a moment their grandmother said, "Is he treating you all right?"

Granddad shifted as if he was uncomfortable. Ginny nodded. Robert said, "Yeah. He's very . . . kind. But we just want to know where we come from."

That was so exactly what Ginny wanted that she could only look at him and nod eagerly. Then Granddad put both hands on the table and stood up.

"Let's go in the front room," he said. "We'll be more comfortable in there. Can't talk comfortably at the tea table. . . ."

IT HAD begun just after the war. Granddad had a great friend, Arthur Weaver, and when they left the army, they set up a little business together, selling motor parts, and then within a month of each other they both got married. Granddad and Grandma—Ken and Dorothy—and Arthur and Kitty became inseparable. They went to the cinema together; they took turns giving each other dinner every weekend after which they'd play bridge; they shared holidays; borrowed each other's lawn mowers and power drills and slide projectors; even took up the same hobbies—golf, camping, wine-making. When Tony was born to Dorothy, and Janet six months later to Kitty, it seemed as if some kind of seal had been set on this wonderful friendship. It was a golden time, Granddad said, and Grandma said separately that they were golden years. . . .

Ginny listened to this recital with powerful curiosity. This was where she came from—half of her: this narrow, prim, cozy, insufferably complacent world of bridge parties and polishing the car and pruning the roses and unfailingly voting Conservative. It was like another planet.

But nothing was more alien to her than that friendship, the obsessive repetition of Arthur and Kitty, Arthur and Kitty, Arthur and Kitty. It was more than a friendship; it was more like a four-way marriage, and Ginny, used to the casual independent freedom she shared with Dad, felt oppressed and claustrophobic as she thought about it. It wasn't natural; it was asking for trouble.

Clearly, though, it had been the biggest thing in Granddad's life, at least. Ginny wasn't so sure about her grandmother; there was something hooded, shadowed, about her manner as she nodded and echoed his words, as if for her there'd been a question at the heart of it all. But she joined in as he got out some photograph albums, with dozens upon dozens of pictures carefully dated and labeled: Arthur and Kitty at Blackpool, Dad as a little boy with a tricycle, Dad in school uniform, Granddad and Arthur playing golf, Dad and Janet . . .

Robert was gazing at the pictures of his mother, his eyes fierce, as if he wanted to drag her back to life. To Ginny's mind she looked willful: dark and pretty and strong-minded, with a tight set to her lips.

"And as time went by," Granddad was saying, "well, we all assumed it would just be the natural thing if the two of them, in the fullness of time, if they were to marry. . . ."

"We never pushed them into it," said Grandma.

"Oh, Lord, no. Absolutely not. It was always understood that they were free to do as they pleased, no pressure on them at all, free agents."

"I know Arthur and Kitty both wanted it, though," she said. "They said so more than once."

"Well, so did we," he said. "No point in denying it."

They were silent for a moment. Then Granddad opened another photograph album.

"Here we are," he said. "The wedding."

"Oh, it was such a happy day," said Grandma. "Everything about it seemed to be blessed, somehow."

The formal clothes, a young Dad with his hair long, Janet queenly and proud, screwing up her eyes against the sun . . .

"It's the bride's parents' place to lay on the wedding, of course," said Granddad, "but we'd gone shares in everything else, we couldn't hold back now. We gave them a wonderful wedding, honeymoon in Tenerife. Then . . . just a short while afterward, it all seemed to go wrong."

"Did Janet . . . did your mum ever talk about those days?" said Grandma delicately to Robert.

"No. Not a word. Honest, I've never heard any of this before. She was very . . . she kept herself to herself, I suppose. We never talked much about anything."

"How did it go wrong?" Ginny asked Granddad.

"Well . . . we still don't know all the details. Because he didn't speak to us, you see. We knew something was going wrong. First thing we knew was Arthur . . ."

"He came to us one day," said Grandma. "Janet had gone home to him and Kitty with some terrible story Tony—your dad—had suddenly told her. Arthur was shaken. He was white, he was . . . We'd never seen him in a state like that."

Granddad nodded. "Naturally Janet wouldn't, she couldn't, well, she, she didn't want anything to do with him anymore, didn't want to see him again, it was all over."

"Broke our hearts," she said.

"Arthur had to come and speak to us on her behalf. Painful. Terrible time."

Ginny was lost. So, she saw, was Robert, who turned to her, frowning in puzzlement. She said, "But why? I don't get it. Dad had gone to his wife, Robert's mum, and he'd told her some terrible story and she wouldn't speak to him anymore? What was this terrible story? It wasn't the car crash, was it? The broken bridge?"

That was a helpless guess. They looked blank, and Grandma shook her head.

"Car crash?" said Granddad. "I'm sorry, my dear, I don't know what you mean. No, it was the old story: it was the other woman. It was your mother. We had no idea; we were knocked sideways by it. Came right out of the blue."

"He wanted Janet to adopt . . ." Grandma began, but went no further.

"Yes, when your mother left you there with the nuns," Granddad said, "he wanted Janet to agree to—"

"What? *Left* me? Left me with the nuns? What nuns?"

"The nuns in the children's home."

"But what d'you mean, *left* me there? I thought she died."

"Well . . ." They looked at each other, alarmed at Ginny's tone.

Then Granddad said, "If that's what he told you, then I'm sure that's . . . You see, we weren't in any position to know; we had it all via Arthur. Tony wanted Janet to agree to adopt you, you see, make it look decent, you know, put a decent face on it, but she said no. Wouldn't budge, wouldn't buy it. Not at any price. So there they were. Breaking up over a thing like that. Not that Tony told us. It all came via Arthur. He—Arthur, I mean—he was very bitter, very cut up about it."

Breaking up over a thing like that, Ginny thought. *So I'm a thing like that. Nice to know at last. A thing like that.*

"Of course, it was the end for the firm," Granddad went on. "Put the skids under the partnership. Thirty years of friendship, lying in ruins . . . Arthur bought out my share of the firm, and shortly after that he sold the whole shoot, the whole boiling. Made a tidy sum. I don't know, I'm not bitter exactly, but . . . We'd see them sometimes, Arthur and Kitty. They'd just pass by without a word. Not the slightest flicker. It was as if those thirty years had never happened. Just been a dream."

That seemed to be the end, as far as they were concerned. They sat looking down at the floor in the furniture-polished silence.

"But . . . what happened then?" said Ginny. "I mean, what about me—what did Dad do? And these nuns—how long was I with them?"

The old couple looked at each other. It was a complicated look: there was a sort of furtive anxiety in it, and guilt, and even a sly I-told-you-so triumph—but which feeling came from which partner, Ginny couldn't have said.

"We don't rightly know," said Granddad. "Tony, your dad, well, he just took off. Left his wife and—" He looked at Robert, and then away again; his eyes never rested on anyone for long. "Well, we thought, naturally, he'd gone off with his fancy woman. Your mother. Left you in the children's home, done a runner. There was no sign, no word from him, nothing."

"But she was dead!" Ginny said again. "And he wouldn't have just *left* me there! It's not like him. I mean, I *know* him, after all. He's not like that. . . ."

But I was fostered, she found herself thinking. *He must have left me sometime. And why do they keep talking about Maman as if she was alive? They're not telling the truth. I don't believe them. They're all liars in this family.*

"What about when Ginny stayed here?" asked Robert, coming to her aid.

"Yes," she said. "Did the nuns bring me here? Or what? I thought it was him, but I can't remember."

Then a strange thing began to happen. Ginny sensed it, and she knew that Robert did too: a change in the atmosphere as instant and definite as if a spotlight had been switched on. She wouldn't have been surprised if there'd been an audible click.

The effect was that her grandmother had suddenly become the focus of the room, like a surprise witness in a murder trial. She hadn't said a word or moved a muscle, but something invisible, some emotional charge—guilt, anger—had leapt to her like a spark crossing a gap and changed her personality. It was a different woman looking out of her eyes, and Ginny quailed.

"That was cruel," said Grandma in a new, louder voice.

Ginny thought: *What? What I said was cruel? Or something else?* Her scalp crawled with a sort of sickening embarrassment.

But Grandma was going on: "We were doing our best. It wasn't much to offer. God knows, it was all we had, but apparently it wasn't enough. . . ."

Ginny was aware of her grandfather sitting up in his chair, his face full of fear. Something bad was in the air.

"But what about my mother?" she said shakily.

The old woman sat up. Her eyes were bright with violence. "Yes," she said, "I'll tell you about her. . . ."

"Dorothy," murmured Granddad.

She turned on him, those eyes full of danger. "Yes, Ken? I was under the impression that Virginia had asked me a question."

He shrank back from the blaze of hatred, nodding, saying, "Yes dear, yes . . ."

"I'm allowed to speak, am I?"

"Of course . . . yes . . ."

Ginny thought: *He's used to this—he's seen her go crazy*

before—he knew it was coming—and now she's going to turn to me—

She did, and Ginny felt a chill at the roots of her soul as those bright eyes found hers. Without knowing how it had happened, she was holding Robert's hand among the sofa cushions, and they clung together like children as Grandma said:

"So I can answer Virginia's question? Well, I'm sorry, dear, but it's got to be said, it's wrong not to tell you, I can't let you live with a stain on your past. It's not a nice word, but I can't help it: your mother is a whore. A black whore. You know what I—"

"A *what?*" Ginny said. "And what d'you mean, *is?*" She thought she wasn't hearing properly. This was impossible, surely.

"Dorothy, please," Granddad whispered.

"Don't you dare interrupt me!" she flared at him. "If you'd had the guts to deal with it at the time, everything would have been all right, but no, leave it to Dorothy, leave it all to Dorothy, that's your motto. Yes, Virginia, God knows it's not your fault, dear, but to think of my boy, my son, my only child, wallowing in colored filth when he had a decent home, a pretty wife, the best background a man could have . . . Well, he'd never have done it if she hadn't tempted him. Stands to reason. She knew a good thing when she saw one, and she grabbed it with both hands. That's her type. If the only way to climb out of the gutter was to steal another woman's husband, then she wouldn't let decency stand in the way. . . ."

The stream of venom continued to pour out, even when Ginny had stood up, even after she'd begun to speak, her shaking voice trying to drown her grandmother's: "Thank you for the tea. It was very nice. I'm sorry I seem to be the wrong color. It must be my mother's fault, like everything else. Spoiling your wonderful golden dream, yes, it must've been horrible for you, but never mind, that's it, I'm going now. Good-bye."

Her grandmother's voice trailed off.

Granddad was trying to get up, but Ginny brushed past him and seized her rucksack from the hall floor. She was fumbling with the front door handle when she heard her grandmother behind her and turned in fury—but the old woman was holding her arms out, just an old woman again, her face blind with tears.

"Virginia—darling—listen: You've always been my dear little grandchild—my first one. If I said anything wrong, I'm sorry, I'm so sorry, I didn't want to offend you. I'm a stupid old woman—stupid. You're my little granddaughter, I love you, I want you to be happy. Is he mistreating you? Is he looking after you? A man can't do it on his own. She shouldn't have left him, it wasn't fair, it wasn't right. My darling, I only want what's best for you. . . ."

And Ginny let herself be hugged and kissed, controlling her disgust at the wetness of tears on her cheek, the smell of stale face powder, the bony looseness of the old woman's body against hers. She stood it for a few seconds and then twisted away. The whole thing was horrible.

"Is she alive?" she demanded. "Is my mother alive?"

"Oh, darling—forget all about her—"

"She is, isn't she? Or are you making it up?"

"Darling, don't say that—stay with us—we'll look after you—she won't want you now—"

Ginny twisted aside and ran out the door and off down the road, trying not to be sick.

THERE was a bus coming; without waiting for Robert, she waved it to a halt, bought a ticket to the town center, sat down trembling.

172

Black whore.
Wallowing in colored filth.

There'd been so many blows, from so many different directions, raining in so suddenly, that Ginny was dazed; and the hardest blow of all was the suggestion that her mother was alive. It was impossible, ridiculous. She dragged *Modern Painters* out of her rucksack and looked again at the advertisement: it merely said "Haitian Painting of the Past Twenty Years," which didn't help at all.

Seeing a railway station, she jumped up impulsively and rang the bell to stop the bus. She felt a faint anxiety about Robert. She'd dragged him all this way; shouldn't she go back and . . .

No. He could find the bus station by himself, surely; for the moment, this was more urgent.

At a phone booth in the station, she dialed the number of the art gallery. There was no answer for a long time, and she began to beat her fist softly against her head.

"Hello. L'Ouverture Gallery."

It was a soft Scottish voice. Ginny, startled by an answer at last, nearly dropped the magazine.

"Oh. Hello. I'm ringing about your exhibition—the paintings from Haiti—"

"Yes. It's opening tomorrow."

"Er . . . one of the painters, Anielle Baptiste . . ."

"Yes?"

"Could you tell me about her work, what you've got there? I mean, I'm a student, you see, and I've seen some of her work before, but only in reproduction. And I'm not here for long. . . ."

"Oh, right. Well, there's a number of paintings from her election series; they haven't been shown here before."

"Election series?"

"She did some pictures based on the Haitian general

election. And there's a quite extraordinary painting called *The Death of Colonel Paul.* It's well worth a visit for that one alone. And some landscapes."

"What election was that?"

"The one they had recently, when it all ended in violence. Two years ago, three maybe. I ought to know—"

"Sorry, when did you say? Two years ago?"

A puzzled laugh. "Yes, that's right. You said you're not in Liverpool for long?"

Ginny was breathless. "Not long, no."

"And you're a student? Well, why don't you come along tonight? We're having a private view, but we're not fussy; it's not formal or anything. Come and join the party. The more the merrier. What's your name?"

"Oh, thanks . . . Ginny Howard. Who would I say told me to come?"

"I'm the owner, Paul Chalmers. I won't forget. You might meet the artist herself. She's coming along later. See you at about seven, then."

Ginny blindly put the phone down. All the golden years had come to this, and there was no going back now.

14

The Death of Colonel Paul

THE L'OUVERTURE GALLERY was situated in a street not far from the docks. Ginny had managed to buy a Liverpool street map at the railway station in Chester before the train left, and she spent the journey alternately poring over it and gazing unseeingly out the train window, smiling from time to time with something that felt absurdly like happiness. The walk from Lime Street Station to the street where the gallery was took twenty minutes. Of Liverpool itself she registered nothing.

She got there at five to seven and made herself stop and look at things in order to calm down. The narrow street seemed to have had three lives, and it still bore traces of each of them: the first as a sternly prosperous area of offices for shipping firms and cotton merchants; the second as a seedy, downmarket collection of flyblown news dealers and dusty tailors' shops; and now its third life was beginning, based on nebulous trendy things like design and lifestyle, with a very expensive clothes shop, an architectural practice, a wine bar, and the L'Ouverture Gallery.

The gallery was a wide glass-fronted place with a display of sculptures in the window. There were paintings on the oatmeal-colored wall, but Ginny couldn't see them clearly from across the street; and there was someone moving about inside.

She crossed the street. Her heart was hammering so hard she thought they must be able to hear it in the wine bar. She looked at a poster on the gallery door advertising the exhibition, and then knocked on the glass. The man inside looked up and waved.

He was in his thirties, plump, wearing the kind of clothes they sold in the expensive shop next door. And he was black, and the moment he spoke, she realized that his was the Scottish voice from the telephone, and she felt surprise, and shame at the white part of her that could be surprised, and a simple curiosity as to whether she herself sounded Welsh.

"You're Ginny Howard," he said.

"And you're Mr. Chalmers? Thanks; this is really nice of you. I can't tell you—"

"That's okay. I was a student once. Come in. You could give me a hand, if you liked."

He was preparing a buffet, or rather peeling the plastic wrapping from one that had been prepared earlier: dishes of salad, plates of cold pizza, fried chicken, and various bits and pieces she supposed were Caribbean. He asked Ginny to take some wineglasses out of a cardboard box and set them on the table, and then to put some paper napkins in between the plates stacked at one end, and altogether it felt like being back at the Yacht Club. She realized guiltily that Angie Lime would have been expecting her, and she hadn't let them know. She realized, less guiltily, that Dad would be wondering where she and Robert were. . . . No, all that was too complicated to think about. Push it out of sight.

Paul Chalmers was asking her a question. She gathered

176

herself and said, "No, my father's English, but my mother came from Haiti, which is why I'm interested in . . . And I saw some of Anielle Baptiste's work illustrated in an article, I can't remember, some American magazine, and I thought I really can't miss this, I've got to see it. It's really good of you to let me come. . . ."

"She's the star of this exhibition, but we haven't made an issue of it; there's a lot of good work besides hers. We've hung her pictures in the large room, through there. Do you want to put your rucksack in the office? Through the door and on the left."

There was a narrow corridor with some unframed pictures in a wooden stand against the wall. It was carpeted in neat oatmeal like the rest of the gallery, and it all looked new and clean. She put her rucksack in the little office, and then, noticing that there was a lavatory next door, gave in to the feeling that had been plucking at her stomach and went in to be sick. She crouched there shivering as if she had the flu, wishing she'd never come, wishing Robert's mother were still alive so that she would never have heard of him, never have disturbed this whole horrible tangle.

But it was no good. Here she was, and in an hour or so she'd meet her mother. She stood up, ran some water, washed, and went back to the gallery.

Paul Chalmers was talking on the phone, so she walked through to the large room, where her mother's paintings were hung.

When Ginny was first becoming interested in art and the history of painting, Dad had given her a big book with hundreds of reproductions in it. She'd pored over it with more than delight—with a kind of greed, in fact. She absorbed everything the book told her about the Renaissance, and the Impressionists, and the Cubists, about Botticelli and Monet and Picasso, and she breathed it all

177

in like oxygen she hadn't known she was missing. And among the pictures in the book, there were two that made her gasp. One was Whistler's *Arrangement in Gray and Black*, his portrait of his mother sitting on an upright chair, and the other was El Greco's *View of Toledo*. She remembered her reaction quite clearly: a sudden intake of breath, caused by sheer surprise at the arrangement of shapes and colors. It was a physical shock.

And when she looked at the big painting that dominated the end wall, the same thing happened. It would have affected her the same way whoever had painted it, because it was a masterpiece. What it showed was a middle-aged black man, in a gaudy uniform with epaulets and medals, in the act of falling onto the red-carpeted floor of a lushly furnished room. He'd been eating a meal, and on the table beside him was a plate of yellow soup. Beyond him, through the open door and at the open window, stood a crowd of people, watching: white people and black, old and young, richly dressed and poverty-stricken. Some of them carried objects that helped you understand who they were: a wad of dollar bills for a banker, a syringe for a drug addict, a clutch of guns for an arms dealer, a chicken for a peasant; and the expressions on their faces told Ginny that they'd all in some ways been victims or accomplices of the man who was dying.

And all that was important, but just as important was the strange discord the particular red of the carpet set up with the particular yellow of the soup, so that you knew it was something significant, and you guessed the soup had been poisoned. And the way the dying man was isolated by that acid red from every other shape in the picture, so that it looked as if he were sinking out of sight in a pool of blood. And mainly what was important was the thing that was impossible to put into words: the arrangement of the shapes on the canvas. These same elements put together differently would have been an interesting picture, but put together like this, they made Ginny catch her breath and put out a hand to the wall.

"Tell me why it's good," said the voice of Paul Chalmers behind her.

She tried to say what was in her mind and how it had affected her. She tried to say that here was a way of painting that was true to everything she knew: to the European fine art tradition, and to the storytelling part of her too, and it was about blackness, about a black society and its experience of itself.

He listened seriously and nodded.

"D'you think a black person paints differently from a white person, then?" he asked when she'd finished.

It was her own question, coming back at her. But in front of these paintings, at last, she thought she could see the beginnings of an answer.

"Not . . . not in the way they'd put paint on the canvas. No. Or in the way they *saw*, even. The rules of perspective would be the same. But . . . but the point is that we never see a picture just as itself. Maybe we should; I don't know. But what we feel and think when we look at a pictures is . . . well, it's part of how we see it, isn't it? We look at it with everything we already know. And we can't ignore that, because it's part of us."

"Go on," he said.

"Well, when I saw this, I thought of El Greco, straight away. The *View of Toledo*, you know? And so that's part of my experience of this painting. The fact that it's part of a European tradition. She speaks the same language. But at the same time . . . You see that mark up there? The man's drawing it in chalk on the wall?"

"What is it?"

"It's the *vever* of Erzulie."

She looked at him, but he didn't know what she meant.

She explained, and then said, "And that's important too. Because I don't know what this man Colonel Paul had done, but one of the things that's going to survive him is . . . love. I think that's what it means. But it's also there like a secret symbol for those people who know what it is. And knowing that it's to do with voodoo . . ." She struggled to find her way back to what she'd started to say. "Well, I can't block out all those things I know and just think of the picture as shapes and colors. So I have to accept them and take in the picture with my mind as well as my eyes, and if my mind knows that the artist is black . . . then maybe there *is* a difference between black art and white art. I mean, if a black person points out that a black politician is corrupt, then at least you know they're not saying it out of racism. But if a white person says it . . . you couldn't be sure. Unless you knew them. I'm not being very clear. . . ."

He was listening carefully, frowning.

"Where are you studying?"

"Oh . . ." She blushed. "I'm still at school. I said I was a student, but . . . I'm a school student."

"What do you want to do?"

"Go to art school and paint."

"Why do you think Baptiste wanted to paint this? To say something about this guy, Colonel Paul?"

"Yes . . . But not mainly. What I think she mainly wanted to do was to see what happened when she put that red and that yellow together. That's what would have started it for me anyway. Some little technical thing like that. And the shape of the man as he falls . . . See, because there's no shadow, you can't sort of see easily where he is in relation to the floor. He seems to be floating in space, almost. But if you work it out by taking a fix on the table and the leg of the chair, you can see that she's got it right, it's technically correct—he hasn't got his foot through the plane of the carpet or anything. She just hasn't given us any clues. Doing that is fantastically difficult, and yet she's just done it without any fuss. It's just . . . Oh, God, I'm amazed. It's brilliant!"

She felt a lump in her throat and had to stop talking. She didn't feel in the least self-conscious with the man. He was part of her world, the world of art.

She looked around at the other paintings, swallowing hard so that she could speak again.

"These are the election pictures? God, what happened?"

"It all went wrong," he said. "After years of dictatorship, maybe it's hard to make a democracy work."

The pictures were uncomfortable to look at: a man mutilated in the dust of a Haitian street, his blood half-dry in the hot sun; a dead child huddled in a doorway; a smiling man with dark glasses firing a machine gun into a crowded church. They were swiftly painted in crude colors, but under each of them Ginny could see that total technical assurance: the artist knew exactly how limbs fitted together, how shadows fell, how the perspective of a sloping street worked, so there was no hesitation between seeing and painting. Not a second of doubt. There was something pitiless there too. A ferocious unblinking stare, like that of a bird of prey.

There was one small landscape that wasn't in the election series, but it had the same fierce quality: sparse green fields bordering a sluggish yellow-brown river. From one side a narrow wooden bridge led out across the water, but it didn't reach the other side because it had collapsed halfway. Clumsy spars of wood trailed in the water.

"A broken bridge," said Ginny to herself in wonder, and then there were other voices from the front of the gallery. The first guests were arriving.

She hurried back through to help. Soon she was pouring wine, hanging coats, offering catalogues as if she belonged there. What would it be like one day to have a show like this, to see her work hanging in a gallery, being admired and discussed and bought? Not as good as doing it, she thought. That was the best part. There was so much to learn.

And all the time she was thinking: *When's she going to come? What's she going to be like? Will she know me?*

At about eight o'clock there was a stir among the people by the door, and without any warning, there she was.

She was shorter than Ginny had expected, and her hair was speckled with gray, though her face was unlined. It was the face in Ginny's photograph, no question about it, but stronger, colder, more austere. She was smiling now, talking to Paul Chalmers and some guests, accepting a glass of wine, and although she was animated and friendly, no one would diminish her by a word like "charming"; she was too powerful for that. She was dressed in what looked like a very expensive cream silk suit, and around her neck she wore a string of heavy bright beads. Her hair was cut short, like Ginny's. Did they look alike? Would anyone notice?

Trying not to stare, Ginny carried on attending to the guests, opening wine, disposing of dirty plates, making conversation. There were about forty people there, white and black, respectable-looking and artistic-looking, and they weren't hard to talk to; they seemed to accept that since she was there, she belonged there.

And at every moment she was aware of where her mother was, of whom she was talking to, of where she was looking. When eventually her mother moved through to the larger room, Ginny followed, and presently she gathered her courage and spoke to her.

"Er . . . Miss Baptiste, can I ask you something? Why

is the man up there, why is he drawing Erzulie's *vever* on the wall?"

"Oh, you know what that is? You know about voodoo?"

She spoke with an American accent, but the word "voodoo" sounded like *vaudou*, as if it were French.

"Well, just a little. Only what someone told me. Am I right? Is that what it is?"

"Yes, that's what it is. But I don't know why he's doing it. It shouldn't be on a wall anyway; it's a sacred thing; it should be drawn in meal on the ground. I guess he doesn't know what he's doing any more than I do."

"Who was Colonel Paul?"

"An army officer. The Americans wanted to extradite him to face drug charges, but he was popular with the army in Haiti. Someone poisoned him with a plate of pumpkin soup."

"I think it's brilliant."

"Thank you . . ."

She was turning away to the two people waiting to talk on her other side. Ginny, desperate, said, "Please . . . Could I show you something?"

She turned back. "Okay. What is it?"

"It's . . . Could you just come in the office a minute? It's in there. . . ."

A slight shrug, an indifferent expression, but she followed Ginny through the door, into the neat cool oatmeal-clean corridor, into the office. Ginny fumbled open the rucksack with shaking hands. She was intensely conscious of the woman in the small room with her, of her expensive clothes, her American accent, her severe manner; they all made Ginny feel small and provincial and unimportant.

She found the photograph in its leather frame, her mother's picture, and held it out.

"What's—" said her mother, and then fell still. Her eyes

glittered as she looked down at the photograph of her younger self. "Where did you get this?" she went on harshly.

Ginny could hardly speak. "It's . . . my mother. It's you. I've always had it."

Her mother looked at her, briefly, and then back at the photograph before turning away.

"You're making a mistake," she said.

"No! I'm not! Dad—my father—he always told me about you. I thought you were dead."

But Anielle Baptiste was shaking her head.

"It has nothing to do with me. This is a mistake. I'm a painter, I'm not a mother. Excuse me, I have to go and see the guests—"

"Oh, *please*—it isn't a mistake—you *must* listen. I'm your *daughter*—"

Her mother was at the door. Ginny was still helplessly holding out the photograph.

"I don't know what you mean. All I can say is you've made a mistake."

She was turning the handle, about to open the door. Ginny rushed forward the three or four steps between them, but stopped before touching her, held away by the formality, that severe, elegant force of character, those cold eyes.

"Just tell me—listen, I promise I won't bother you, I swear I'll go away right now and never see you again, you won't ever hear of me—but just *tell* me, for God's sake: Is it true or not? Are you my mother?"

The woman looked away. Her hand on the doorknob, strong, square, with paint ineradicably staining the rims of her nails, was the only thing about her that didn't look glossy and fashionable. Ginny lowered her eyes and looked at that hand; it was the only place she thought she'd be able to make contact.

184

She reached out to touch it. Her mother let Ginny's hand rest there but gave nothing back, neither moving to hold it nor taking her own away, and after a second or so Ginny dropped hers to her side.

"What's your name?" said her mother.

"Ginny. Howard." It was a hoarse whisper through the lump in her throat.

"You're interested in painting?"

"It's the only thing—"

"It's not the only thing. It's not even the most important thing."

"What—" Ginny still couldn't speak properly. "What is the most important thing?"

There was a long, long silence.

Then Anielle Baptiste slowly turned away and opened the door.

She said, "Painting isn't the most important thing, but it'll have to do till we find out what is."

Ginny held out her hand again.

"Please! You haven't answered my question! You can't— you mustn't—"

But the woman was halfway out of the room, and then she'd left it entirely. Her back was turned. The soft neon strip light above her in the narrow corridor gave her figure the look of the dying Colonel Paul—weightless, without a fixed position, either floating or sinking but in any case out of human reach. Without looking back, she opened the door to the gallery and went through.

Ginny was left in the office doorway. Holding herself with great care, like someone trying to avoid spilling a glass that was filled to the brim, she turned back inside, put the photograph into the rucksack, slung the jacket over her shoulders, and went out through a back entrance into a little yard, into the street beyond, into the city.

15

Arrangement in Pink and Yellow

TWENTY-FOUR HOURS later, Ginny got off the bus in Porthafon, and stiffly, reluctantly made her way through the town to the row of council houses by Mr. Alston's garden furniture factory, and stood by the gate of one of them.

Most of its neighbors had been sold to their tenants; they had stone cladding over the front, or new ranch-style porches, or fancy diamond-paned windows. This one didn't. The window frames were in need of painting, and the garden was a tangle of long grass and weeds. It was Joe Chicago's house, and Ginny was going to return the jacket.

She'd come to that decision in the early hours of the morning, on a bench near the station in Liverpool, at the moment when the street light nearby began to weaken as the sky soaked up the first hints of day from the hidden sun. She'd been wandering around all night, working things out, and she thought she was beginning to see them clearly at last.

And as she'd known, there would be a price to pay. And

the price was simply this, that she had to take back the jacket and apologize.

So she'd phoned Helen's number from Liverpool first thing that morning and got Joe's address, without explaining why. Nor had she phoned Dad, nor had she found Robert. There was no shortage of things to feel guilty about, she thought, but one thing at a time, and this one first.

She pushed open the gate and went up the cracked path to the front door. The bell didn't work, so she knocked, and almost at once a high quavering cry arose from inside, like that of a mad child. She took a step back in fright.

Then there was the rumble of Joe's voice saying something in Welsh, and a key turned, and the door opened.

As far as his sullen features could manage it, they took on an expression of surprise. Before it could turn to anger, she said, "I've brought your jacket back. It's all right. It's not damaged or anything. I've got it here in my rucksack. I just needed it for a few days. I'm sorry I took it like that. Can I—"

She faltered and stopped, because behind Joe she could see another figure, something out of a nightmare: a corpse, a ghoul, swathed in graveclothes, with a vacant mouth and hollow staring eyes. It plucked at Joe's sleeve, whimpering, and he turned and said in Welsh, "It's all right, Mam, don't worry."

A mother? Joe had a mother? Ginny could only stare. He turned back to her, and she said clumsily, "Look, I'm sorry to bother you, but I really need to ask you something. Can I come in? It won't take long, honest. . . ."

He considered heavily for a moment or two and said, "Wait there."

He shut the door again, and she heard their voices going back into the house. After a minute the door opened again, and she stepped inside, to the smells of fried food and cigarette smoke and unwashed clothes, and worse.

Joe's mother was sitting on a torn and greasy sofa, clutching a cushion as if it were a baby. She was wearing nothing but a pink nylon nightdress, the front of it stained with food, and a pair of yellow Garfield slippers. Her hair hung like gray rags from her bony head; she was toothless and senile and, Ginny saw, terrified of her.

"It's all right, Mam," Joe said in Welsh. "She won't hurt you. The little girl's come to see Joe. She won't hurt Mam. Don't worry."

Ginny's head was swimming. She dragged the jacket from the rucksack and held it out wordlessly, and he took it and slipped it on at once.

"Well?" he said.

"I wanted to ask you about my dad," she said. "Tony Howard."

His mouth fell open. He was astonished, breathless. He couldn't speak.

She went on: "It was you that told Benny that he'd been in jail, wasn't it?"

"Aye."

"How did you know?"

"Because that's where I met him. *Duw.* It's *you.* . . ." Tony Howard . . . *Duw annwyl,* I never guessed. . . ."

"What . . . ?" Ginny's mouth was dry. She looked at the old woman on the sofa. "Does your mam speak English?"

"She won't understand nothing. What d'you want to know?"

"What was he in prison for?"

"For kidnapping you," Joe said. "That was it, see."

"*What?*"

"He stole you from somewhere and ran off with you. It

was in all the papers. Everyone in the prison, they thought he was a nonce, till he fought back. Then they found out the truth."

"What's a nonce?"

"You know, a man who molests kiddies. They thought he was one of them. But then the story come out that it was his own kid, like, and there was nothing bad about it, and it was all right after that. See, prisoners, they hate men like that. Kill 'em if they could. You ought to ask him, not me. What did you take my bloody jacket for, anyway?"

"Because I . . . Oh, it's too complicated. I can't . . ."

"What d'you mean? Think I'm thick or something? Think I'm stupid?"

Behind Joe, sensing his slow-rumbling anger, his ancient mother was rocking back and forth, making crying sounds with her gaping mouth. Ginny looked from one to the other.

"No, it's not that—honest—I thought you got it from the broken bridge, Pont Doredig, and I—"

"The what? Pont Doredig? What's that?"

Ginny closed her eyes. "It was a mistake. I heard this story about a car crash and someone stole a jacket from the car, and I—I thought it was that jacket. So I was going to take it back and . . . that's all. But I was wrong, I see now. I got it all wrong. I'm sorry. I shouldn't have taken it."

"I bought this jacket," he said. "I never stole it."

Ginny wondered if she could ask about Andy and why Joe was chasing him, why Andy had paid that money at the fair; but she was already feeling sick from the closeness and the smell, and besides, whatever business Andy had with Joe was dark and private. And Andy would always know how to look after himself.

Joe's mother was saying something in a high, tremulous voice. Ginny couldn't understand much, but she made out the word "*black.*" There was no getting away from it. Were all people crazy? This old woman was just another version of Grandma, a bit further gone, but fundamentally the same.

She turned to leave and heard Joe say in Welsh, "Don't worry, Mam, she's not going to hurt you. She's a friend, she's Joe's friend, see, she's come to give Joe his jacket, she's a kind girl, don't you worry. We'll take you up to bed in a minute, make you happy again. Have some cocoa. Don't worry, now. . . ."

Ginny quietly made her way to the front door and left. What he'd told her about Dad was less of a revelation than his tenderness to the deranged old woman who was his mother. That put everyone to shame. Why did everyone but Joe Chicago treat their relatives so badly?

But she itched to draw her. Like the picture Whistler made of his mother: the formal composition, the cool colors, but instead of the dignified old lady in her clean white bonnet and apron, this poor stained wreck in her nylon nightdress, the flesh withering on her arms, her swollen feet treading down the sides of the cheap yellow slippers.

To draw her grandparents. Granddad: The Man Who Looked Away. Her grandmother, possessed. The need to put them down on paper was almost an ache; she would, she would . . . And Joe, his great coarse giant's features, his greasy skin, the infinite gentleness in his eyes . . . How do you draw gentleness? What shape was that? What color? Look at Rembrandt. Learn.

There was one more phone call to make. She found a booth by the harbor, put her phonecard in, and dialed. He snatched it up on the first ring.

"Dad?"

"Ginny—where the hell are you?"

"I'm in Porthafon. I'm coming home. Is Robert—"

"Robert's here, yes. Whereabouts are you?"

"By the harbor. There's a bus—"

"I'll come and get you. It'll be quicker."

"We're going to have to talk, Dad."

"I know. I know. . . ."

"I'll be waiting in Davy Jones's Locker, okay?"

"I'll be there in half an hour."

"Dad, can I talk to Robert? Is he there?"

"Yes, here he is. See you soon."

The phone changed hands.

"Ginny?"

"Robert . . . Has he gone?"

"No, not . . . Yes. That was the front door. Where the hell did you go? Where've you been?"

"Oh, God, Robert. I'm sorry, leaving you and running out like that. I was just so confused. . . . What did you do? You didn't stay there?"

"Not for long. She was crying and hitting herself with her fists—I've never seen anything like it—and he was just . . . He was dead scared; he was terrified. He gave me ten quid, you know. He . . . Just after you'd left, he called me into the front room while she was crying in the hall, and he shoved this money at me and said it was for both of us—"

"I don't want it."

"Well, whatever. It was the only thing he could think of to do. . . . But she said your mother was alive, didn't she? Was that why . . . and all that racist crap . . . ?"

"Yeah. She's alive. I've seen her, Robert. I met her last night."

"What? Where? What happened?"

She told him everything that had happened, and she

found herself thinking: *It's true, he's my brother. I can tell him this, and he understands.*

She got to the end and said, "And then . . . I just wandered about, thinking. It's crazy, you know. All my life I've been wondering about my mother and then I find her and you know what? I can't feel anything at all. I thought I'd be so happy, I thought everything would be wonderful. . . . And it isn't. Nothing's changed. Well, I've seen her paintings, and that's important—"

"Are they good?"

"They're . . . Oh, God, yes. She's the real thing. No question. But I mean, having seen them, right, I know how I've got to paint. Not because she's my mother, but because they . . . I can't explain. But as for her being a mother, forget it. Oh, and I found out why Dad was in jail. He kidnapped me. Probably from those nuns or whatever. At least, that's what Joe Chicago said."

"You've spoken to Joe Chicago?"

"I've just been there. Robert, he was so kind to his mother. . . . He looks after her. I never knew; I bet no one knows. She's senile, she can't feed herself or anything, and there he was, being all gentle. . . . God, it's stupid; I'm crying just thinking about it. . . ."

He was silent while she tried to gather herself together.

"So when did you get back?" she said. "And Dad, what did you tell him?"

"I phoned him last night. I told him where we'd been. I stayed the night with someone I know up near Liverpool and came back first thing this morning. I thought he'd be angry, but he was just worried."

"Yeah . . . Robert?"

"What?"

"I'm sorry."

"What for?"

"Oh, that quarrel we had. Calling you whatever I called you."

"Yeah, you went to town, didn't you."

"I don't mean it anymore. I didn't mean it then."

"Nor did I."

"I was just so wrapped up in *my* stuff, I couldn't . . ."

"Yeah. Well, I thought we . . . when we were there, at the grandparents' . . ."

"We were understanding each other then. Yeah. Right."

"But what a pair . . . She's mad, isn't she? I mean insane?"

"Yeah. She must be. And all that Arthur and Kitty stuff . . . Do you remember Kitty?"

"Yeah. I hated her. I think *he* was the one, Arthur, he was the one who was bound up in it all, emotionally. . . . She was as hard as nails."

"Arthur and Granddad. It's so weird. And when, you know, when he was saying about Dad and my mother—it was as if no one had ever done that before, as if it was the end of the world. . . ."

"The end of their world. Yeah, that's right. And the way she turned on him—"

"I remember that from when I was a kid," Ginny said. "You know I told you I'd seen her hit him, when I was staying there before, I saw them through the glass in the kitchen door? Well, I've just remembered she turned on him then exactly like that. If she'd had a knife, I swear she'd have used it. I can remember it so clearly, him just turning away holding his arm and saying, *Hush, for God's sake.* If he knew she was going to kill him, he'd ask her to do it quietly so they didn't disturb the neighbors."

"Yeah, and spread some newspaper on the floor to catch the blood," he said.

They were silent for a moment.

"It's really strange how different Dad is," Ginny said. "He's not like them at all."

"Are you going to ask him about this kidnapping business?"

"Bloody right. Before I come home, I'm going to get *everything* out of him. I mean it. If not, that's the end for him."

They talked a little more, but it didn't matter what they said; it was enough to be talking like friends. They said good-bye, and Ginny went to have some coffee in Davy Jones's Locker, sipping it slowly, looking out across the parking lot until she saw the white VW Golf come to a halt at the far side.

She shouldered her rucksack and went out to meet him.

16

Golden Years, Part Two

"HELLO, DAD."

"Hello, Ginny."

She clicked the seat belt on and settled the rucksack down between her feet as he put the car in gear and drove away. It was a good thing the night was hot; she would have missed that jacket otherwise, she thought.

He was silent beside her as they went out over the toll bridge and took the flat road south along the coast. There was a bright moon shining on the great hills to the left, the distant endless dunes far off to the right. Ginny realized that she was going to have to speak first, but at the very moment she thought that, he surprised her by saying, "Robert told me you'd been to your grandparents'. And what happened. Was it much of a shock?"

"Dad . . . I've seen Maman. I spoke to her last night. You knew she was alive all this time, didn't you?"

Silence. His profile was clear in the dim light reflected from the road, and she stared at him mercilessly, trying to see any wavering, any weakness, any similarity to those doomed people in Chester. There was hardly any. He was quite different from them, and all she could see in his expression was sadness.

He slowed the car down, looking for somewhere to stop, and finally pulled up in the gateway to a field beside the road. He switched off the engine and the lights. All around them the wide night was silent; and then he began to speak.

"We should have done this years ago, shouldn't we? Talk, I mean. But things were okay for such a long time; I suppose we just talked about easy stuff like what are we going to have for supper and where shall we go on vacation. . . . Anyway, we've come to it at last. The reason for all of this is quite simple, Ginny: it's fear. Fear is why it happened, fear is why I haven't talked about it. That's the reason for everything.

"I grew up afraid, Ginny. I was frightened every day of my life till I left home, and sometimes I'm still frightened now. Frightened of different things, but once you're marked . . .

"What was I afraid of most . . . Well, I was afraid my father would hit me, which he did. But not very afraid of that, and that stopped anyway as I got bigger. I was mainly afraid my mother wouldn't love me, I think. What would happen to me if she didn't love me anymore I couldn't imagine, but it would be . . . it would be terrible.

"Some of the things that happened . . .

"I think the earliest memory I have, the very first thing I remember, is her beating me. Not smacking me or clouting me round the head but spanking me, and in public. I must have been about three. It was in a shop, some department store, and I'd taken something from one of those child-height displays and refused to put it back. I can't remember what it was, even, but I remember her tearing down my trousers, and my pants, and bending me over right there in the middle of the crowd and lashing at me with her open hand. And I remember screaming, 'Daddy! Daddy!' and twisting my head to look for him, and reaching out with both arms, and I remember him standing a little way off looking in the other direction, though I knew he could hear me. I remember it all now, as if it had only just happened.

"Then when I was six or so she found me with my cousin Lucy. Lucy was a bit younger than me, and we were playing in the bedroom. And like all kids, I suppose, we were curious about each other's bodies, and we were comparing ourselves with each other in the most innocent way when the door opened suddenly and there was my mother. And her expression changed in a second. She seemed . . . it was as if she'd instantly gone mad, in a kind of explosion."

He stopped. Ginny murmured, "Yeah. We saw her do that. . . ."

"That's the part that stays with me," Dad went on, "not Lucy's little body but the sheer terror I felt when my mother leapt at me. She sprang at me and snatched me up, half-clothed as I was, and she ran with me into the bathroom. I remember what I did, and this'll sound strange, but I swear it's true. I flung my arms around her neck and kissed her again and again and I cried, 'I love you, Mummy, I love you. . . .' Terror, you see. But it was no good. She tore my hands away and flung me down into the tub so hard I thought she'd killed me. Then she wrenched at the hot tap, and as the water came out, scalding, splashing down at me, she held me under the stream of it and said I was filthy, I was dirty scum inside and out, she was sickened and disgusted, I was unwholesome, I stank . . .

"But I loved her, Ginny, you see, I loved her because she was my mother, and because I loved her I thought she must be right, it must be true what she said. So all the time I was struggling to protect myself from the hot water I remember hoping that she wouldn't think I was struggling because I didn't love her, or that I was trying to hurt her, and I remember grabbing her sleeve, her red cardigan sleeve, and sobbing out that I was sorry, I was sorry, I was sorry. But she looked down at her arm with my tears and snivel all over it and she snatched it away, and pulled off the cardigan, and plunged that under the tap to scrub off the mess.

"Then she made me wait downstairs, out of the way, in the dining room, still without trousers and pants, and she rang my Auntie Mary, my father's sister. And a little later Auntie Mary came to take Lucy away. I've never seen her from that day to this. We were so friendly and happy together. I remember waiting at the dining room door, hoping to hear Lucy's voice, and not wanting to touch any of the furniture in case I dirtied it.

"One more memory. I had a teddy bear, the only soft toy I had. The rest of my toys—I had plenty of them—the rest were cars and trains and guns and construction kits. I was never short of things to play with, but I didn't love them like I loved my bear. He slept in my bed till . . . I don't know when it happened, but I'll never forget it, never. Not till I die."

He swallowed hard. Ginny couldn't move. He was clutching the steering wheel with both hands, staring ahead down the empty road. He went on:

"It was a winter night. I'd stolen a bar of chocolate from the news dealer's shop round the corner. I'd never done it before and I don't know why I did it then, but there I was, lying in bed with the light out, eating this chocolate, feeling smug because I had it and guilty because I knew I shouldn't. I stayed awake for a long time. And bit by bit the guilt grew and took over, and I hid the rest of the chocolate under my pillow and clung to Teddy.

"Then I started to cry. And my mother, who was coming up the stairs, she heard me and came in, and she saw the chocolate on my face and pulled the pillow away, and I knew what was going to happen, because her eyes flicked to Teddy and then she snatched him away from me.

" 'He doesn't want Teddy anymore,' she said. 'He wants chocolate instead. He's too old for Teddy. Teddy will have to be killed.'

"Then she was gone, down the stairs in a flash, and I ran screaming after her, but she went out the back door into the darkness and locked it behind her, and I heard terrible chopping sounds. They kept a little ax there, to chop the kindling wood. I clung to the back door, trying to drag it open, and then I fled, I ran into the sitting room, absolutely incoherent with terror, couldn't breathe, hardly, and I threw myself at my father, who was watching the television.

"But all he said was 'No, no, go back to bed, there's a good boy,' and even in the state I was in I could tell he was frightened too. Then he looked up at the doorway and quickly pushed my hands away, because there she stood.

"D'you know, her face was full of sorrow. She opened her arms to me and because it was what I needed I ran to her and sobbed, and I found myself saying, 'I'm sorry, I'm sorry. . . .'

"She took me upstairs and laid me back in my bed and explained—I remember her soft voice and the perfume she used to wear—she explained how when teddy bears weren't loved properly anymore they had to be killed. Teddy had had to be chopped up, and it was very sad, but if I'd loved him more I wouldn't have wanted to eat chocolate instead. Then she kissed me and wished me happy dreams, and went out and shut the door and left me in the darkness.

"Till the moment I die I'll never forget that, that desolation, that misery. You might think I'd hate her, but feelings, I don't know, they're not that predictable, are they? In fact, after that, I was desperate with love and fear. I clung to her, I smothered her with affection, terrified that she'd think I didn't love her.

"Now I can see what she did to me, now I can see that she made me want to apologize to her for not loving her enough. . . . Well, there are times when I could willingly go there and kill her. I still wake up now, a grown man, I still wake up in the night sweating with fear and rage and hatred. I can only excuse her by thinking that she's mad. But I can't forgive him. I'll never forgive him.

"Well . . . Anyway.

"So somewhere in the middle of all that they broke my confidence in myself, Ginny, and they never showed me how to repair it. Never thought to. They stamped me with fear so deep, so early on, I couldn't get rid of it."

He stopped for a moment to pull out a handkerchief and wipe his eyes. Ginny wanted to touch him, to say something, but she felt helpless.

Then something absurd happened. The car windows were open, because of the heat, and at the same moment both Ginny and her father became aware of someone watching them, a presence. There was a face looking over the gate—a huge, solemn cow's face.

They laughed as the tension went, and hearing them the cow lumbered away nervously. Dad got out of the car and went to lean on the gate. Ginny joined him and presently the cow, curious again, came up slowly to gaze at them.

"I thought they put them inside at night," Ginny said.

"It's having a strange night, like us. Ginny . . ."

He was looking away from her, and his voice was quiet in the wide night.

"I'm glad you went to Chester," he said. "It's made me tell you all this. You're like your mother."

"How?"

"You make your mind up and then you act. It's what I should do. Should have done. I will . . . Thank you, Ginny love. I'm telling you all this because you deserve to know it, and to explain it to myself, I suppose . . . So you can see why I married Janet. There's no reason otherwise; I didn't love her. . . . But her parents—Uncle Arthur and Auntie Kitty, as I had to call them—and mine, they had the whole thing worked out years in advance: I'd marry Janet, take over the firm, supply them with grandchildren. Oh, they didn't say it aloud, but it was there in everything they said and everything they did.

"And I didn't dare go against it, you see. It sounds incredible, I know, a grown man obeying his parents like a puppet, even against his own judgment. But that fear built into me over years, it was impossible to resist, it was like defying gravity. Janet herself . . . I never knew what she thought. A smug, prim, narrow girl she was. A hard little nature, closed and greedy and . . . I could *see* it, and still I went through with the marriage. What a dream I was living in! A grown man, and the only thing I longed for was my mother's approval. I thought I didn't, but I did. I thought I'd grown beyond it, but I hadn't.

"So we got married, and then I met your mother. Anielle Baptiste. She was studying art. Came from a wealthy family, apparently. There'd been some kind of political trouble in the time of Papa Doc Duvalier; Anielle's father and mother had been exiled: they were living in Canada, I think. . . . I don't know. She . . . I thought she was American at first, but she was intensely Haitian. An artist.

My family thought art was something for women, or lefties, or homosexuals. Oh, and liars. They couldn't see what there was in it, so they thought people who said they could see something in it were lying. I suppose I'd thought that too, until I met Anielle. I knew she wasn't a liar. She was too honest for that. Too honest for me.

"I'd never met, never imagined there could be, anyone like her.

"And if I'd had the strength, if I hadn't had my confidence broken some long long time before, I'd have thrown Janet over and lived with Anielle. Maybe persuaded her to marry me. But I didn't. It was such a tangle: Janet was pregnant, Anielle was pregnant . . . and I didn't dare tell anyone about it until it was all too late. And then I told Janet. You can imagine the reaction."

"They told us," Ginny said. "They said it knocked them sideways. It shattered everything."

He nodded.

"Anielle was a Catholic, and there was no question of abortion, thank God. She disappeared and went into a Catholic nursing home to have you, and then . . . She just left. You see, my not leaving Janet, that was a betrayal she couldn't forgive. I don't forgive myself for it. If I'd lived with Anielle she might not have gone, might have stayed to be a mother. . . . I don't know. There was the painting as well. She lived for that. Being a mother was something that happened to her; being a painter was something she was born to. She . . . she wasn't rejecting you, love. Don't blame her for leaving you.

"But she was so contemptuous of me that she didn't tell the nuns—the nuns who ran the nursing home—she didn't tell them my name. She just vanished. I didn't know where she'd gone, I didn't know if you'd been born safely, didn't know anything.

"And so when I finally found the children's home where

they were looking after you and turned up claiming to be the father of this child . . . Well, six months had gone past. Why should they hand over a baby girl to a total stranger? Naturally they wouldn't, not until they'd made all kinds of checks. But I thought that if Janet . . . I thought that if she agreed to adopt you, if there was a home for you to go to, they'd be more likely to release you into my care. So that was when I told her about it.

"Ha. Fat chance. All that came of it was hysterics. I'd been unfaithful to her, I'd got a mistress, a black mistress, that was it, got a pickaninny child—that's the way she talked. She went straight round to her parents, and he, Uncle Arthur—I still called him that—he came to my parents as if it was something to do with them, as if I'd been a naughty boy and it was up to them to punish me for it . . . Or as if he'd bought me, one son-in-law, and I was faulty, and he was coming back to complain . . .

"Yes, when I look at it now, Ginny, it seems incredible, it seems impossible that grown people should behave like that, like Janet and Arthur and Kitty and my parents, and me, too, that we should all be acting like—what? Puppets? Not people, that's for sure. I was actually summoned, actually told to come and explain, come and apologize, they meant, come and grovel for forgiveness.

"But I couldn't stick that. I wouldn't behave like that. I told them all that you were my child, that I was going to look after you, and damn the rest of them. Janet could divorce me as soon as she liked; I'd pay her whatever maintenance she wanted to look after Robert. I . . . I didn't want him, any more than she wanted you. Then I walked out. I felt free. For the first time in my life, I felt free. Can you imagine that?

"So . . . I kept on struggling to get the social services to let me have you. All kinds of obstacles, all kinds of tests and questions and queries. Since it was a Catholic society looking after you by that stage, and since I wasn't living with my wife, that didn't make it any easier.

"In the end they agreed—the social services and the Catholic society between them and the courts and the priest and the bishop and the Pope for all I know—they agreed to let me have restricted access. I could have you for the occasional weekend, but no more. You were growing up, my little one, you were two and then you were three, and going from one foster parent to another and back to the home again. . . . And then suddenly it stopped. I went to collect you one weekend and you were gone. You were with someone else, they said. A permanent placement.

"I've forgotten all the details, but it turned out that the difficulties I'd been having about getting you permanently were due to someone reporting me to the social services for . . . oh, cruelty, baby battering—that was the phrase then. The social services were in a cleft stick. They could see you were all right, but on the other hand they couldn't ignore rumors like that in case they turned out to be true. So they wouldn't let me have you. I couldn't believe it. I tried to get the name of whoever it was who'd been telling these lies, but of course they wouldn't pass on a thing like that.

"So there I was. Someone had stolen you. And once I'd calmed down and thought about it, I knew who it was at once."

"Granddad? Grandma?" Ginny could hardly whisper. "Was it them?"

"It was her."

"And was that why I was staying with them?"

"That's right. What they thought they were doing, God only knows. They'd lied about me and then persuaded the fools in charge to let them look after you. After I'd walked out, after Arthur and Kitty had deserted them, they had nothing left, I suppose. Desperate. Well, I went mad. Thinking of the way I'd grown up . . . you going through all that . . . I couldn't bear to think of it. So I went straight there and took you away."

"Joe Chicago said . . . he said you were in prison. You kidnapped me and went to prison."

"Oh, you've seen Joe? That's right, that's what happened. I kidnapped you. We traveled all over the country under different names. Six months, going from place to place. You probably don't remember any of it. Cheap rooms, flats, landladies, up and down the country . . . It couldn't last. And when I finally ran out of money and couldn't hide anymore . . . Do you remember that cold morning in Norwich? Autumn morning, full of mist? No, probably not. The police station, the curious police-woman, the social worker who snatched you away and insisted on examining you there and then to see if you were being abused.

"Anyway, the arrangement my parents had had, that was a court order, and by taking you I'd violated it, you see. Contempt of court. More than that; I'd knocked the old fool down. Him. When I saw them I was shocked. Shrunk, they'd physically shrunk; they were huddled in this little narrow house where I'd spent my little frightened childhood; they were frightened themselves now. . . . But he tried to bluster, tried to threaten me, and I lost my head and hit him. I should have done it years before. Still, it didn't sound good in court. They gave me six months, which my solicitor said was a bit steep. Lot of help he was. I was out after four, then I started the whole business again, only legally this time. I was determined. You were everything, you were my life. I wasn't going to give up.

"And eventually, at long last, eventually it came to the

High Court and there was a sympathetic judge—what a miracle! He decided it once and for all. You were my child, I was your father, no question, I had custody, that was it. After four years, all finished in about four minutes.

"So we . . . started living, I suppose. Struggled. But at least we were together. Ginny . . . Tell me the truth now: was there ever a moment when you thought I didn't love you?"

She couldn't speak. She could only shake her head.

"And when you were with them, when you were little . . . They didn't mistreat you, did they? They didn't frighten you?"

"No," she said, swallowing hard. "They didn't mistreat me."

"I didn't think they would in just a few days. It would still be new for them; they wouldn't have time. . . . And she could be kind, she could be generous sometimes. There was something to love there, under the madness. . . .

"So time went by.

"I never told you the truth, because I was afraid to, you see. Ashamed. Everything I did before I decided to be your father, be responsible for you, I was ashamed of. I didn't want you to know about Janet or about any of it. So I invented a story and told you as much of the truth as fitted it. I told you that Maman had died because I thought it would be easier for you than thinking you had a mother who abandoned you. And now you tell me you've found her. . . . It was bound to happen, I suppose. How was she? How did you find her?"

"I saw this advertisement in an art magazine," Ginny said, brushing her eyes with the back of her hand. "She was having an exhibition in a gallery in Liverpool. I rang them up, and the owner said I could come to the private view last night. And I saw her and I . . . I showed her the photograph. It was stupid of me, really. It wasn't the time. She knew it was her picture, but she wouldn't admit it, she wouldn't admit who I was."

"Did that upset you?"

"I thought it did. It's funny, I really thought it did, until I stopped wandering about feeling sorry for myself and realized what I did feel. And what I felt was: So what? It doesn't matter. I've never had her, so I can't miss her, really. Her pictures are wonderful; that's the important thing. I don't have to be her daughter to see those, though."

"Did she look well?"

"Oh, yes. She looked . . . very strong and independent."

"Yes. She was that. I'm glad she's doing well. And I'm glad she's seen you too, even if she didn't want to. She'll be proud of you."

Ginny doubted that. Dad went on:

"And anyway, that's how it would have stayed. But then Janet got ill and Robert was going to need somewhere to go. . . . He could have gone to his grandmother, Kitty, in Spain. But she didn't want him; she made that perfectly clear. She was a detestable woman. My mother was mad, perhaps, but Kitty was just cold, hard, greedy . . . both of them much stronger than their husbands. Arthur and my father, they were the real marriage. That was the real bond. The wives weren't nearly so close."

"That's what Robert said," Ginny told him.

"He's right. He sees a lot, Robert. . . . What was I talking about?"

"About Robert," Ginny said. "Needing somewhere to go."

"Oh, yes. Well, he wasn't wanted with Kitty, and as for my parents, that was out of the question. The only option was to live in some residential home up in Liverpool while he did his A Levels. When Wendy Stevens came that day and told me about it, I knew I'd have to offer to have him here. I was responsible for him. So that's when it all began to unravel. I should have told you everything straight away. I should have told you everything from the beginning. Stupid of me. But I was afraid, you see. That's at the heart of it."

They stood for a while in silence. Not a single car had gone past; they had the night to themselves. The cow had wandered away, and far away over the flat fields Ginny could hear an owl cry.

"Actually," Ginny said, "there was something else that started it for me. Rhiannon's sister, Helen, she'd heard from someone that you'd been in prison. When I heard that, I thought no, it's impossible. But it made me start wondering. . . . I went to see Joe Chicago tonight, before I rang home. I . . . I pinched his jacket, you see. I thought he'd stolen it, and I wanted to . . . give it back in some way. But I realized he hadn't stolen it after all, so I went to see him. He was looking after his mother. He told me why you were in prison. I suppose I could have asked him a long time ago if I'd dared. I just thought he was so dangerous."

Dad didn't speak for a while. Then he said, "Yeah . . . Helen. I had no idea she was Rhiannon's sister. Well, it's a small place. And poor old Joe. I see him sometimes in town and give him a few quid. He's harmless. But looking like that, he hasn't got much in his favor. Ginny . . . I'm sorry."

She was a little surprised. "What for?"

"For not telling you." He paused. "For all this."

She thought of the years when there'd just been the two of them, when she'd been the queen of the world and he'd been the king; she thought of the breakfast ladies; she thought of that little boy her father had been; she thought of the desolation of his parents, knowing themselves abandoned and hated, and knowing why; she thought of Robert and his cold, hard, dying mother; she thought of Dad in jail for her sake, and her not knowing anything about it; she thought of Joe Chicago's mother. A sense of the vast loneliness and sadness of being human brushed past her. The world was huge, after all. She'd been very lucky.

Then without knowing how it happened, she was crying on his shoulder, sobbing for all of them, and his arms were round her as they'd always been.

After a while Ginny sighed a shaky sigh and they stood apart.

"You know," she said, confessing, "I thought I was so hard done by . . . and I wasn't at all. Robert's much worse off than me. So were you. I just didn't realize. But once I felt things were shaky underneath . . . well, I couldn't trust anything. There were all sorts of other people who knew things about me that I didn't, and I had to find out, Dad. I had to. And now I see. . . ."

They got back in the car. Ginny found herself yawning. The lights of a truck lit up the interior from behind them, and the heavy vehicle roared steadily past on its way to the south, laden with Mr. Alston's garden furniture to pay for more bricks for his beach house, perhaps, or with cases of wine for the Yacht Club.

"You know," she said, "I never even asked if they did the ton."

"The what?"

"In the Yacht Club. A hundred dinners. They probably did, though. I think they need another waiter. D'you think Robert would like a job?"

"You better ask him," he said, starting the engine. "Let's go home."

17

The Morning Train

GINNY WOKE UP long before six. She knew it was early before she looked at the clock; the sun was already shining in through the gap in the curtains, but the air was cool and fresh, fresher than it had seemed for days.

And because it was so long since she'd been on the beach, Ginny found herself longing for the edge of the water once more, the shore of her kingdom. She got up quickly, washed her face and cleaned her teeth, and put on shorts and T-shirt and sneakers. The house was still, the others both asleep. She left through the kitchen and ran down the lane.

In the pearly light, her kingdom looked like one of those dreamy beaches painted by Salvador Dalí: tiny bizarre details in an infinite limpidity. The ribs of the old fishing boat sticking up out of the mud in the estuary, the station cat curled up asleep on a beer barrel outside the Yacht Club kitchen, a washing line strung between the rafters of Mr. Alston's house, with Dafydd's or Andy's dingy shirts and socks hanging in the open loft—she saw them all bathed in the same benevolent clarity. There was no one about, no one awake, and hers were the first footprints on the beach.

She took off her shoes and left them at the edge of the soft sand before going down to the water. The tide was nearly out, and the air was so still that there was nothing to stir the sea into waves. It was smooth and glassy as far as Ginny could see; in her imagination she saw this surreal calm extending out past the southern coast of Ireland and on into the ocean, south and west for thousands of miles, through the Sargasso Sea and over the lost continent of Atlantis, where sea serpents coiled among the ruined temples, until it touched the shores of Haiti.

Where the *loa* lived. Where Baron Samedi had come from. They were real; you had to respect them, even when they were wrong about things. All of that was dark and confusing, but it was part of what she was. Maybe art itself was a kind of voodoo, possessing you, giving you supernatural power, letting you see in the dark.

With the sun on her back, she waded into the chilly water, wriggling her toes down into the sand, sensing the presence of little curious nibbling things deep out of sight. She wandered slowly along, knee-deep, thinking about the broken bridge, and about why she'd been so affected by the story.

Because it *was* about her. She was the baby, the warm fur-lined jacket was her mother, and Joe Chicago . . . Joe Chicago wasn't death; he was art.

She stood still. Now the story made perfect sense. It was art that had taken her mother away, because art had no conscience; it demanded, it was cruel, it took what it wanted brutally and paid no heed to the consequences. Or (as Rhiannon would say) it wasn't kind, it was sexy.

Ginny wandered a little farther, the mild water stirring around her legs, and reached down to cool her hands, lifting it and letting it trail down in glittering drops. Kind or sexy—was this a division that split the world in two? Was Rhiannon right? Did everything have to be either kind and ineffective or sexy and heartless?

And as for her, she'd protested to Rhiannon that it must somehow be possible to be both. Well, how did she rate? She remembered trying to comfort Helen in the little spare room at Jubilee Terrace and moving her leg to improve the balance of the composition: nothing very kind there. She remembered Robert's words in that terrible quarrel—bitter hurting words, but they were true. Part of her *was* cold and arrogant; part of her *was* indifferent to those who were untalented.

Arrogant, indifferent . . . But sexy, as in sex? She thought of her one attempt to become a lover, and grimaced.

How unlikable she was.

But at least, she found herself arguing feebly, there was no envy in her. When she saw talent or genius she didn't resent its not being hers; she rejoiced in it wherever it was. It was the most important thing in the world. . . .

She heard her mother again: *Painting isn't the most important thing, but it'll have to do till we find out what is.* She'd meant *for us. For people like us. For artists.* She'd acknowledged that connection, if nothing else.

Ginny turned around and walked slowly back the other way, the sun now full on her face and breast and arms. She wasn't alone on the beach anymore; there was someone at the far end, coming toward her. A boy. Robert. She waved, and he waved back.

Well, even if she was an artist, she could still be a sister, do whatever sisters did. She wondered whether to tell Robert about what Dad had said in the car, in the dark and silence of the night, but she swiftly decided not to. That was a secret. It was acknowledgment of the closeness they'd had, she and Dad, and she'd respect it. Besides, there was no need for Robert to hear anything that reflected badly on his mother, who might have been narrow and prim and greedy like Kitty but who had just painfully died, after all.

Or was concealing it from Robert no better than Dad's concealing things from her for so long? It was hard to say. She hoped she could get it right.

She bent to pick up her shoes as his shadow fell across them.

"Hi," she said.

"Hello," said Glyn Williams.

She looked up, blinking in astonishment. Yes, it was Glyn, not Robert at all, and for a moment she didn't know what to say.

"What's the matter?" he said.

"I thought you were someone else. Sorry, I didn't mean . . ."

He shrugged, smiling, and half turned away, and she fell in with his unspoken invitation and walked along beside him to the mouth of the estuary.

"You're up early," she said.

"I help out with the horses," he said. There was a riding stable in the village, where tourists paid to sit in hard hats and be slowly led up into the hills and down again by girls in jodhpurs.

"I can't see you doing that, somehow," she said.

"I don't do the pony-trekking stuff. I go there first thing before the tourists come. I'm in the shop most of the day anyway. I do it so I can get free rides."

"D'you ride, then? I didn't know. . . ."

"Yeah. What about you?"

"I've never tried."

"You ought to come. I'll take you out. You won't have to go in a line with a lot of little kids."

She looked at him. Was this a date? Was someone asking her to go out with him? She was suddenly conscious of her bare legs, her thin T-shirt with nothing under it; and of his dark-red curly hair, his half-innocent, half-sardonic smile, like Andy's but more complicated, stronger, more subtle. And she was conscious of her unlikableness. She felt so shy that she could hardly breathe.

"Well, why not?" he said. "I'll teach you to ride."

"No reason. Thanks. Yeah. I'd like that."

They walked on slowly.

"How's your brother getting on?" he said.

"Oh, Robert. Yeah, fine. You know his mum died recently? That's why he's here. It was hard at first. It probably will be for a while, but he's okay."

They reached the breakwater, a stone wall with a concrete path on the top just wide enough for two people to walk abreast. She stopped to put on her shoes before jumping up to join him, and they wandered along toward the end. To their left was the glistening sand of the empty lagoon, to their right the seaweed-covered rocks at the foot of the breakwater. Ahead, across the narrow mouth where the river entered the sea, was the widest stretch of dunes on the whole coast: miles of high tumbled sand hills laced through with marram grass, and a beach where you could find a billion perfect shells. Ginny seldom went there, near as it was, because swimming across the mouth was safe only at low tide and the journey all the way round by land was miles. But now they had a boat, she remembered suddenly. It would be easy.

"Can you sail?" she said.

"No. Why?"

"Well, I can't either, but my dad bought a boat a couple of weeks ago. When I've learned to sail, I'll teach you," she said, daring. "In exchange."

"All right! That's a bargain. Hey, I haven't seen you around for a few days. You been away?"

"Yeah. Robert and I went to Chester to see our grand-parents. But I've been busy, you know. . . ."

"What, drawing?"

"How d'you know about my drawing?"

"Well, don't sound so defensive. *Cet animal est très méchant—*"

"*Quand on l'attaque, il se défend!*" she finished. "Yeah. Sorry. You weren't even attacking me."

"Anyway, you're not an *il*, you're an *elle*."

"Yeah, but that wouldn't work, 'cause it'd be *méchante*, and it wouldn't rhyme."

"*Touché*," he said. "I know about your drawing because, first, Rhiannon told me, and second, I saw your stuff in the Art Room, and third, I saw you out on the top road drawing the other evening. I was going to come and say hello, but you'd scarpered by the time I got there."

What a difference that might have made, she thought. What a difference this was making now. They reached the end of the breakwater, and Glyn sat down.

"I brought you a present," he said, and she noticed that he was carrying a paper bag.

"What? Me? Oh . . ."

Is that all you can say? she thought. *Don't be so bloody incoherent, girl. Inarticulate. Whatever. Say thank you.*

"Thanks," she said, sitting down awkwardly beside him.

He was taking out two kiwifruit and a clasp knife. "I saw you from the stables," he said, "and I thought you looked hungry, so I raided the shop." He cut the fruit in half and gave her two pieces, and they ate the delicate flesh out of the skins, wiping away the juice with the backs of their hands.

"I love kiwifruit," she said. "How could you see I looked hungry?"

"I couldn't. It was just an excuse. You didn't look very happy, though."

He was close enough for her to see the flecks of green in his eyes, and for a long confusing moment she couldn't tell whether he was kind, or sexy, or both.

"Well, I am," she said. "Honest. I wasn't, but that's"— she gestured vaguely—"over now," she finished.

"You're coming back to join the rest of us?"

"Did it seem like that?"

"Yeah. Rhiannon said it was your artistic temperament."

"There's no such thing!"

"Well, it can't have been that, then," he said, "but I won't ask if you don't want me to."

She looked at him again. "Do you really want to know?"

"Yeah. I'm interested. 'Cause I like you. And I mean, now we've had breakfast together, we ought to get to know each other better. Wouldn't be proper otherwise, would it?"

"No," she agreed smiling. "So you want to know what I've been doing?"

"Well, not *now*, necessarily. Not all at once. You could start this afternoon when we go riding."

"This after*noon* already?"

"Why not?"

There was no reason. She shrugged, quite unable to keep that smile off her face.

"Okay," she said.

This was novel. This was better than unexpected kiwifruit, even. Ginny saw something flash beyond Glyn's shoulder and watched as the sun caught the windows of the morning train crossing the little bridge outside Stuart's house and slowing down to stop at the station.

He saw where she was looking. "*Duw*, is that the time?" he said. "I'll have to get a move on. I'll see you later, then. At the stables, about two o'clock, all right?"

She nodded, feeling dopey from her smile to her sneakers, and watched him go.

Glyn. Well. Wow.

She sat at the end of the breakwater hugging her knees as her kingdom came to wakefulness around her, intact, rich, alive in all its details, from the scuttling little crabs among the rocks below her to the station cat yawning and stretching outside the Yacht Club, from the mother-of-pearl water to the great green presence of the hills.

There was so much to do.

Apologize to Angie Lime and Mr. Calvert, first, for missing a couple of days without letting them know.

Talk to Rhiannon. (That could last for days.)

Get to know Robert. Learn to sail.

Write to her mother. No. Yes. Maybe. Or write, but not mail it. Sort out what she thought. Talk to Glyn about it. . . .

Go and see Helen. Explain.

Think about her grandparents. Maybe it would be possible to meet them with Dad somewhere neutral, somewhere safe and public, where Grandma would feel constrained to be rational. They were so desperate and unhappy; maybe she and Robert and Dad were strong enough to take charge of bringing the family together. Perhaps it was time to start healing.

Talk to Stuart about her mother's paintings.

Those paintings . . . She realized that she was still dazed

by them. *The Death of Colonel Paul* was an arrangement in red and yellow, a stunning one, but it wasn't only that; it was about human beings as well, about suffering and justice and greed. It cut through all the jargon and the labels and the boxes of abstraction and post-modernism and neo-expressionism; it was technically dazzling and it showed something true; it was the way a person could paint and be faithful to everything she knew, to Europe and to Africa, to academic discipline and to voodoo. If her mother's absence all these years had made it possible for her to show Ginny that, then it had been worth it, Ginny thought.

Her hand itched for a pencil. And that afternoon she was going riding with Glyn. . . . She marveled. Maybe she wasn't so unlikable. Maybe you could be an artist *and* have a boyfriend. Anything was possible, really. Even being kind as well as sexy.

She stood up and stretched. The sun was hot already; the morning train, having unloaded its newspapers, was moving out toward Porthafon, and in the bright clear air Ginny could hear a crate of bottles being put down somewhere outside the Yacht Club, the news dealer's van turning into the station, distant voices calling.

She turned to run up to the house. As she passed the station, she waved to the porter and the news dealer, and to Harry Lime, who stood there scratching in the Yacht Club kitchen doorway, and their voices mingled. *Bore da,* good morning, *bore da,* Ginny, good morning, good morning.

Philip Pullman

is the author of the popular Sally Lockhart trilogy: *The Ruby in the Smoke*, winner of the IRA Children's Book Award for Older Readers, *Shadow in the North*, and *The Tiger in the Well*. All three titles were named ALA Best Books for Young Adults. His most recent book is *Spring-Heeled Jack*, a comic thriller, and he has also written one novel for adults. A former schoolteacher, he lives with his family in Oxford, England.

ISABELLE
Shows Her Stuff

ALSO BY CONSTANCE C. GREENE

ISABELLE
Shows Her Stuff

BY CONSTANCE C. GREENE

VIKING KESTREL

1722750

VIKING KESTREL
Viking Penguin Inc., 40 West 23rd Street, New York, New York 10010, U.S.A.
Penguin Books Ltd, Harmondsworth, Middlesex, England
Penguin Books Australia Ltd, Ringwood, Victoria, Australia
Penguin Books Canada Limited, 2801 John Street, Markham, Ontario, Canada L3R 1B4
Penguin Books (N.Z.) Ltd, 182–190 Wairau Road, Auckland 10, New Zealand

Library of Congress Cataloging in Publication Data
Greene, Constance C.   Isabelle shows her stuff.
Summary: Anxious to change his "goody-goody" image,
eight-year-old Guy is delighted when Isabelle the Itch
offers to teach him the art of being a funny pest. Her
lessons end up teaching them both what being a tough
guy really means.
1. Children's stories, American. [1. Behavior—
Fiction] I. Title.
PZ7.G8287Ju 1984   [Fic]   84-40255
ISBN 0-670-41103-5

For Nora

Chapter One

The day Guy Gibbs moved to Hot Water Street was the best day of his life. How could he miss getting into hot water now? What a stroke of luck! What a neat house! What a neat street!

The house, tall and thin and graying, leaned a little into the wind. There was a birdbath in back, a huge old maple tree in front with a vacant bird's nest swinging from its branches, and a path to the front door made of big round stones that reminded Guy of oversized hopscotch potsies.

1

All in all, that house was just about perfect.

Living on Hot Water Street was going to change Guy's life. He was sure of that. His heart swelled with excitement as he thought of himself marching down to the principal's office.

"Not *you* again!" the principal would exclaim, clutching his head. "What have you done now?"

Guy hugged himself with delight as he imagined himself pulling up to his house in a police car, the street lined with kids watching, mouths open wide in astonishment. He'd been caught snitching apples. Or pumpkins. Or for shooting out streetlights with a BB gun. Which he didn't have. The important thing was, he'd been caught.

No more goody-goody Guy. That was behind him now. From here on in, he, Guy Gibbs, was on a high roll.

The movers were messing around, trying to figure out how to get the piano into the house without bending it, when a girl wearing a red hat with a ripply brim and carrying a newspaper bag on her shoulder came up the path.

She and Guy stood watching.

"A little to the left, Len!" the head mover hollered. "Easy, now, don't break nothing."

Back and forth they went, trying this way and that.

"You might have to take the legs off," the girl said at last.

The head mover was hot and tired and ready to call

it quits. "Cool it, girlie," he said. "I been in this business twice as long as you been alive. I know what I'm doing. I don't need no upstart kid telling me my own business."

"How long have you been in this business?" the girl asked.

The man yanked a gray handkerchief out of his pocket and wiped his forehead. He cleared his throat and said in a very raspy voice, "How long you been around, toots?"

"I asked you first," she said.

He cleared his throat a second time and, turning his head to one side, sent a glittering ball of spit onto the grass. Then he turned his back on the girl and shouted, "Let's try it another way, Len, see how that works."

"How about if you leave the piano outside and when somebody feels like playing, they can open the window and stick their hands out and play from the inside?"

The mover's thick chest moved mightily as he took a deep breath. His little helper, Len, watched anxiously. Guy kept quiet, waiting for the next move.

"That way," the girl explained, "even if it was winter, even if there was a blizzard, they could put on gloves, wipe off the snow, and still play that old piano."

"It's not old, it's new," said Guy. From far away, a dog barked. Trucks rolled on the turnpike. Guy swallowed noisily.

No one spoke. Then the head mover said, "You belong here?" jerking his thumb in the direction of Guy's new house.

"Nope, I'm the paper boy," the girl said.

"They don't want no paper right at this minute, girlie." The man spoke slowly, carefully, biting off each word as if it were a piece of tough meat. "Why don't you do us all a big favor and get lost, huh? Take off. Vamoose."

"I was only trying to help." She did a little jig.

"Yeah," Guy chimed in, "you don't hafta get a red nose."

"Right," the girl agreed. "What's that mean?"

"My father says it means you don't hafta get riled up," Guy told her, pleased he knew something she didn't.

"I'm gonna pull that on Herbie," she said. "How about asking your mother if she wants the paper delivered?" She whipped out a pencil and pad from her bag. "Philip'll kill me if I don't write everything down."

"Who's Philip?"

"My brother. It's his route. Well, sort of half mine. I'm subbing for him on account of he sprained his ankle. He's got crutches and everything. You'd think he was the first person who ever had crutches." She sighed. "Boys make such a fuss. He won't even let me try 'em out. And you should see the way my mother waits on him. It's enough to make you puke." She rolled her eyes. "What's your name?"

"Guy," he said. "What's yours?"

"Isabelle. Go ask your mom, will you? I'm in a hurry. Herbie's waiting for me. We're fighting at my house today. He might skin out on me if I'm late."

"Why are you fighting with Herbie? Are you mad at him?" Guy asked. To meet a paper boy like Isabelle his first day in the new house was another sign his luck was changing. He could've talked to her all day.

"Heck, no. We're friends. We just like to fight. We fight every day after school. Go ask, will you? I've got to blast off."

Guy raced inside, and Isabelle, snapping her fingers and whistling, began to dance. The movers stopped to watch.

"Whaddya call that?" the little mover asked, scratching his head.

"It's a dance," she said. "I made it up."

"Loony-bin time," the big mover said. "Get to it, Len. Time's a-wasting."

"You said it," Isabelle agreed.

"She says you can start tomorrow," Guy shouted, racing back.

"Okay." Isabelle was all business. "Name and address, please," she said, pencil poised.

"Guy Gibbs," said Guy.

"Father's name, dodo," she said.

"Peter Gibbs, Twenty-two Hot Water Street," he answered proudly.

"Lucky you. I always wanted to live on this street,"

she said, tucking her pad and pencil into her bag.

"Don't forget what I said about the legs," she hollered to the moving men, and then she was off and running, on her way to fight with Herbie.

"Sonny," the big mover said, "count your lucky stars that kid ain't related to you."

"Right," the little mover agreed.

"But maybe she's got something," he said. "Maybe the legs unscrew or something. Let's give it a try."

The big one gave the little one a black look, and they went back to trying to figure out the best way to get the piano into Twenty-two Hot Water Street.

Chapter Two

Guy hadn't made a lot of important decisions in his short life. Should he have chocolate or vanilla, or should he wear his red shirt or his blue—things like that.

But when he decided to follow Isabelle that first day in his new house, he acted as if he'd been making big, important decisions all the days of his life.

She traveled fast. Guy managed to keep up, but only just. He got a bad pain in his side. He wanted to stop and rest. But he was afraid he might lose her. That wouldn't do. So he kept going. When he was at the end of his rope, his tongue hanging out like a dog who'd been chasing cars or sheep, when his heart was pounding so hard it threatened to pop out of his chest, Isabelle got where she was going.

"Where ya been? I almost left!" he heard someone shout.

Guy hid behind a narrow tree, bulging out from behind it on either side. A baby could've spotted him, but neither Isabelle nor Herbie (for surely this was Herbie) seemed to notice him. He watched Isabelle throw down her newspaper bag, settle her hat firmly on her head, and leap like a tiger upon Herbie. Herbie howled as his head hit the ground. They rolled around in the dirt, exchanging blows. Guy came out from behind the tree and squatted at a respectful distance, watching them, entranced. It was like watching a TV Western, he thought. They weren't wearing high-heeled boots. Or ten-gallon hats. And they weren't even breaking chairs over each other's heads, and there wasn't any shooting. But Herbie and Isabelle were making the same noises the TV cowboys made, grunting, groaning, sending up shouts of rage. And it was all live, real—much more exciting than watching TV.

"No feet!" Isabelle hollered suddenly. "We said no feet!" She had relaxed her grip for a second. That was all Herbie needed. He flipped her over, with the aid of his feet. He was winning.

"How come it's okay if *you* use feet but it's not okay

if I do?" Herbie asked quietly. Herbie always got quiet when he was winning.

Isabelle had big feet and she was proud of them. Her feet came in handy, both for fighting and for running.

"Besides," Herbie explained, "I only used one foot. And that's because you were crushing all the bones in my stomach."

"You don't have bones in your stomach," Isabelle said scornfully. "You've got guts. Gobs and gobs of guts. If you stretched 'em out, those guts of yours would probably reach down to the end of the street and around the block."

Herbie didn't like to hear about guts, his own or anyone else's. Guy didn't either, but he listened anyway.

Slowly, lovingly, Isabelle described Herbie's guts to him. "They're all pink and wobbly," she said. "Like giant worms, miles and miles of giant worms, all pink and wobbly, squiggly and slippery."

Guy's stomach began to do flip-flops. Herbie's must've too, because he jumped up and ran over to the curb and began heaving.

Isabelle, a small smile of triumph on her face, went over to investigate.

"You're a faker, Herb," she said. "You didn't throw up one drop. Not one. Some faker you are."

"Leave me alone," Herbie said crossly. "Maybe you

don't have bones in your stomach, but I sure do in mine. Who's that?"

Guy had blown his cover and was practically breathing down their necks by now.

"He's my new customer on my paper route," Isabelle said.

"Wait'll I tell Philip you called it your route!" Herbie howled.

Isabelle assumed her boxer's stance: knees bent, fists held close to her face. She bobbed in circles around Guy, punching at the air around his head. His eyes, shiny and still as two pebbles at the bottom of a pond, followed her. The rest of him was still.

"How old are you?" Isabelle said, still punching.

"Eight," he said softly.

"I'm ten!" Isabelle crowed. "I'm in fifth grade and doing fine in life. How about you?"

"I'm in third grade," he said.

"So? So?" she said, as if he was trying to start trouble. "Hey, Herb, this kid lives on Hot Water Street."

Herbie hooked his thumbs into the waist of his pants, partly to appear tough, partly to hold them up. His mother bought his pants a size too big to allow for shrinkage in the dryer. Herbie was constantly in danger of losing his pants. He sauntered over to Guy, eyes narrowed, sneering a little.

"You look like a straight shooter, pardner," Herbie said. He wiped his hand on his pants and said, "Shake." Guy shook.

"How about you and me wiping up the floor with her?" Herbie suggested. "Two against one? How about it?"

"Okay, you little twerps!" Isabelle roared, advancing on them, fists ready.

At that very moment a voice cried, "Isabelle! Time!"

"Coming!" Isabelle shouted, still advancing on Guy and Herbie.

"I didn't say anything," Guy said in a quavery voice. For the first time he thought perhaps he should've stayed at home.

"You better go, Iz," Herbie said. "I can tell when your mother means it or if she's only fooling around."

"My mother never fools around," Isabelle said.

"Isabelle! Last call!"

Isabelle took one last lucky swing and decked Herbie. He howled as she took off, her Adidas a blur in the gathering dusk.

"She fights dirty," Herbie said, rubbing his ear. "They don't call her Isabelle the Itch for nothing. She's always punching out people. She didn't really hurt me. I always holler and she stops. I was only pretending. If I holler loud enough, she lays off. See you," and Herbie was gone too, flying low.

It was almost dark.

I hope I don't get lost, Guy thought. I hope no monsters are hiding in the bushes. Excitement crowded him. He had made two new friends—big kids, tough kids. Isabelle the Itch and Herbie.

11

Noises came from the shadows, but he kept going. At long last the street sign said Hot Water Street. He was home.

Chapter Three

"Where'd they put the piano?" Isabelle asked, mashing her face against the screen door, mouth open, enjoying the slightly bitter taste of metal.

Without moving her chin from its nesting place in her hand, the little girl looked at her and said, "Who're you?"

"The paper boy. Where's the piano?" Isabelle opened the door and, uninvited, eased herself inside.

"You looked like a guppy," the little girl said. "With your mouth open like that. Just like our guppy when I feed him."

"How do you know it's a him? I told the movers they might have to take off the legs if they wanted to get the piano inside. Either that or leave it outside, and when your mother wants to play, she could open the window and play from inside."

"My mother doesn't play the piano," the child said. "I do. I take lessons."

"I can play 'Chopsticks,' " Isabelle said. "What's a little twerp like you doing taking piano lessons?" She opened the refrigerator door absent-mindedly and looked inside. It was amazing what some people kept in refrigerators. She knew a girl whose mother was a writer and kept her manuscripts in the refrigerator, in case the house burned down. That way her manuscripts would be safe.

"My mother says you should never open somebody's refrigerator," the little girl said. "It makes her mad when kids do that."

Isabelle closed the door. There was nothing good in there anyway. "Have you got an ice maker?" she asked. Isabelle's father said they were expensive and unnecessary, but she longed for one. They made such neat noises. Little clinking sounds, like fish coming up for air. Or mice having a party.

"We only moved in yesterday. We haven't got settled yet," the little girl said. "I'm not a little twerp. I'm a child."

"You could've fooled me," said Isabelle.

"What's your name?" the child asked.

"Isabelle. What's yours?"

"I'm Becca. I'm six. Do you want to see my chains?"

"Sure. Are they gold?"

"No, silly." Becca got down off her chair. "Come on, I'll show you."

There was nothing Isabelle liked better than inspecting other people's houses. Closets were her specialty, but she also liked cellars, attics, bathrooms, rec rooms, and master bedrooms. So far she'd never seen a master in a master bedroom, but she kept trying. My daughter the real-estate lady, her mother sometimes called her.

"They're in here." Becca opened the door to a small room off the kitchen. "This is our playroom, except when my grandmother comes to visit."

The room was crowded with paper chains. The ceiling was festooned with them and they decorated the walls, moving in a slow dance as the draft from the open door stirred them to action. They hung every which way.

"They're like cobwebs," Isabelle said, brushing the chains away from her face. "How come you've got so many?"

"Every time I read a book," Becca said, "I make a chain. That way, I keep count of how many books I've read."

In spite of herself Isabelle was impressed. "I bet you didn't read this many," she said, starting to count Becca's chains.

"There are forty-three," Becca said. "And I read them all. How many books have you read?"

"Oh," Isabelle said, waving her hands in the air, "I don't have time to read. I've got too many things to do. I play soccer. And tap-dance. And fight and do Philip's paper route. And practice the fifty-yard dash. That's my specialty, the fifty-yard dash."

"Everyone has time to read books," Becca said, unimpressed by Isabelle's busy schedule. "If they want to, that is."

This little squirt sounded like Isabelle's teacher, Mrs. Esposito, or like Isabelle's own mother, for Pete's sake.

"What grade are you in?" Isabelle wanted to know.

"I'm in first," Becca said. "I'm a gifted child."

"Okay," said Isabelle, "say something gifted."

"You're cuckoo!" Becca replied, laughing.

"If you're so gifted, how come you're not in high school already? I read about a thirteen-year-old kid who was so smart he was going to college. What's holding you up?" Isabelle demanded.

"I'm too little to be in high school," Becca said calmly.

"Becca, who are you talking to?" a voice called from upstairs.

"I'm talking to Isabelle, the paper boy," Becca called back. "My mother's up in the attic, unpacking things," she told Isabelle.

"Where's your brother? Did he have to stay after school or something?" Isabelle asked.

"Of course not. Guy never has to stay after school."

"He doesn't?" Isabelle asked, amazed. Staying after school was as natural to her as breathing.

"Guy never gets into trouble," Becca said, leading the way back to the kitchen.

Loud noises from outside interrupted them. Isabelle went to the window. "Looks like he's in it now," she said.

Guy came running up the path. Behind him was a gang of boys, all bigger than he. They were singing and shouting and waving their arms. Guy banged in and slammed the door, standing with his back against it, breathing hard. His sweater was torn and his pants were muddy. Tears made tracks through the dirt on his face.

"They followed me," he said.

Outside, the boys sang, "Goody-goody-goody-goody," imitating a train picking up speed. "Goody-goody Guy, wouldn't hurt a fly!" they sang with enthusiasm.

"I thought it would be different, living on Hot Water Street," Guy said sadly. "But it's no use, it's no use at all."

"I'll get 'em for you!" Isabelle cried, exploding out the door and into the midst of the gang. "Pick on somebody your own size, why don't you!" she shrieked, fists flying, feet churning.

Someone stuck out a foot. Isabelle tripped and fell

17

to the sidewalk, where she lay, feeling sick to her stomach.

"Izzy, Izzy, tin-lizzy Izzy!" they sang. "Izzy, Izzy is a bear, in her flowered underwear!" They must've picked that up from Chauncey Lapidus, Isabelle thought. He'd made up that verse. "Izzy's in a tizzy!"

Then, in the flick of an eye, they disappeared—as if a gigantic eraser had wiped them off the board. As if a trap door had opened and swallowed them all whole.

From where she lay Isabelle watched as a taxi pulled up and a woman wearing a large black hat got out and paid the driver.

"Who are you, little girl?" the woman asked.

"I'm the paper boy," said Isabelle, for what seemed like the tenth time.

"From my experience," the woman said, "that is not the proper way to deliver newspapers." She reached down a hand to help Isabelle to her feet. Then they both marched up the front path, and the woman opened the door to Guy's new house as if she belonged there.

"Who are you?" Isabelle asked the woman, figuring tit for tat was fair.

"I'm Guy's grandmother. I've come for a visit, to help out until they get settled. They're not expecting me, but I'm sure they'll be glad to see me. I haven't been to visit them in ages."

A woman was standing at the sink bathing Guy's dirty face. "Good heavens, Mother Gibbs!" the woman cried. "I certainly didn't expect to see you!"

Isabelle wanted to stay to see what was going to happen, but her canvas bag still bulged with unde-livered papers. She laid one on the table and took off.

Chapter Four

"How's my angel?" Guy's grandmother pursed her lips and pointed them in his direction.

"I'm not your angel," Guy said, backing off. "How long are you staying?"

"I just got here," his grandmother said, sitting in the most comfortable chair and crossing her legs. She looked around.

"No ashtrays?" she said.

"Nobody smokes."

"I do," she announced.

"I knew you weren't an angel," she continued. "I'm a little rusty at being a grandmother. That's the way they're supposed to talk to their grandchildren, isn't it? Give me time." She and Guy stared at one another.

From the kitchen Guy's mother called, "Be right out, Mother Gibbs."

"I wish she wouldn't call me that," Guy's grandmother said. "Makes me feel like an old lady in an apron."

"What should she call you?" Guy asked, thinking she *was* old, even if she didn't wear an apron.

"My name."

"What's your name?"

"Maybelle." She looked pleased. "I was born in May and I was a beautiful baby."

"You were?" Guy said, not believing her. He didn't think a whole lot of Maybelle as a name, but he kept quiet, studying her. He hadn't seen his grandmother since he'd been a tiny baby. At least, that's what they told him. He was pretty sure he could remember her peering down at him and saying, "Skinny little shaver, isn't he?" If it wasn't her, it was somebody just like her.

"Hello," said Becca, appearing in the doorway.

"Who's that?" Guy's grandmother said, squinting through the smoke of the cigarette she'd lit.

"That's my sister, Becca," Guy said.

"Oh, right. I forgot about her. How's it going, Becca?" Guy's grandmother said.

"This is my grandmother, Becca," Guy said.

"She's my grandmother, too, don't forget," Becca said. "Your lungs will turn black if you smoke."

"Who said?" Guy's grandmother asked, raising her eyebrows.

After a short silence Becca said, "I'm a gifted child."

"Who said?" Guy's grandmother asked again.

"Who said what?"

"That you're a gifted child." Guy's grandmother blew out a huge cloud of smoke, and Becca went into a coughing fit.

"I'm in a special class for gifted children," Becca said, when she'd finished her coughing fit.

"And what about you, Guy?" his grandmother asked.

"I'm an underachiever," Guy said in a loud voice. "What's more, they call me goody-goody because I can't get into trouble."

"Everybody in school calls him Goody-Goody Guy," Becca put in her two cents.

Guy clenched his fists and shouted, "Shut up! Who asked you?"

"How about an ashtray?" Guy's grandmother said. Guy raced into the kitchen and returned in the nick of time with an old orange-juice can. They all watched as the ash trembled and fell into the can.

"Here we are, Mother Gibbs," Guy's mother cried, carrying in a tray of refreshments.

"Call her Maybelle, that's her name," Guy said.

22

"Guy," his mother said sternly, "she's your grandmother."

"How long is she staying?" Becca asked.

"It depends. Maybe a week, maybe a month." Guy's grandmother looked around at them. "Depends on how much you need me."

"A month," Guy's mother said, handing round a plate of little cakes. "How nice."

Guy's grandmother took out another cigarette. "How about a match?" she said.

"I can't stand the smell of smoke," said Becca. "It makes me sick."

"Well, don't go getting a red nose about it." Guy's grandmother put the cigarette back in her handbag.

"I got a copy of *Grimm's Fairy Tales* for being the best reader in my class," Becca said.

"That beats a sharp stick in the eye. Read that," and Guy's grandmother snatched up the newspaper and pointed to the headline.

Becca said, "Oh, I only read books," and twirled out of the room.

Guy's grandmother turned her dark, deep-set eyes on him. He lifted his shoulders as if to say, "What can I do?"

"She's something." Guy's grandmother tapped her fingers on the table, then dove into her handbag and came up with another cigarette. They both looked at it. She put it back in her bag.

"So they call you goody-goody, do they?" she said.

23

Guy squeezed his hands between his knees and clicked his feet together rhythmically.

"That's not the worst thing in the world," she said. Guy's feet clicked, lickety split, faster and faster.

"I'm glad I came," Guy's grandmother said.

Chapter Five

If my name was Jake, things would be different.

Guy stared at himself in the mirror.

If my name was Jake, they would never chase a person named Jake, hollering "Goody-goody Jake!" It would never happen. A person named Jake wouldn't take any guff from anybody. "Everything's jake," his father said when he meant everything was fine and dandy. Catch him saying "Everything's Guy." Just catch him.

Guy lifted his lip and sneered at himself. Jake

sounded tough. Already he looked different. Mean. Tough. Beware of Jake, they'd whisper. Don't rub Jake the wrong way. You know Jake. He'll take off your ear in one bite.

He turned sideways and sneered some more. He reminded himself of a pro football player he'd seen on TV. Yup, he was definitely a Jake. The thought cheered him as he put on his socks and sneaks. Then the jeans. Oops. He always forgot. The jeans wouldn't go over the sneaks. Off with the sneaks, on with the jeans.

The minute he woke up that morning Guy had smelled Saturday—crispy, spicy, fragrant, as if his mother had taken a freshly baked apple pie from the oven. He planned to spend today with Isabelle, only she didn't know it. He'd better hot-foot it over to her house before she and Herbie went somewhere.

Guy wet his hands and smashed down his cowlick. People named Jake who were mean and tough didn't have cowlicks on the top of their heads. But in its own way, the cowlick was mean and tough, too. It sprang back up like a jack-in-the-box.

On weekdays, Guy dawdled. On Saturdays, he dressed with the speed of a volunteer fireman. Down the stairs he went, two at a time.

"For a little boy," his mother said in her soft voice, "you make a great deal of noise. Cereal's ready."

"I'm not eating cereal," Guy said in a loud, rude

voice. "I don't have time for cereal," Guy/Jake said. "I gotta get going."

"Have to, not gotta," said his mother gently. Everything she said and did was gentle.

"Too bad," she told him. "The cinnamon doughnuts are almost warm."

He *knew* he'd smelled Saturday. He ate his cereal fast, wishing, not for the first time, for a dog. A dog would sure love that bowl of cereal, Guy thought. A dog would be company, would lick his hand, and would sleep at the foot of his bed at night. A dog would guard the house. A dog would be a friend. But a dog was messy and a lot of trouble. And expensive—to feed, to take to the vet's.

"Guy," his mother said. He almost said "My name's Jake," but didn't. "Guy, if those boys bother you again, I want you to promise to tell me. I'll do something about it. That's not right. Dad wouldn't like it either." They tried never to bother Dad with tales of Guy being teased. Dad didn't like to hear this—he liked to think Guy was an all-around-American-boy-type who was never called names and made fun of. Guy's father was the football coach at the high school. He planned on Guy being a football player someday. Being a football player was way down at the end of Guy's list of favorite things to think about.

"I'm done." Guy showed his mother the bottom of his dish. The doughnut was his. Cradling it in his hand, he headed for the door.

"I'm going to Isabelle's," he told her.

"Who is Isabelle?"

"The paper boy. She was here yesterday "

"She called me a twerp," Becca said.

"You are," said Guy.

"Guy," his mother said, "that's not nice."

"Isabelle asked me over to her house today." Guy looked at his mother from under lowered lids. He almost never lied, and he was surprised when she seemed to believe what he said. "Isn't Isabelle a trifle too old for you to play with?" was all she said.

"She's only ten," he said. *Only* ten! She was practically a teenager, that's what. He didn't tell his mother about Isabelle and Herbie fighting every day after school. She wouldn't like that, he knew.

"Don't wear out your welcome," his mother told him as he said good-bye.

When he got to Isabelle's, there was no answer to his knock. Guy sat on the back step to wait. Presently the door opened and a man carrying a bag of garbage almost fell over him.

"Oops!" said the man. "Sorry, didn't see you."

"Is Isabelle up yet?" Guy asked.

"No, thank God," the man said. "I have the place all to myself. If you promise to be quiet, not say a word, you can come in and wait."

"I promise," Guy said.

Once in, the man pointed a floury finger and said,

"Sit there. And remember, no talking. I can't cook and talk at the same time."

Guy sat. The man whistled happily, sifting flour, checking a cookbook spread open on the counter. "I think I've got it!" he cried out once or twice. "I really think I've got it! It's not easy, making pizza from scratch," he told Guy. "And it's not cheap either. Cheese, sausages, anchovies, all that stuff. But the real trick is the dough. That's the tough part. You have to be quick when you toss it up and catch it. You ever seen 'em throw it up in the air in a pizza store, then catch it on its way down?" Guy shook his head no. "Fantastic! Absolutely fantastic!" the man said. "They never miss. Toss it up, twirl it around, then toss it up again. I wish I could do it. I'm learning, though. Don't want to rush it. Easy does it, eh?"

Guy nodded, smiling. He was enjoying the conversation, even if he hadn't said a word.

Isabelle zoomed into the kitchen and headed straight for the refrigerator. "Hi," she said to Guy, not at all surprised to see him there. "Dad," she said to the pizza man, "I've decided to leave my body to science."

"That so?" Isabelle's father leaned over his cookbook, muttering to himself. A large boy on crutches appeared. Philip, Guy figured, as clever as any detective. That's Philip.

"I'm leaving my body to science," Isabelle told Philip.

"Suppose they give it back?" Philip speared a pickle

from a jar. "What do they want with a wimpy little bod like yours?"

Isabelle gave it one more try. "I'm leaving my body to science," she told Guy in a loud voice, as if she thought he might be deaf.

Guy nodded to show he'd heard and then laid a finger against his lips.

"Who's he?" Philip aimed a crutch in Guy's direction. "Where'd he come from?"

"He's a new customer on my . . . I mean, your paper route. Better treat him nice or he might cancel. His name's Guy," said Isabelle.

Guy opened his mouth to say his name was Jake, then remembered his promise to keep quiet.

"What's your prob, kid? Cat got your tongue?" Philip asked.

Isabelle's father ran his hand through his hair, leaving white tracks. "I've been at this since dawn and I'm still a long way from finishing. You can talk now," he told Guy. "I'm tired of making bread," he said to them. "I'm letting my imagination soar and making pizza instead."

"Go for it, Dad," Philip said.

"My father always makes bread on Saturday," Isabelle explained. "I take a loaf to my teacher. She's on a diet, but she eats my father's bread anyway because it's so delicious."

Guy, who had been wondering what to say now that he no longer had to be silent, said, "My father gave blood once. After, they gave him a glass of orange juice. And my grandmother said she might donate her organs."

Then he tapped his feet and stared at the ceiling, having talked himself out.

"Cool," Isabelle said. "I wouldn't mind donating my organs."

"Which organ did you have in mind?" Isabelle's father asked, pausing in his pizza-making.

"Which one do you think would be best?" Isabelle asked, not having the faintest idea what organs were.

"How about your brain?" Philip suggested. "If you donated your brain to science, they could give it to a monkey and that old monkey would be the smartest monkey on his block."

"Har-de-har," Isabelle said.

"The brain isn't an organ," Isabelle's father said, kneading his dough. Isabelle pointed a finger at Philip, laughing hugely and silently at his mistake.

"Make it your liver or your kidneys," Isabelle's father said.

"Liver and kidneys!" Isabelle made throw-up noises. Then, as if she'd just made it up, she did an elaborate dance, crooning "excellent, excellent" to herself, praising her own talents.

"I'm off to Angelo's now. Hands off my dough. Your mother's still asleep, so keep the noise down, please. Angelo's giving me a lesson in how to toss the dough up and catch it coming down. I'll be back in an hour."

The telephone rang and Isabelle raced to answer. Philip gave her a hip check and sent her crashing against the wall.

"Hello," their father said. "No, I'm sorry. They're both busy misbehaving. Call back, please." He hung up. "Shape up or ship out," he said. "You both behave like troglodytes."

"What's that?" Isabelle asked.

"Cave men. And they didn't have telephones."

"Who was it?" asked Philip.

"I didn't ask. The young lady didn't leave her name."

"I knew it was for me!" Philip howled.

"I bet it was Mary Eliza Shook. She always checks up on me on Saturday."

"Remember what I said. Hands off the dough." They listened as their father started the car and drove away.

"Turkey," Philip said.

"I'm telling Dad you called him a turkey!" Isabelle cried.

"Not him, scuzz. You."

"Dinosaur breath," said Isabelle.

Guy scrooched down in his chair and folded his hands on his stomach, like an old man taking the sun on a park bench, enjoying himself.

Disgusted, Philip crutched his way out, muttering "spoiled brat" and "stink baby" and other endearments.

Isabelle took a can of Reddi Wip from the refrigerator and shot some into her mouth.

"Open," she said to Guy, like a dentist. He opened and she shot some into his mouth.

"It's sweet," Guy said, surprised.

"What'd you expect, sour?" Isabelle took something out of a drawer and pulled it on over her head.

"What's that?"

"It's my mother's old pantyhose. I'm trying it out on Herbie's mother. I like to freak her out. Robbers wear pantyhose masks when they don't want people to know who they are. I bet Herbie's mother won't know who I am. Maybe she'll think I'm a robber. That oughta really get her," she announced with satisfaction.

"It makes your voice sound funny," said Guy. "And it makes you look funny, too."

"Good." Isabelle lifted the cloth her father had placed over his pizza dough and poked it with one finger. "I'm just testing to see if anything's happened yet," she said.

"You father said hands off," Guy reminded her.

"I only touched it a tiny bit. He won't know. Not unless you tell him," she said, scowling at Guy.

"Cross my heart," he said. "I won't tell."

"All right," she said. "Let's go."

Chapter Six

"Herbie can't come out today. He's got a cold." Herbie's mother looked straight at Isabelle and didn't scream once. Not even a tiny little scream.

"He didn't have one yesterday," Isabelle said indignantly, from behind her pantyhose mask.

"Well, he has one today." Herbie's mother opened the door a fraction and said to Guy, "What's your name?"

"Guy," said Isabelle.

"Jake," said Guy.

Herbie's mother looked surprised. "You kids better get your act together," she said.

"Don't you notice anything?" Isabelle slowly turned her head from left to right, right to left.

Herbie's mother narrowed her eyes and studied Isabelle carefully. "Now that you mention it," she said, "I *did* think you were Mary Eliza Shook for a minute."

Isabelle crossed her eyes and tried to stick her thumbs in her ears and waggle her fingers to show how she felt about looking like Mary Eliza Shook, but the pantyhose got in the way.

"But when I heard your voice," Herbie's mother said, smiling, "I knew it was you."

"Let 'em in, Mom!" Isabelle heard Herbie shout. She looked through the door and saw Herbie teetering on the top step. He had on his astronaut pajamas and his crash helmet. He didn't look the least bit sick.

Herbie's mother turned her head and shouted, "Get back to bed!" And in a flash Isabelle thrust the toe of her Adidas in the crack in the door, an opening wedge.

"Hey, Herb!" she cried, her mouth against the crack. "How about a game of Crazy Eights or Monopoly?"

Isabelle and Herbie hadn't played Monopoly since the time when she'd made some counterfeit money and tried to pass it off as the real Monopoly stuff. Herbie was still sore about that.

"Sorry." Herbie's mother almost shut Isabelle's nose in the door. "Herbie's off-limits today. He had a tem-

35

perature last night." She shut the door firmly in their faces.

"Maybe it's catching!" Isabelle cried. "Let us in! It might be catching!"

But Herbie's mother slid the lock into place and waved good-bye to them. "Boy," said Isabelle, "I bet Herbie's drinking orange juice by the quart today. His mother feeds him vitamin C to keep him from getting colds. He gets colds anyhow. Let's wait out front. Herbie'll come and talk to us out the window. Come on."

Guy hadn't said a single word except "Jake" when asked what his name was. "I changed my name to Jake," he told Isabelle.

"When?"

"Yesterday. I figure if my name's Jake, it'll make me tougher, and they won't call me goody-goody Jake, that's for sure."

"Maybe." Isabelle looked doubtful. "Don't put any money on it, though. There he is! Hey, Herb," she called.

Herbie opened the upstairs window and leaned out. "What's that on your head?" he croaked.

"My mother's pantyhose. It's a mask like the ones robbers wear when they rob a bank. So nobody'll recognize 'em. Your mother knew who I was right away, though. By my voice, she said," Isabelle told Herbie.

"If you rob a bank," Herbie said, "you write a note and shove it to the person you're robbing. That way you don't have to talk and give it all away." He coughed loudly to prove he was sick.

"Send some germs down to us," Isabelle called up. "Me and Guy could use a few germs."

Herbie opened the window further and breathed out a lot of germs.

"Too bad you can't come with us," Isabelle said. "My father's making pizza today. I have to go home and help him throw the dough up in the air."

"What kind's he making?" Herbie said.

"Onion and pepperoni," she said. It was Herbie's favorite kind.

"Ooh!" Herbie wailed. His mother came up behind him and slammed the window down. Herbie disappeared.

"Let's put the show on the road," Isabelle said, whipping off her mask and stuffing it in her pocket.

Mary Eliza Shook materialized as if she'd been waiting for them. She wore her jogging suit, a sweatband, and leg warmers.

Isabelle made a face. "Your legs are all wrinkly," she said.

Mary Eliza looked at her legs with great fondness. "Those are leg warmers," she said. "All ballet dancers wear them. Other people wear them too, but they're not professionals. Only ballet dancers should really wear leg warmers. If their legs get cold, they might get cramps."

"Then what?" Isabelle said.

"Then they can't dance, dummy." Mary Eliza's arms arched over her head as she prepared her next *pas de chat*.

"Plenty of people wear leg warmers and they're not ballet dancers," Isabelle told Mary Eliza. "My brother Philip says girls who wear 'em have elephant legs. That's what he calls 'em, Elephant Legs, because they make your legs look all wrinkly, like an elephant's. Who needs it?"

"Who's the boyfriend, dear? Aren't you robbing the cradle?" Mary Eliza let out a blast of her most irritating laughter. Isabelle silenced her with a direct hit from her ring.

"Cut it out," Mary Eliza said. "If he's not your boyfriend, who is he?"

A line from a TV movie she'd recently seen popped into Isabelle's head.

"He's me little brudder, that's who," she said. Guy's mouth dropped open in astonishment as she laid a protective arm on his shoulder. He flinched, thinking she was going to belt him.

"Pooh!" said Mary Eliza. "You don't have a little brother and you know it."

"We just adopted him," said Isabelle, getting a firmer grip on Guy. All of a sudden, the idea of a little brother was very attractive. She could boss him around and everything. A little brother, Isabelle suddenly decided, beat a big brother all hollow.

"What's his name, Miss Smarty?"

"His name's Jake. Say hello to the lady, Jake." Isabelle dug her elbow into Guy's ribs.

"Hello," said Guy, dipping his head and staring at the sidewalk, trying to work free of Isabelle's clinging hands. In case she was going to nudge him again, he'd rather be far away from her.

"Well, all I can say is, it's very strange, very strange indeed," Mary Eliza muttered. She darted at Isabelle, ready to link arms, a terrible habit of hers. But Isabelle was too fast for her. She stuck out her fist with the point of her friendship ring aimed straight for Mary Eliza's nose. That did it. Mary Eliza backed off. But she didn't take defeat lightly.

"All right, then!" she shouted. Words failed her.

"You shout too much," Guy said.

"She sure does!" Mary Eliza said, at the top of her voice.

"Not her, you," said Guy. "You make me tired, you shout so much."

"Let's go get some of Dad's homemade pizza," Isabelle said. "I'm hungry, Jake. How about you?" They left Mary Eliza doing a perfect *entrechat* for anyone passing by to see.

"Thanks for calling me Jake," Guy said.

"That's okay. Anytime," said Isabelle, filled with a glow of well-being.

Which didn't last long, for the minute she saw her father's face, she knew he'd discovered her fingerprint in the pizza dough.

"You just can't keep your hands off, can you?" he said. "I ought to put you over my knee and give you an old-fashioned spanking. That's what you deserve. I should've known better than to leave it within your reach." He swatted her with his rolling pin. It wasn't a very hard swat, but it left flour on her rear end.

Isabelle's mother, washing her hair at the kitchen sink, peered up at her and asked, "Who's that?" meaning Guy.

"He's me little brudder," Isabelle said, fooling around.

"What did you say?" her mother asked, through her dripping hair.

"He's Guy from my paper route, Mom." Isabelle didn't want to push either of her parents any further today. "I brought him home for a piece of Dad's pizza."

"The pizza won't be much good," her father said. "The crust's ruined. When I said 'hands off' I meant exactly that. But Angelo gave me a lesson in throwing the dough up and catching it, so I'm going to go ahead."

The telephone rang. "That's for me," Isabelle's father said. "I'm expecting a call." He wiped his hands on his pants and went into the hall to answer the phone. Isabelle looked at the large circle of dough lying on the counter. Isabelle's mother wrapped a towel around her head and disappeared. The kitchen was very still. Isabelle listened to her father talking on the telephone.

It would be so easy, she thought. Toss it up, catch

it coming down. She'd watched Angelo plenty of times. The way he did it, it looked like a snap.

"Oh, no," Guy said very softly, as she scooped up her father's dough from the counter and held it in both hands.

With a flourish, Isabelle flipped it up into the air. She and Guy watched it go, circling lazily overhead, moving slowly, like a miniature flying saucer. Perfect. Absolutely perfect.

Things got out of control. The circle of dough descended much faster than it had risen. Swift as a falling star, it came down to earth and landed smack on Isabelle's head.

Guy put his hand over his mouth to hold back his giggles. "You look so funny!" he said. Isabelle's father stood in the doorway. Isabelle's mother came downstairs. Silently, she handed Isabelle a hand mirror.

She did indeed look funny. The dough hung limply around her ears, covering her hair and most of her face.

"Tell you what, Isabelle." She heard her father's voice, although she couldn't see him through the curtain of dough. "We'll make the pizza anyway. Just gather it together off your head and roll it out again. It'll be terrible, probably very tough, but it's the best you're going to get today. And you know what?"

"No, sir," Isabelle said.

She could hear her father smiling.

"You get the piece with the most hair in it," he said.

Chapter Seven

Guy sped toward home. After they'd eaten the pizza, which turned out to be not bad after all, he'd helped Isabelle deliver papers. An old lady named Mrs. Stern wasn't home, which disappointed Guy. Isabelle had told him Mrs. Stern painted her front door, as well as the rooms of her house, a different color any time she felt like it—sometimes just to cheer herself up. Guy liked that idea and thought about painting his room dark blue so he could paste some stars on the walls and ceiling. Then he could lie in bed and see the stars shining above and around him and pretend he was camping out.

The wind was rising, making whispery noises in the trees. "Tell your mother I'll collect next week," Isabelle had said. "I'm hoping Philip will still be on crutches. Then she smiled and added, "If his hurt ankle gets better, I can always put a skate at the top of the stairs, and he might fall over it and hurt his other ankle. We'll see." She would, too, Guy thought, full of admiration. Even if Philip was a teenager, Isabelle could handle him. She was awesome.

The sky was smeared with scarlet and gold and looked, Guy thought, like a finger painting he'd done last year. It was his favorite and still hung above his bed. When he grew up, he was going to be an artist. He'd seen paintings done by grown-up artists that looked like finger paintings and which had been sold for a lot of money too. If they could do it, why couldn't he?

The dark clumps of bushes took on the shape of people. "Here he comes," the wind whispered. "Here he comes," they sighed.

Here who comes?

A small, dark shape rushed out at him, and Guy let out a little shout of fear.

"Oh," he said, drawing a deep breath when he saw the little brown dog. "It's only you." He knelt down and patted the dog's soft fur. The dog licked Guy's hand with his rough tongue, and they became immediate friends.

"You're just the right size," Guy told the dog, who wriggled with pleasure. "You could come home with me if my mother would let you," Guy said. "She might let you stay. I'm not sure. If you're good. If you don't go to the bathroom on the rug. Or chew the furniture. Or eat a lot. A dog is a big responsibility, you know." The dog tilted its head to one side and considered this information. It was a frisky little dog, with a tail like a feather duster and eager amber eyes. It would be a good dog to play Frisbee with, Guy thought. It would be a good watchdog, even though it was small, because it could be fierce when fierceness was needed.

"I could hide you in the attic," Guy said aloud. "Keep you a secret until I talked her into loving you. Why don't we try it?" The more he thought about hiding the dog in the attic, the better the idea seemed.

The dog laid a stick at Guy's feet and backed off, barking. So Guy threw the stick and the little dog brought it back, triumphant. Guy threw the stick a second time and the dog went after it again. Guy heard him barking but he didn't return. Guy called and called—"Hey, I'm over here!"—but still the dog didn't appear.

"All right for you!" Guy shouted at last, when he could hardly see the outline of the trees, it was getting so dark. He scurried homeward, turning now and then, checking to see if the dog was following him. But he was alone.

"It's late, Guy," his mother said. "You should have been home long ago. I was very worried."

"I had to help Isabelle deliver her papers," he said. "Here's ours," and he handed over the paper.

"She called," his mother said.

"Isabelle?" he asked, surprised.

"She said for you to come over tomorrow. She said she and Herbie are probably going to fight and you could watch. What's that all about?"

"Oh, they fight all the time. They're friends but they just like to fight," he said, making it sound perfectly normal to like to fight.

"I don't want you fighting, Guy," she said. "You might get hurt."

"I don't know how to fight," he said, and went up to his room and lay on his bed, looking at the ceiling, trying to imagine how it would look pasted all over with stars. His mother found him there.

"I would like to paint my room dark blue and paste stars on it so it would be like the night," he told her.

"Guy." She laid an anxious hand on his forehead. "Do you feel all right?"

"I feel fine," he said, bounding up and down to prove he felt fine. "I just want to paint my room dark blue to cheer myself up. That's all."

Chapter Eight

"Aunt Maude, this is my friend Guy," Isabelle said.

"How do you do? I'm happy to meet you," said Aunt Maude, who had stopped in after church, as usual, to show off her new hat. Guy said hello. Aunt Maude turned to Isabelle's mother and said in a loud whisper, "Hasn't he shrunk?"

"Shrunk?"

"Yes. The little boy, I mean. He seems to have gotten smaller."

"Oh, you've got him confused with Herbie, Maude.

This is a different boy. His family has just moved into a house on Hot Water Street."

"Oh, my." Aunt Maude's eyes rolled, and she said, "I've always thought that would be a very hazardous place to live. All that water boiling around, don't you know." Aunt Maude settled herself on the couch like a hen on its nest.

"My hair seems to be getting thin," she said, patting her freshly washed, newly blonde coiffure.

"Who wants fat hair?" Isabelle said, poking Guy and avoiding her mother's eye, knowing it would be shooting daggers at her.

Fortunately, Aunt Maude's hearing wasn't what it had once been. "I'll take a bald man any day," she continued, "but I do think there's something rather unattractive about a bald woman, don't you agree?"

Isabelle's mother murmured something about having to see to dinner. On her way out she stepped over Isabelle, who was lying on the floor, reading the comics. "Watch it," she said, putting her foot in the middle of Isabelle's back.

"What smells so good?" Aunt Maude sniffed the air delicately.

"Roast pork," Isabelle's mother called out.

"Nobody noticed my hat," Aunt Maude said, getting up and revolving slowly, showing off her hat from every angle. It was made of pale felt and had a wide brim.

"Where on earth did you get it?" Isabelle's mother said, coming back into the room.

"At a tag sale. I don't know what I did before someone invented tag sales. They are a marvel. Absolutely a marvel. There's nothing you can't find at a tag sale."

"If only you had a black mask," Isabelle told Aunt Maude, "you'd look like the Lone Ranger."

"My stars! The Lone Ranger! I haven't heard anyone mention him in donkey's years. Where'd you hear about him?"

"My friend Mrs. Stern told me about him and his horse Silver. They were always doing good deeds, she said. She used to listen to them on the radio. She showed me a picture of him and his friend Tonto. After the Lone Ranger did a good deed, he hollered, 'Hi yo, Silver, away!' and you heard the sound of galloping hooves."

"Sounds like a drag to me," said Philip, in his super bored voice.

"Then a voice said, 'Who *was* that masked man?' like he was the Incredible Hulk or something," Isabelle went on, "and a voice said, 'That was the Lone Ranger.' "

"And Tonto called the Lone Ranger 'Kemosabe,' " Aunt Maude put in. "I remember that much, although of course I was very young at the time." She gently patted her thin hair.

"El Wimpo Kemosabe," Philip said under his breath.

"I always say roast pork isn't roast pork without

applesauce," said Aunt Maude, getting back to the matter at hand. "Are you having applesauce?"

"If it isn't roast pork, what is it?" Philip asked Isabelle. Philip got away with murder around Aunt Maude. Never having had any children of her own, she was partial to boys.

"Of course, darling, we're having applesauce. I've set a place for you—I hope you'll stay."

"Oh, I couldn't possibly!" Aunt Maude cried. They went through this every Sunday. She always stayed.

"Would you like to stay for dinner, Guy? We've plenty of everything," Isabelle's mother said.

"I've already aten," Guy said. "Eaten, I mean." He blushed furiously, embarrassed at having mixed up his words. He hadn't eaten dinner, he was just too shy to say he'd like to stay. Plus, he was a very picky eater, and he couldn't remember whether he liked roast pork or not.

"Why," Guy said, really looking at Aunt Maude for the first time, "you look just like my uncle!"

"How so?" she said in a somewhat haughty manner, not at all sure she liked being told she looked like Guy's uncle.

"He's a state trooper," Guy said, "and he has a hat just like yours. Plus, he carries a gun."

Aunt Maude gave a little scream of pleasure at this interesting information. "Perhaps this is a state trooper's hat and I didn't even know it," she said, running her hand over her hat's brim.

When dinner was announced, Guy sat with the family, even though he wasn't hungry. The roast pork certainly smelled good. Maybe he'd never had any. Suddenly, he was starving. But he didn't have the nerve to say he'd changed his mind.

As if he knew what Guy was thinking, Isabelle's father said, "Send this down to the young man from Hot Water Street," slicing off some pork and putting it on a plate. Guy ate it in one gulp. It was delicious. He folded his hands in his lap and kept an eye on the other plates. "Help yourself to applesauce and pass it down," Isabelle whispered, giving him an elbow in the ribs. Then the corn pudding was passed, and Guy had a spot of that. All in all, he did pretty well, especially for someone who'd already eaten.

Aunt Maude asked Philip what he was up to these days. When his ankle was better, that is.

"Well, I'm on the Y swim team," Philip said. "I'm a Webfoot. I do the butterfly in record time. I won a race last month. Next month I swim against the state champs."

Each time Philip said "I" Isabelle counted, mouthing the numbers "One, two, three, four, five" so everyone would know Philip had said "I" five times.

"Isabelle, we can do without that," her mother said. When dinner was over, Isabelle's father said, "Why don't you repair to the parlor, Maude, and put your feet up and rest so we can clear the table."

Aunt Maude always got out of KP duty because she

broke things. When Isabelle caught on to this, she broke a plate (old) and a cup (new) the next time she was called upon to clear. All she got was yelled at.

"You take out the salt and pepper," Isabelle told Guy. "You didn't eat much so you don't have to do much."

"I ate quite a lot. I had two pieces of meat and some applesauce and—"

"Just do what I say, and when we're finished, I'm going to give you a lesson."

"Doing what?" Guy asked.

"In fighting," Isabelle said.

Guy dropped the salt shaker on the floor. Isabelle picked it up and said, "Lucky for you it didn't break. Wait'll I crumb the table, then we'll head out." Crumbing the table was Isabelle's favorite part of Sunday dinner. With a large napkin and her usual enthusiasm, she brushed all the crumbs that had fallen on the table during the meal into a tray. The floor needed crumbing, too, after she'd finished.

"Okay." She regarded the clean tablecloth with a practiced eye. "Mission accomplished. Let's go."

"Is Herbie still sick?" Guy asked, longing for Herbie to be up-and-at-'em so *he* could fight with Isabelle.

"I called him up this morning," Isabelle said, "and his mother said he was in bed. But I could hear him hollering in the background that he was fine. He called his mother a mean old witch because she wouldn't let him out. If I called my mother a mean old witch, she'd wash my mouth out with soap. Come on," and she dragged Guy behind her as she left.

"Don't go far," her mother said.

"Why not?"

"I don't know," her mother said, surprised. "If I call you, I want you to be able to hear me."

Outside at last, Isabelle said, "Okay, put up your dukes."

"I don't have any dukes," said Guy. "I just remembered—I didn't thank your mother. I better go back in and thank her."

Isabelle grabbed Guy's sweater and wouldn't let go. "You don't have to thank her," she said. "We better get going. Dukes are fists, dummy. You got fists. Make a fist." She showed him how. "That's right. Now hit me. Here." She stuck her chin at him. "Hit me as hard as you can. I can take it."

He swung at her and missed.

"Again!" Isabelle shouted.

Fists flailing, Guy stirred up the air around Isabelle's head, but he never hit her.

"You're not trying," she said, sounding like Mrs. Esposito. "You're not concentrating. How can you fight if you don't try?"

"I don't know," Guy said.

Suddenly, two creeps from the fourth grade came swooping down the street on their bikes. They headed straight for where Isabelle and Guy were standing.

"Guy, schmy, couldn't hurt a fly!" one of the boys

bellowed. Guy darted behind a tree and Isabelle took off after the boys. But as fast as she could run, their bikes were faster. One of them spit at her and the other cackled and called names all the way to the end of the block and around the corner until they were out of sight.

When she came back, panting and out of breath, Guy was still behind the tree, waiting for her.

"I don't know what we're gonna do," she said. "You don't want to fight. You can't get into trouble. It's hopeless."

He nodded. "I know," he said. "I thought you could help me."

"I'll think of something," Isabelle said. "But it won't be easy. You're a tough case. I'll need a couple of days. But I'll think of something."

Chapter Nine

The next morning Guy pounced on Isabelle as she came out of her classroom.

"Did you think of anything yet?" he said.

"Give me a break. That was only yesterday," she told him.

"Isabelle, may I see you for a minute, please?" Mrs. Esposito said from the doorway.

"Uh-oh." Isabelle knew that meant trouble.

"Look at this." Mrs. Esposito waved a paper marked with a large red F in Isabelle's face. "Last week's test.

Multiplication tables, the ones I drilled you in. The ones I told you we'd have on the test. There's no excuse for the number you had wrong. Absolutely no excuse. You don't concentrate. You don't pay attention. Your mind is always someplace else. I want to help, Isabelle." Mrs. Esposito's pretty eyes were troubled. "But I can't do it without your cooperation."

If Mrs. Esposito felt bad about Isabelle's F, Isabelle felt worse. Already she could hear her father saying, "Pull yourself together, Isabelle, or we lower the boom." Lowering the boom meant no television, no fun, no nothing. She could see her mother's disappointed face as she said, "I thought you were going to do better."

Isabelle spent a lot of time trying to do better, but it was like running in place. She never got anywhere.

And worst of all, she could hear Philip singing under his breath, singing songs about Scuzzy Izzy. And worse.

"I tried," Isabelle said, jigging first on one foot, then the other. "I really tried."

"No, Isabelle, I don't think you did. If you had, this wouldn't have happened. What am I going to do with you?"

"I know." Isabelle snapped her fingers, delighted with the idea that had just occurred to her. "I could come home with you and stay at your house a while. A week or a month, maybe. Then you could drill me on my multiplication tables every morning before school. How would that be?" Isabelle had never been to Mrs. Esposito's house and had always wanted to see what it was like.

Mrs. Esposito shuddered slightly. "No," she said, "I'm sure your mother and father would never permit that."

"They might," Isabelle said. "They get fed up with me. Maybe if I went to live with you, they'd be sorry they were so mean to me."

"I'm sure your mother and father aren't mean to you, Isabelle."

"Oh, yes, they are. They say I'm a pest and a terrible itch and they make me go to my room until I simmer down. My mother says I'm making her old before her time, and my brother kicks me in the stomach when they're out and locks me in the bathroom and steals my candy. Even when I hide it in my shoes, he finds it and eats it. He says it smells of feet but he eats it anyway."

Mrs. Esposito laughed. "One thing about you, Isabelle, you always cheer me up. Even when I'm cross with you, you cheer me up."

"That's good." Isabelle danced around Mrs. Esposito. "My father made pizza Saturday. The crust was a little tough but he said to tell you next time it'll be better and you can have some."

"Tell your father I'd like that." Mrs. Esposito handed Isabelle her test paper. "Take this home," she said, "and go over it. Correct all the mistakes you made and bring it back tomorrow."

"Do I have to have my mother or father sign it?" Isabelle asked.

Mrs. Esposito sighed. "Not this time. This will be between you and me. Just this once."

Isabelle threw her arms around Mrs. Esposito and almost knocked her down. "I love you!" she cried. "You're the most excellent teacher in the whole world!"

She raced out of the room and almost bumped into Jane Malone.

"Sally Smith is moving," Jane said. "My mother said I could give her a farewell party."

"Neat. Who're you going to ask?"

"The class."

"The whole class!" Isabelle said, astonished.

"Yep. My mother says she doesn't think it would be nice to leave anyone out."

"You mean Chauncey and Mary Eliza and everybody?" Isabelle said, remembering parties she'd been left out of.

"Yep. Everyone," said Jane.

"That's a lot of mouths to feed," Isabelle said. "Maybe my mother could help."

"That'd be nice."

Isabelle raced back and caught Mrs. Esposito just as she was putting on her jacket.

"How many people are there in the class?" Isabelle cried.

"Twenty-one, I think." Mrs. Esposito did a little

mental arithmetic. "Yes, that's right. Not counting me," she said, smiling.

Isabelle charged back into the hall.

"There are twenty-one people in the class," she told Jane. "Not counting Mrs. Esposito. Don't forget her. You don't want to leave her out, do you?"

"Oh, no," said Jane. "Thanks for reminding me."

Isabelle felt she had done her good deed for the day. Sort of like the Lone Ranger.

"You're welcome, Kemosabe," she said.

Chapter Ten

"*Have you heard the news?*" Mary Eliza popped out from behind her locker. "Sally Smith is moving!"

"I know. Jane told me," said Isabelle. "She's having a farewell party for Sally. She's inviting everyone."

"Everyone?" Mary Eliza drew herself up haughtily. "That's a lot."

"It's twenty-two, including Mrs. Esposito. My mother's helping Jane's mother." Isabelle aimed a neat blow in Mary Eliza's direction. "Only one cupcake to a person," she hissed. "That's the rule."

Mary Eliza backed off and hissed back, "I'm getting Sally's job!"

"What job?" Isabelle asked, knowing perfectly well what job.

"Art editor of *The Bee*." *The Bee* was the class paper. Some kids wanted to call it *The Bumble Bee* but that was voted down as being too buzzy.

"It just so happens I have a picture with me I drew only this morning." Mary Eliza dove down into her briefcase and pulled out a drawing of a girl in a ballet suit.

Mary Eliza was the only person in the fifth grade, maybe even in the entire school, who had a briefcase.

Isabelle squinted at the picture. "It looks just like you," she said, "only not as ugly." Then she put out her arms and soared in circles around Mary Eliza, making airplane noises, preparing for takeoff.

Insults bounced off Mary Eliza like bullets off Superman. "It's interesting you should say that, because it *is* me," Mary Eliza said with pride. "A good likeness, if I do say so. Notice the placement of the feet, how the arm is extended. Perfect form. I am the artist as well as the artist's model. You might say I'm a shoo-in to be the new art editor of *The Bee*."

"*You* might but you won't catch me saying it," Isabelle said. "I wouldn't say you were a shoo-in if you tied me to a tree and poured honey on my nose so the ants would lick me to death."

"Ants can't lick you to death," Mary Eliza said,

crossing her arms on her chest and slitting her eyes, getting ready to pounce.

Isabelle backed off. She wondered if it was possible to run backwards. She'd never find out until she gave it a try. Moving backwards, she picked up speed.

"Hey! Watch where you're going!" Herbie hollered, as she bumped into him.

"Oh, hi. I thought you were still sick," Isabelle said. "I thought maybe your mother locked you in so the germs couldn't find you."

"She wanted to, but I told her if I missed any more school, I might get left back. So she wrote a note to excuse me from recess and gym so I wouldn't get overheated," Herbie explained.

"I thought only cars got overheated," Isabelle said. "I didn't know people did too."

"There's your little brother!" Mary Eliza shouted as Guy came down the hall.

"She doesn't have any little brother," Herbie said, scowling.

"I knew it! I knew it!" Mary Eliza cried.

"You can come to my house today if you want," Guy said. "My mother said it's all right."

"Today's my last day to do the route," Isabelle said. "Philip owes me a buck fifty times two."

"A buck fifty times two!" Herbie whistled. "Whose little brother is he, then?"

"Go paint yourself into a corner, why don't you?" Isabelle suggested.

Mary Eliza twirled a few times to clear her head. "I might just do that," she said. "A portrait of the artist sitting in a corner. Another first for me."

"How about sitting on a tuffet, eating your curds and whey?" Herbie said.

"What's a tuffet?" Mary Eliza said.

"You don't know what a tuffet is?" Isabelle exclaimed, popping her eyes out.

"I bet you don't know what a tuffet is either, smarty pants. What's a tuffet, then?" Mary Eliza yelled.

"I'm not telling," Isabelle said. She made herself stand quietly and smile at Mary Eliza. It was easier to smile than it was to stand quietly. Much easier. But she did it. Then she turned and walked away— walked, not ran. All the way down the hall, she felt Mary Eliza's eyes on her.

Slowly, slowly. Walk, do not run.

Once around the corner she broke into a fifty-yard dash.

"Slow down!" she heard someone yell.

A sixth-grade traffic cop, the worst kind. Isabelle slowed down, feeling, in some way, victorious.

What *is* a tuffet anyway?

Chapter Eleven

"Mother, this is Herbie and this is Isabelle," Guy said.

"I've met Isabelle," Guy's mother said, not exactly unfriendly, but not exactly friendly, either. "Hello, Herbie," she said.

Herbie was not at his best in front of strangers. He mumbled hello back and hid behind Isabelle.

"Would you like some juice and crackers, children? Guy, you may pour the apple juice and Becca will get the crackers."

"Read any good books lately?" Isabelle asked Becca, joking.

Becca sighed elaborately and handed Isabelle a graham cracker.

Isabelle felt Herbie tugging on her. She reached around and slapped at him to cut it out.

Herbie drank two glasses of apple juice as if he'd just come from the desert. "Okay, where's the hot water?" he demanded, wiping his mouth on the back of his hand.

"If you'd like to wash your hands, Guy will show you to the lavatory," Guy's mother said.

"Outside, I meant." Herbie slid halfway under the table as all eyes turned on him.

"There's no hot water outside, only inside," Becca said.

"I know what he means," Guy said, coming to Herbie's rescue. "When my father first said we were moving here, I dreamed that I fished out of my bedroom window. Just let the line down and lots of fish swimming under my window bit and I hauled 'em up and ate them right there on the rug. They were delicious," he said dreamily. "I thought that was the way it was going to be, a little stream filled with hot water running under my window. I was disappointed for quite a long time."

"That's what I meant," Herbie said. "I thought hot water ran down the street." He didn't say he was disappointed too, but Isabelle thought he was.

"You want to see my chains?" Becca asked Herbie, having taken a sudden fancy to him.

Herbie blinked. "What kind of chains?"

"Chain chains," Becca said. "Come on."

Herbie went reluctantly, sticking his thumbs in his belt and walking like a cowboy, which wasn't easy considering he was wearing his old sneakers. Wait'll he found out what all those dangling chains meant! Herbie'd freak out, Isabelle was sure. He'd only read about one book in his whole life. Every time he had to give an oral book report, he got up and said, "This is a story of a boy who was raised in the wild."

Last time he'd pulled that, the class had groaned in unison.

"That will be quite enough, boys and girls," Mrs. Esposito had said, trying not to smile.

Guy went upstairs to change his clothes before going out to play. That left Isabelle alone with Guy's mother. Isabelle considered doing a tap dance to entertain Guy's mother and started moving her feet, getting them warmed up.

"You're not in Guy's class, are you?" his mother said.

"Nope. I'm in fifth grade," Isabelle replied.

"I thought you were too tall to be in the third grade. And Herbie? Is he in fifth grade too?"

Isabelle nodded.

"I would like Guy to have some friends his own age," Guy's mother said.

"Oh, he will," Isabelle said grandly. "Just wait. Once he gets toughened up, he'll have plenty of friends his own age."

Guy's mother raised her eyebrows. "Toughened up?" she said.

"Can I go up and see if he's ready yet?" Isabelle asked, wishing Herbie would come out of Becca's chain room and that Guy would come down in his old clothes and they could get the show on the road.

Guy came clattering downstairs just then, and Isabelle breathed a sigh of relief. Herbie came back too, looking stunned by his experience.

"He's only read thirty-five books," Becca told her mother. Isabelle glared at Herbie but he refused to meet her eyes. They both said "Thanks" to Guy's mother and traipsed outside.

"Thirty-five!" Isabelle leaned on Herbie so hard he almost fell. "Who are you kidding?"

"How many books have you read?" Herbie asked Guy.

Guy looked at the sky, counting. "Oh, about a hundred, I guess," he said.

"Have you got paper chains, too, in your room?"

"Some. Not as many as Becca. She's a show-off."

"How come you read so many books? How come your sister can read and she's only six?" Isabelle asked.

"Well, she's a gifted child," Guy said.

Herbie's eyes popped. "You shoulda told me!" he

66

wheezed. "I never woulda gone into her room to see the chains if I knew that."

"And also," Guy said, "my mother read to us while we were still inside her stomach. That way, she figured we'd get started early."

Astounded at this piece of information, Isabelle said, "Could you hear her?"

"I don't remember," Guy said truthfully. "I must've, though. My mother's a librarian, too."

"Oh." Isabelle nodded wisely. "That explains it." Herbie nodded wisely, too. They both felt better, knowing Guy and Becca's mother was a librarian.

"Bet she's always telling you to be quiet, huh?" Isabelle said, laughing.

Guy put his hand over his mouth and laughed through it, the way he did when he didn't get something.

"Don't you like to read?" he asked.

"I'd rather fight," said Isabelle.

"Can't you do both?"

Isabelle looked at the ground, then up at both boys. The thought had never occurred to her.

"I guess," she said, doubtfully.

Chapter Twelve

"I corrected them all, like you said. Check it." Isabelle thrust her arithmetic test under Mrs. Esposito's nose. "Please."

With her coat still on, Mrs. Esposito checked.

"Perfect," she said. "Now I want to see you do this the first time around next time. You can do as well. Can't you?"

"I'm not sure. I guess." Isabelle thought a minute "Sure."

"That's the way. Now would you mind opening the

window a trifle? This room smells like bologna sandwiches."

"Don't you like bologna sandwiches?"

"Not enough to smell them all morning."

Isabelle flung open the window, sending the papers
on Mrs. Esposito's desk flying.

"I said a trifle, not the whole way."

Isabelle closed the window to a slit and picked up
the papers.

"If they called you a goody-goody because you never
did anything wrong, never even had to go to the principal's office once," she said suddenly, "and kids teased
you and chased you and called you names, what would
you do?" Isabelle watched Mrs. Esposito with her bright
brown eyes and waited to hear what she'd say.

"That's a tough one," Mrs. Esposito said, frowning.
"I assume you're not talking about yourself, Isabelle,"
she said, winking.

"It's a friend of mine." Isabelle didn't feel like joking. "It's this really nice little guy. He's, well, he's sort
of, well, sweet. I really like him. I feel bad because
these crummy creeps make him miserable and there's
nothing he can do about it. I tried to teach him how
to fight so he can punch 'em out, but he doesn't like
to fight. How can he be mean and tough if he's not
mean or tough?"

"He probably can't. How old is he?"

"He's only eight."

"Give him a while. Maybe he'll figure out something in a couple of years."

"Yeah, but what does he do for a couple of years? Just stand there and take it?"

"Perhaps the best thing would be to tell his mother and father, and they could handle it," Mrs. Esposito suggested.

"He doesn't want to do that. You know how mothers and fathers are." Isabelle lifted her shoulders and turned her hands palms up, trying to explain mothers and fathers to her teacher.

"They're supposed to protect children until children are big enough to take care of themselves," Mrs. Esposito said. "I think eight is too little to handle something like this by himself. Why don't you tell your friend to tell his parents and they might be able to help."

Isabelle shook her head from side to side, letting her brown hair swing across her cheeks. "He won't," she said firmly. "I know this kid and I guarantee you, he won't."

A little knock came at the door. "Come in," the teacher called. The door opened and Guy stood there, hair slicked down, cowlick waving from the top of his head. His cheeks were shiny with soap.

"I came to talk to her." Guy said, pointing to Isabelle.

"Well, talk then," Isabelle said. He looked very

small to her. Very clean and very small.

"Did you figure out anything yet?" He came right up to her and whispered, so Mrs. Esposito wouldn't hear. "You promised. Did you?"

"Not yet," Isabelle said.

"I thought so." Guy stuck his hands in his pockets and dug the toe of his sneaker against the nearest desk. "I was counting on you." He looked at her with his enormous eyes. "If you can't figure out something, then I guess nobody can."

Isabelle's face got warm. She was blushing. She tried to think of something to say to make Guy feel better and couldn't.

"Guess what!" Chauncey Lapidus charged into the room like a bull. Or a steamroller. "I'm invited to a party!" He looked around at their faces, wanting them to share his joy and pleasure at this singular event. "I'm invited to Sally Smith's farewell party! I never been invited to a party before. But I'm going to this one!" Chauncey's face glowed.

"Oh, everybody's going to the party for Sally Smith," Isabelle said airily. "The whole class is invited."

Chauncey's face fell.

"How nice, Chauncey!" Mrs. Esposito cried. "I like parties, too."

When Chauncey stomped to his desk at the back of the room, Mrs. Esposito said in a low voice, "That wasn't nice, Isabelle. That was unkind and you know it. Why couldn't you let him enjoy his invitation without telling him everyone was going? I'm ashamed of you."

Isabelle's head drooped like a wilted flower on a stalk. Tears stung her eyes. She knew she shouldn't have said what she said. Chauncey felt special, being invited to the party. And she'd destroyed that feeling. Isabelle raised her head, peeking up at Mrs. Esposito's feet tucked neatly under her desk. Mrs. Esposito didn't raise her eyes. Isabelle checked out the hall. It was empty. Guy had gone. The day had just begun.

When the recess bell rang, the entire class rose as one and exited, shouting and screaming their joy at being released. Isabelle stayed behind.

"I didn't mean to be mean," she said to Mrs. Esposito.

Mrs. Esposito regarded her steadily. "Are you sure?"

"I'm sure I'm sure," Isabelle said, enjoying the rhythm of her words. "I'm very sure I'm sure."

"This is not a joke, Isabelle. This is serious. Think about it for a while. On the one hand, you're trying to help your friend Guy out of his problem. And on the other, you're making another boy unhappy. To be mean for meanness' sake is a terrible thing. You wanted to put Chauncey down. You knew exactly what to say to bring this about. I'm disappointed in you. Now, I'm afraid I have work to do." Mrs. Esposito bent over her desk, shutting Isabelle out.

What do I care? Isabelle thought. She ran, shouting and screaming as loud as anybody, out to the playground, looking for some action.

Chapter Thirteen

"How do you like it?" Mrs. Stern asked, pointing to her tomato-red front door. "I think it's the best I've ever done. Mixed it myself, too. Mr. Brady across the street told me when he comes out on his way to work and sees that door, it makes his day. Come on in, both of you."

Isabelle and Guy followed her down the hall to the kitchen. "This is my friend Guy Gibbs," Isabelle said. "He's a customer on my route. This is my last day to deliver. Philip's off his crutches, darn it. I was hoping he'd have to use 'em a lot longer."

"Hello, Guy. One or two?" Mrs. Stern bustled about, getting down a bag of marshmallows.

"What are they?" Guy whispered.

"Marshmallows, dummy." Isabelle said. "Take two, I'll eat yours."

"Two, please," Guy said.

"Well, this is indeed a pleasure." Mrs. Stern's silver eyes twinkled. "I haven't seen you in so long I thought you'd forgotten me."

"I've been here but you were always someplace else," Isabelle said.

"To tell you the truth, an old friend is in town," Mrs. Stern said. "He's been taking me dancing and to the movies and the museums. Oh, it's been grand!" She clasped her hands, a dreamy expression on her face. "It's been lovely," she said.

Isabelle was astonished. She had thought Mrs. Stern was an old lady. A very sharp old lady, but nevertheless an old lady. And now she was behaving like a teenager. Well, the dancing and the movies were teenage things. She wasn't sure about the museums.

Mrs. Stern poured out the cocoa and sat down with them. Marshmallows bobbed cozily on the hot cocoa. "Is he your age?" Isabelle asked, having decided it was better not to say, "Is he as old as you?"

"No, he's older." Mrs. Stern punched down her marshmallow with her spoon. Isabelle let out a little gasp. Mrs. Stern grinned.

"I knew that'd get you!" Mrs. Stern laughed. "He's the older brother of my dearest friend. When she died, she left me a ring in her will, and he came to deliver it personally."

"Did that make you sad?" Isabelle asked.

"We had been friends for almost sixty years," Mrs. Stern said simply.

Isabelle and Guy looked at one another and said nothing.

"Tell me about you," Mrs. Stern said briskly, looking straight at Guy. To put off answering her, he put both marshmallows into his mouth at once. It was more than he could handle. Mrs. Stern tactfully left the table.

"Spit 'em out!" Isabelle ordered. Guy's aim was good. The slightly soggy marshmallows landed neatly in his cup.

"More cocoa?" Mrs. Stern said.

Guy nodded, incapable of speech at the moment.

"He lives on Hot Water Street," Isabelle said. "He's in third grade. His sister is six. She reads books. His father is a football coach. His mother is a librarian."

"Well," Mrs. Stern said, after a small silence, "I guess that takes care of Guy. How is life treating you, Isabelle?"

"So so," Isabelle said, shrugging. "Pretty good. Not great."

Guy sat up very straight. "Maybe you and my grandmother could be friends," he said suddenly.

"She's about your age. She comes and stays with us sometimes. Her name is Maybelle Gibbs."

"I hope someday we may meet," Mrs. Stern said. "That's very kind of you to think of, Guy."

Isabelle rolled her eyes at Guy. "We better go now," she said. "I have lots of papers to deliver."

"Don't be such a stranger, Isabelle, even if Philip is back on his feet," Mrs. Stern said. "I've missed you. You come again too, Guy."

"What'd you say that for?" Isabelle demanded when they were outside. "What a dumb thing to say. Telling Mrs. Stern she was about the same age as your grandmother. Sheesh!"

"What's so dumb about that?" Unexpectedly, Guy defended himself. "She said her best friend died, didn't she? So I thought my grandmother and her could be best friends. What's so dumb about that?"

"Oh, come on. Quit dragging your feet." Isabelle stalked ahead angrily. Mrs. Stern had said that Guy was kind. She'd never said Isabelle was kind. Isabelle wished she'd thought of suggesting Guy's grandmother and Mrs. Stern might be friends. Then Mrs. Stern might've smiled at her and told her she was kind.

"Tell your mother I'm collecting today," Isabelle directed when they reached Guy's house.

"She's not home. My grandmother's staying with us. My mother's working," he said.

Isabelle heard Becca playing the piano. She tiptoed

to a window and peeked in. I wonder how they got it inside, she thought. If I ever run into those moving men, I'll ask. I wonder if they took off the legs.

When she turned, Guy was right behind her.

"Did you think of anything yet?" he asked.

"Nope," she said. "Maybe you better ask your mother and father if they can figure out how to make those geezers stop teasing you."

Guy's face crumpled. "My mother and father?" he said in a cracked voice. "I counted on you." All of him drooped, including his cowlick. "I counted on you, Isabelle," he said.

Isabelle hoisted her newspaper bag from one shoulder to the other. Guy held one hand over his mouth. Over it, his huge eyes looked at her, unblinking.

"Well," she said in a gruff voice, "maybe I'll come up with something. But don't stand on one leg until I do, okay?"

The corners of Guy's mouth turned up a little. He put one hand on Isabelle's arm where it rested, as weightless as a leaf.

"You're my friend," he said. "My best friend, Isabelle."

"Pooh!" Isabelle cried. She turned and ran, as fast as she could, as if she were running in the fifty-yard dash, the canvas bag thumping rhythmically against her back. Guy waved at her but she never once looked back.

"Jane Malone's mother is having a farewell party for Sally Smith. The whole class is invited. I said you'd help," Isabelle gasped, bursting into the kitchen.

"You remember Mrs. Stilson, Isabelle," Isabelle's mother said in her "mind your manners" tone.

"Sure. Hello, Mrs. Stilson."

"Hello, Isabelle." Mrs. Stilson's stomach billowed under her maternity dress.

"I didn't know you were having a baby," Isabelle said. "When's it coming?" She almost pointed at Mrs. Stilson's stomach but stopped herself in time. Beside her, she heard her mother sigh.

"In five weeks," Mrs. Stilson replied.

Isabelle pondered this information.

"You want me to read to it?" she said at last.

"That would be nice." Mrs. Stilson looked startled.

"Isabelle loves babies," her mother said. One never knew what Isabelle might say. One often wished Isabelle would keep her trap shut.

"I'll read to it right now," Isabelle announced.

"Okay," Mrs. Stilson said.

"I think I'll go down to the cellar and do a load of wash," Isabelle's mother said. She sometimes did this when Isabelle got to be too much for her. Isabelle dashed up to her room and dashed back, bearing her favorite Dr. Seuss.

"Did you know if you read to your baby while it's still in your stomach, it'll probably be an ace reader when it gets out?"

Mrs. Stilson digested this information while Isabelle sat and aimed herself at Mrs. Stilson's stomach. In a loud and penetrating voice, Isabelle pronounced each word very clearly so the baby would hear each one.

"There you are," Guy's grandmother said.

"Where'd you think I was?"

She raised her eyebrows. "Something wrong?" she asked.

"No," Guy said.

Becca came in and said, "Did you hear me practicing the piano?"

"Yeah," Guy said, "you stink."

"Guy, what's come over you?" his grandmother said.

Becca sat down at the table with her crayons and began coloring Snoopy's nose bright red.

"He's just mad because he doesn't have any friends," Becca said.

"That'll be enough, miss," Guy's grandmother said.

Calmly Becca colored Snoopy's ears purple.

"You may be a gifted child but you sure are a lousy colorer," Guy told her.

"I have three friends. Their names are Donna and Michelle and Amy." Becca colored Snoopy's arms and legs yellow.

"Yeah, well, I have three friends too," Guy said. "Their names are Isabelle and Herbie and Mrs. Stern."

"Friends are supposed to be the same age you are,"

Becca said. "Isabelle and Herbie are older'n you. I don't know any Mrs. Stern."

"Yeah, well, she's the same age I am," Guy said.

Becca opened her mouth, then closed it and went back to her piano.

"Well done," Guy's grandmother told him.

Chapter Fourteen

The day of the party dawned bright and clear. Isabelle bounded out of bed, wrote PARTY! for the fifth time on her blackboard, then bounded downstairs.

Isabelle's mother stood at the sink, stabbing at a floating eggshell. "What time's the movie let out?"

"I can walk home," Philip said.

"Where's he going?" Isabelle rested her elbows on the table.

"It's none of your business!" Philip shot one of his laser-beam stares at her, guaranteed to cut her in half.

"There's a bunch of people going. We'll walk home together."

"Does he have a date?" Isabelle asked her mother.

Philip's face went from pink to red to purple. Once, years ago, Philip had had a tantrum. He might be having another, Isabelle thought, shivering in anticipation.

"Shut your face," he ordered, from the corner of his mouth.

"I forgot," he said, remembering. "Billy's brother is picking us up when it's over."

"Is he the one who's been arrested for speeding?"

"No, that's Chuck's brother," Isabelle said. "He plays cool disco," and she did a brief disco dance to illustrate.

Philip unclenched his hands and went for Isabelle's throat.

"Good morning." Isabelle's father, all suited up for work, greeted his happy little family. "What's up?" he asked, snapping open his newspaper, reaching for his coffee.

"Philip has a date," Isabelle said. "With a girl."

Philip made a gargling noise. Isabelle picked up her bowl and drank the remaining milk. No one told her not to. This day was off to a fine start. Invigorated, she jogged outside, looking for Guy. He wasn't there. She jogged all the way to school, turning now and then to see if he was following her. He wasn't in the playground either. Just as well. She still hadn't come up with a solution. After the party she would. She promised herself she would.

"Class, we all know today is the big sendoff for Sally," Mrs. Esposito said. "Tomorrow, we're going to hold an election to see who will fill Sally's shoes." Chauncey stuck one leg straight up in the air and wiggled his foot. Everybody laughed, then looked at Sally. She only smiled and bent over her book. Sally Smith was a star. She not only was art editor, she was lots of other things. Everyone wanted to be Sally Smith.

Mary Eliza flipped back her hair and preened like a peacock. Isabelle studied her Adidas. Sally's feet were small and hers were big. Still, she knew she could fill Sally's shoes nicely. It would be grand to be an art editor. Even if she didn't know what one did.

"Each of you is allowed one vote," Mrs. Esposito went on. "Drop your votes in here," and she pointed to the box on her desk. It was the box that served as a Valentine box on Valentine's Day, and it had a large, faded red heart pasted on its front.

"I want you to vote for the person you think will do the best job," Mrs. Esposito told them. "Don't vote for yourself unless you're prepared to work hard." A wave of snickers rolled over the room. Isabelle shot one of her laser beams in Mary Eliza's direction. But Mary Eliza was so busy looking modest, she didn't notice.

The party got off to a good start. Chauncey kicked a soccer ball which landed smack in Mary Eliza's mouth, jarring her retainer and sending blood spurting down her chin. Mary Eliza was brave and poor Chauncey felt terrible. When the excitement had died down, refreshments were served. Isabelle's mother's cupcakes were a big hit. Isabelle was extremely proud of her mother and told everyone whose cupcakes they were. The high spot was when Mrs. Malone brought out a large chocolate three-layer cake with FAREWELL, SALLY written on it in pink icing.

"Here, Sally," she said, handing Sally a cake knife, "you do the honors."

With a big smile, Sally cut the first slice. Then, to everyone's amazement, she burst into tears.

"Oh, dear," Mrs. Malone said. "What's wrong, dear? Do you feel all right?"

"I feel fine," Sally blubbered. "It's just that I hate to move. I'm sad about leaving. I don't want to go."

Isabelle was dismayed by Sally's tears. She didn't think Sally ever cried. Sally was a leader. Leaders didn't cry.

"Nothing will ever be as nice as here," Sally snuffled. "This is the best place in the world. Nothing will be as much fun."

"Don't worry, Sally," Isabelle said. "You'll make friends. I bet you'll be the art editor at your new school. I bet you'll be the best speller and the best in arithmetic, too."

"I don't want to be a baby," Sally said. "But I couldn't help it."

"I'll miss you," Isabelle whispered at the edge of Sally's ear. "You are my friend, Sally. You are the best person in the entire world. You are the best . . ." she paused, trying to think of other comforting words to offer Sally. Herbie arrived and stepped hard on Isabelle's Adidas.

"Knock it off," Herbie said, scowling. "We're having a game of musical chairs, so come on and stop being a jerk."

Musical chairs! Isabelle's favorite. All the pushing and shoving! Lovely.

"Come on, Sally," and Isabelle dragged her new friend's hand and pulled her into the game.

Isabelle had never even been to Sally's house. She had not been invited to Sally's birthday party, which took place in Sally's rec room. Sally had one toe out the door, so to speak, and here they were, best friends. She promised to write her every day.

That night, before lights out, Isabelle wrote on her blackboard SALLY SMITH IS COOL. SALLY SMITH IS MY PEN PAL. SALLY SMITH IS MY NEW BEST FRIEND.

And underneath, written in letters so small she had to push her nose against the blackboard to read them, Isabelle wrote: YEAH! ISABELLE, NEW ART ED. OF THE BEE. YEAH!

Chapter Fifteen

"They followed me home from school yesterday," Guy said. "Calling me goody-goody Guy, Mama's boy, all that. I went to your house and you weren't there. I sat and waited for you and you didn't come."

"I was at Sally Smith's farewell party," Isabelle told him. "I told you about that. You knew I was going to her party. I can't just not go because you want me to figure out a way to make 'em stop, can I?"

"No," said Guy.

"I thought about it, though. A lot. I thought and

thought. How about if you throw a stone through the principal's window. And it breaks. Not a big stone, only a little one, so if it hit Mrs. Prendergast, it would only bounce off her head and wouldn't even cut her or anything. Only scare her a little. How about that?" asked Isabelle, who had only just that minute thought of this plan.

"My father'd get awful mad at me if I did that," Guy said. "Besides, I like Mrs. Prendergast. She never did anything to me. Why'd I want to do that to her?"

"For crying out loud!" Isabelle cried. "What difference does it make if you like her or not? You want them to stop calling you names, don't you? You want to do something bad so they won't call you a goody-goody, don't you?"

"Yes," said Guy.

"Well then. If you did that, everybody would find out about it and they'd say, 'Hey, that's the little creep we were always calling a goody-goody. Guess he's not one after all.' Isn't that what you want?"

"I'm too scared to do something like that," Guy said.

"Well, you could break into the school on Saturday when it was empty and write stuff on the walls and mess up the classrooms." He looked at her with great, sad eyes and was silent.

"Sheesh! I'm running out of ideas," Isabelle said.

"That's okay. I know you tried. Maybe my grandmother will think of something."

"Your grandmother?" Isabelle stood on her head. "Your grandmother?" She liked the way the words came out when she talked standing on her head. They sounded odd, not like her at all. "I'll bet she doesn't know squat about getting into trouble."

"She was a child once," Guy said.

"Yeah, like about a hundred million years ago." Spots began to dance in front of Isabelle's eyes, but she stayed put.

"She may be old," Guy defended his grandmother, "but she's young at heart." He'd heard that in a song on the radio once and thought it described his grandmother perfectly.

Isabelle collapsed and lay outstretched on the ground. At that instant Herbie's mother drove by. Herbie leaned out and yelled, "Hey, you finally got her! Yippee!" and the car kept going until it was out of sight.

Made bold by this, Guy planted one of his feet firmly on Isabelle's stomach, holding her down. "How about you and me fighting?" he asked, tempted to put both feet on her and take a little walk. But he wasn't *that* bold.

"You whippersnapper!" Isabelle hollered, struggling to get up. Guy removed his foot and started running. He wanted to put distance between himself and her.

When he looked back, she was standing there, shaking her fist at him. "You bozo!" she cried.

Elated by an unaccustomed feeling of power, Guy waved and kept on going. He'd never stepped on anyone in his entire life. It was an exhilarating experience.

When Guy got home, his grandmother was soaking her feet in Epsom salts.

"My dogs are barking," she said, rubbing one dripping foot against the other.

Becca turned her head, listening. "I don't hear anything," she said.

"She means her feet hurt, you whippersnapper," said Guy.

"You're getting feisty," his grandmother said. "I detect the influence of the paper boy."

"When you were a child, were you ever bad?" Guy asked suddenly.

"Once in a while. The worst thing I ever did was try to sell my baby sister to some new people who moved on our street." She threw back her head and laughed. "I wasn't very old, only about four. And I was very jealous of my sister. She was getting entirely too much attention, it seemed to me. So when the new people moved in, I bundled up the baby and pushed her in her pram down the street. I rang the bell, and when the lady of the house came to the door, I said, 'Would you like to buy this baby? She's for sale. Cheap.' I'll tell you, they never let me forget that."

90

"Did they buy the baby?" Guy wanted to know. He was entranced with the story. If only he'd thought of that when Becca was little. It was too late now, of course. Nobody would want to buy a gifted child.

"No. They had children of their own. I would've tried it again but they kept a close eye on me from then on. Then there was the time I took my brother's bicycle. Molly McCabe and I wanted to go on a picnic. I guess I had a bicycle, but the tires were flat or some such thing. Anyway, I took Bob's. He was older than I and had a terrible temper. As luck would have it, he came home and wanted to ride his bicycle. And it was gone. Well, there was some fracas when Bob discovered I'd taken it, I can tell you. I was shut in my room without supper that night. We'd always been taught to respect other people's property, you see. That was a fair old time. What fun we had! We never did anything really bad. Not like some of the things that happen these days."

Guy sat still, hoping she'd think of some other tales of her childhood. None of them were of any use to him, of course, except for the baby-selling one. If only he'd thought of that before Becca could talk. Come to think of it, she'd been born talking. Life was full of missed opportunities, it seemed to him.

"This water's getting chilly," Guy's grandmother said. "I better dry my feet before I take cold. Bring me a towel, would you please, Guy?"

He sat on the floor and watched while she dried her

feet. Her legs were very white. Blue veins ran every which way up and down them, then trailed a slender tracing across her feet.

"Did you ever get sent to the principal's office?" Guy wanted to know.

"Once or twice. Our principal was an old lady who wore glasses and her skirts to the floor. She looked like somebody's grandmother. But she was tough." Guy's grandmother rolled her eyes at him. "My Lord, but she was tough. Nobody got away with anything with her. She was allowed to cane the boys and not the girls. Those were the days, you see, when girls were supposed to be the gentler sex. We both know that's not the case, don't we?" Guy nodded, afraid to speak, afraid to break the spell.

"She'd say to me, 'Maybelle, it pains me to see you here again,' meaning her office. She knew my name, you see, knew the name of every child in the school. And their family situation, too. She was a very smart woman. Hand me my slippers, will you, Guy?"

He handed them to her and said, without thinking, "I like you."

"I like you too," she said.

"I'm not much for kissing," he told her, so there'd be no misunderstanding.

"How about hugging?"

He thought about that. "I guess hugging's okay as long as you don't hug too hard or too much."

"Listen," she said, "I've had lots of experience. I

92

always hug just right." He allowed her to give him a
sample.

"How was it?" she asked.

"Just right," Guy said.

Chapter Sixteen

The afternoon stretched slowly, slowly, like Rip van Winkle waking from his twenty years' sleep. The clock seemed to have stopped ticking. A fat black fly beat its head against the window. Outside, someone tried repeatedly and unsuccessfully to start a car's engine. Inside, Isabelle read about how many coffee beans there were in Brazil.

Something was crawling around inside her T-shirt. Isabelle pulled it away from herself with one finger and peered down. There was nothing there except her undershirt. She hooked the T-shirt over her nose and looked out at the room over it, hoping someone was watching her.

Mary Eliza Shook was paying close attention to her book. Isabelle made a few faces in that direction, but Mary Eliza never once looked up. So Isabelle crossed her eyes at Herbie over her T-shirt. But Herbie was involved in making a spitball and didn't even notice.

Mrs. Esposito cleared her throat loudly. Everyone jumped. Mrs. Esposito glared at Isabelle, who took her T-shirt down from her nose and went back to Brazil.

"All right, class. You can put away your books now." At last Mrs. Esposito took pity on them. A great crashing and banging followed her announcement. They were ready.

"I have counted all the votes and I'm happy to announce the name of the new art editor," Mrs. Esposito said.

Everyone sat up very straight, trying not to look self-conscious. A couple of kids in back starting horsing around.

"There will be no announcement, class, until everyone comes to order," Mrs. Esposito said.

I bet she'd make a good army person, Isabelle thought in admiration. They wouldn't dare disobey Mrs. Esposito.

When at last the class was totally still, Mrs. Esposito said, "When I announce the winner's name, I would like that person to stand, please."

Isabelle got her feet ready.

"Our new art editor is . . ."

Isabelle closed her eyes and clasped her hands in front of her, as if she were praying.

Mary Eliza lifted her backside off her chair, ready to spring.

Mrs. Esposito's voice seemed to come from the end of a long tunnel.

"Our new art editor is . . ." Mrs. Esposito liked to tantalize them.

"Herbie!" she cried.

Isabelle's eyes snapped open, and she said, "Herbie?"

Herbie looked as if he'd been hit over the head with a shovel.

"Herbie!" yelled Herbie. "That's cuckoo! I don't want to be no art editor! I won't—"

"Will the winner please stand?" Mrs. Esposito said, in measured tones. The boy sitting behind Herbie punched him in the back and growled, "Stand up, wonko."

Hitching up his pants, Herbie staggered to his feet, his orange-juice mustache giving him a somewhat sinister look.

"Congratulations, Herbie," said Mrs. Esposito. "We know you'll do a good job. And class, it's my pleasure to tell you that Herbie had more votes than any other candidate. Let's give him three cheers."

"Hip hip hooray!" the class thundered, three times. Herbie sat down and his expression was one of total amazement.

"I don't know what happened," he mumbled. He shook his head once or twice, like a boxer down for the count. "I don't want to be no art editor. I don't know what an art editor's supposed to do, so how can I do it?"

"I'll give you a hand, Herb," Isabelle soothed him. "I'll be your right-hand man."

"Yeah, but how about my left hand? My left hand needs help, too." Herbie was definitely in the pits.

"If you ask me," Mary Eliza stormed up, "it's a put-up job."

"So who asked you?" Imitating prizefighters she'd seen on TV, Isabelle dabbed at her nose with her thumb several times.

In a rage, Mary Eliza flounced away without speaking.

"All I know is," Herbie said glumly, "it musta been somebody who hates me. Who else would vote for me? They knew I didn't want the job. I have an enemy and I didn't even know it." Herbie's face wore a hunted look.

"It wasn't me, Herb," Isabelle said. "You can count on that."

"You're a pal, Iz." Herbie called Isabelle Iz when his emotions were stirred. "Thanks for not voting for me. You voted for yourself, right?"

"Sure. Who else would've?" She took a few pokes at him, trying to cheer him up. Herbie was not in a laughing mood, however.

"Wait'll my mother hears I'm art editor," Herbie said. "She'll flip."

"How about if we have a good fight? That'll make you feel better," Isabelle suggested.

"No, thanks. I'm not in the mood," Herbie said. "I'm going home."

"What're you gonna do when you get home?" Isabelle wanted to know.

He looked at her, his eyes full of woe. "Think," he said.

"Think?" Isabelle echoed.

"Yeah, think."

"Awesome," said Isabelle.

Chapter Seventeen

"Take that! And that! And that!" Guy shadow-boxed his way around his room, ferocious, fearless, unbeatable. Bouncing on the balls of his feet, fists held up the way Isabelle had taught him, Guy smiled quietly at his own power.

Last night he'd watched a karate exhibition on TV. Those guys knew what was what. He'd seen a girl smaller than he was break a board with her bare hands. Imagine that. If she could, he could.

"I'm gonna knock you out of your socks," Guy muttered. "I'm gonna bash in your head and stick my thumb in your eye, and when it falls out I'm just gonna leave it there. I'm not gonna pick it up or anything, just leave it there." He shivered, thinking of all those eyes lying on the ground, looking up at him.

It was all very well to be mean and tough in your own room, in your own house with all your family there. It was another thing entirely, Guy knew, to be mean and tough out in the real world, when and where it counted.

Karate was the answer, no question. All he had to do was talk his mother and father into letting him take a karate course. They had one at the Y.

Someone knocked. Guy said, "Come in," in a deep and hairy voice. It was Herbie.

"Your mom said I could come up," Herbie said.

"I was just practicing," Guy said.

Herbie sat on the bed. "I got elected art editor of *The Bee* today," he said.

"That's nice," Guy said. "You wanna do anything? Look through my microscope or anything? Look at my stamp collection?"

Herbie shook his head no.

"My favorite animal is frogs," Guy said. "What's yours?"

"Zebra," Herbie answered, after some thought.

"I never saw a zebra," Guy said.

"Me either," said Herbie. "Except on a jungle special."

"Want some Jell-O?" he asked Guy, pulling a packet out of his pocket.

"What color?"

"Green." Herbie ripped open the inside wrapping and poured out some green Jell-O into his hand. "Once I used it to brush my teeth with," he said.

"What'd it taste like?"

"Green," Herbie said. He poured some into his mouth and some more into Guy's open hand. Guy wondered if he really wanted some Jell-O that bad.

"My second favorite animal is unicorns," he said.

"I never saw one, never heard of one either," Herbie said, chewing and making a face.

"It's got one horn growing out of its head. If you see one, it means good luck."

"One horn," Herbie said. "Crazy."

"I never even saw one in the zoo. That's because it's only mythical," Guy explained.

"What's that mean?"

"It isn't real. It doesn't really exist. It's just in your imagination."

"Crazy," Herbie said again.

There was a companionable silence as the two boys stared into space.

"I'm going to paint my room dark blue and paste stars on the ceiling," Guy said at last.

"Cool," said Herbie. "My mother put wallpaper on mine. It's stupid. It's stripes that go up and down, up and down. That's it. I wouldn't mind pasting stars on mine. Where you getting the stars?"

Guy shrugged. He hadn't thought it through. "Maybe from school," he said. "Like the ones they give you if you get an A. Silver stars. That way, I can look at 'em at night and pretend I'm sleeping out."

"Yeah. You can also get a jar full of mosquitoes, and when it gets dark, let 'em out. They'll dive-bomb you all night and bite the stuffing out of you. That way, you'll *really* think you're sleeping out." Herbie laughed and scratched himself on the leg.

Guy covered his mouth with his hand and smiled around it at Herbie. He liked the idea of sleeping out under the stars, but he wasn't too hot on the idea of mosquitoes.

Becca knocked and opened the door.

"Supper's ready," she announced.

"You wanna stay for supper?" Guy asked.

"What's for supper?"

"Tuna fish," said Becca.

Herbie only liked to stay at people's houses for supper if they were having spaghetti.

"No thanks," he said. "My mother said I should be home early. See you," he said.

Guy listened to the sound of Herbie's feet clattering down the stairs. Then he started punching his way around the room again.

"Take that and that and that!" he muttered.

Pow, pow, pow!

Not one mosquito escaped his deadly blows.

"Supper's ready!"

Stepping carefully around the mosquito bodies littering the floor, Guy went downstairs.

The first thing I have to do, he thought, is get some stars. Then I get the paint.

Chapter Eighteen

"It was me voted Herbie in," Chauncey bragged. *"I started* the landslide. Just the way when somebody runs for president. Some presidents win by only a couple of votes, and some win by a landslide. I told it around that Herbie was our man. I told 'em Herbie was the best person for the job. I landslided Herbie into office, I did." Chauncey beamed. Isabelle felt like wiping off Chauncey's smile. She got her fists ready.

"It was a good deed, huh?" she asked. "You Lone Ranger, me Tonto. Who Kemosabe?"

"Talk English, why don'tcha?" Power had already gone to Chauncey's head. He wasn't letting any grass grow under *his* feet, Isabelle thought.

She opened her mouth, ready to let him have it. Unbidden, Mrs. Esposito's words about being kind popped into her head. She shook it, trying to clear the words out. But they stayed, they wouldn't go away.

Chauncey was not an easy person to be kind to. But she had promised herself she'd try. So try she would.

She cleared her throat and said, "You did a good job, Chauncey."

Stunned by praise, to which he was a stranger, Chauncey puffed out his chest like a baby robin who's just caught the first worm of the season.

"I'm thinking of going into politics," he said. "I was going to be a tennis player or maybe a pro ball player, but now I've decided to go into politics. I'm even writing a speech."

Talk about getting the ball and running with it! Isabelle thought. "What about?" she said.

"Whaddya mean, what about?" Chauncey had lost his train of thought.

"The speech. What's it about?"

"Oh." Chauncey shrugged. "Lots of things."

"Name some."

Chauncey stared at a spot just over Isabelle's head. "Well, peace on earth, for one."

"Are you for it or against it?" Isabelle asked, dangling her hands loosely, the way Philip did before a swim meet.

"I'm for it," Chauncey said stoutly. "Plus, we oughta have more open spaces and less pollution. I think weekends oughta be longer. I think kids oughta have the same rights parents have. I think . . ."

"You're all right, Chauncey," Isabelle cut in. Once started, Chauncey had fallen in love with the sound of his own words.

"We should also have bigger lunches and not so much homework," he continued, glassy-eyed with joy at her attention. "I also think kids oughta be allowed to pick out their own shoes when they go to the shoe store. They have to wear 'em, not their mothers."

Chauncey was getting out of hand, Isabelle decided. "I'm late," she said. "See you."

"Hi," said Guy, as she rounded the steps to the playground. "Did you?"

"No," she said. "Not yet."

"Well, you don't have to. You said you were going to think of something. I didn't ask you, you said you would."

"I know. I will. I'm real busy right now." The sight of Guy looking woebegone made her feel guilty. "Listen, wait here. I've got something for you." She wanted to make him look happy so she wouldn't feel so bad. "I'll be right back."

And she was. "Here, these are for you."

Guy's eyes shone as he saw the five silver stars

she handed him. "Gee, thanks," he said.

"Mrs. Esposito said it was all she had left. She said she ordered some more. Maybe you can ask her later and she'll fork over some more. So long," and she left him in the hall, smiling at his stars.

After school Guy kept an eye out for Isabelle. Maybe they'd go see Mrs. Stern again. She was, Guy knew, a good mixer of paints. He knew just the shade of blue he wanted—a deep blue, the color the sky got just before total darkness fell, before the moon showed its face.

A boy named Bernie barreled out the door.

"Hey, Bernie," Guy said shyly. Bernie sat across the aisle from him. Bernie was small, smaller even than Guy. Bernie was very smart, too, but he didn't make a big deal out of being smart.

"My cat had kittens this morning," Bernie said, out of breath. "I was eating a piece of toast when the first one was born, right in our kitchen in my mother's old laundry basket."

"How many did she have?" Guy asked, envious, wishing he'd been there in Bernie's kitchen, eating toast when the first kitten was born.

Bernie held up three fingers. "My mother said to hurry home, maybe there'd be more. Gotta go!" and Bernie went.

Guy watched him go, wishing he was going too, running home to see Bernie's new kittens.

I don't need Isabelle, Guy thought. I can find Mrs.

Stern's by myself. I've been there once. Just keep an eye out for the tomato-red door.

Follow the yellow brick road. He'd seen *The Wizard of Oz* four times on television and wondered if he'd ever have the luck to find a yellow brick road. He thought not.

A solitary walk on a sunny day was not a bad thing. He'd find some violets, pick a bouquet for Mrs. Stern. This was violet time. He'd seen their little faces peeking out in empty lots he'd passed on his way to school. He was in no hurry. He liked being alone. Sometimes, not always. This was one of those times when he liked it a lot.

Guy started to skip. He was quite a good skipper, if he did say so himself.

This is the turn. Is this the turn? Surely this was Mrs. Stern's street. He wished he'd paid more attention when Isabelle and he had come here.

Still, he could find it on his own. He knew he could. But suppose Mrs. Stern had painted her front door another color? Isabelle had said she changed the colors of her rooms and her front door at the drop of a hat.

What then?

No, that door was still tomato-red. Hadn't Mrs. Stern said she liked that color, it was the best she'd ever done?

Guy investigated a spot of color he thought might be a clump of violets. No, it turned out to be only a piece of paper, crumpled up and thrown away.

Up ahead, a group of people were making a lot of noise, shouting and hollering. Guy heard loud voices, loud music. One of them had a big radio turned up high. They were too far away to give him any trouble, but Guy kept an eye on them anyway, just to make sure.

With a surge of relief Guy saw the red door. It shone at him like a beacon lighting his way. And even though he'd found no violets for Mrs. Stern, he hurried toward that red door, empty-handed and joyful. Would she ask him in for some cocoa? Maybe not. Maybe she only asked Isabelle in. No, she'd ask him in. He was positive.

He knocked, getting a big smile ready to greet her. Maybe she wouldn't remember him. He knocked twice, getting anxious. Sure she would. She was a nice lady. She'd remember him. If she didn't, he'd tell her he was Isabelle's friend. Then she'd ask him in. For sure.

Should he knock again? Someone was watching him. He felt eyes. Maybe Mrs. Stern was hiding behind the curtains, watching him, wishing he'd go away. He stared at the windows. They stared back. He decided to try the back door. Maybe Mrs. Stern was deaf. She was old. Old people were often hard of hearing. If she was in the kitchen, she might not have heard his knock.

He pressed his face against the kitchen window, shading his eyes against the glass to get a better look. The room was neat and tidy. There were no dirty dishes in the sink, no pots on top of the stove. A newspaper was spread out on the table as if someone had been reading it there. A bunch of flowers nodded at him in a friendly fashion. Guy breathed a circle on the windowpane and wrote GUY in big letters.

He sat down on the back steps to think. Maybe Mrs. Stern had just nipped down to the corner on an errand and she'd be back any moment. He picked up a handful of pebbles and tossed them in the air one by one.

Minutes passed. Isabelle had told him Mrs. Stern sometimes climbed up on her roof to clean out the gutters.

"At her age!" Isabelle had said admiringly.

The roof was empty today except for a cluster of starlings roosting on the TV antenna, chatting nervously among themselves, passing the time of day.

Then Guy heard someone coming, someone whistling gaily. He hid in the bushes under Mrs. Stern's front windows. If it was Isabelle, he'd pounce out on her and scare her. He hoped it was Isabelle.

It was Philip, delivering his papers. Guy was scared of Philip. Isabelle said Philip was always doing bad things to her, socking her in the stomach, calling her names, stealing her candy. He crouched low, spying on Philip.

Two girls appeared. They stood at the yard's edge talking, watching from the corners of their eyes as Philip folded his newspapers in the special, intricate way he had. Philip frowned and twitched and carried on, Guy thought, like a mad scientist about to blow

110

up the world. The girls acted as if they didn't know he was there. They whispered behind their hands and waited for Philip to notice them.

A caterpillar crawled slowly up Guy's leg, under his jeans, looking for something to eat, maybe. Guy dug his hands in and moved his fingers, looking for the caterpillar so he could pull it out and hurl it onto the grass.

Guy heard a thump nearby. Philip had thrown Mrs. Stern's paper. It had landed right on target, on the stoop. Still whistling, Philip got on his bike and prepared to ride away.

"Oh, hi," he said to the girls, noticing them for the first time.

The girls, looking a little frayed around the edges from all their efforts, said, "Oh, hi!" back.

With fanfare befitting a high-powered motorcycle, Philip took off in a cloud of dust. The girls watched him go. Then they too went on their way. The street was quiet.

Reluctantly, Guy crawled out of his hiding place. He pulled up his jeans to see if the caterpillar had left any marks on him.

He'd come back later, Guy told himself. He was disappointed about not seeing Mrs. Stern. It had been an adventure, coming to her house by himself. But now his adventure was over.

Chapter Nineteen

Guy skipped his way down Mrs. Stern's street and, wouldn't you know, soon came upon a vast clump of violets, growing wild. They were fragrant and delicate, colored white and purple. He picked all his hands could hold. Tomorrow he'd return and pick more.

"Well, hello dere." The large boy, larger even than Philip, loomed in Guy's path, blocking the way. He had slick, dark hair and an earring in one ear. He smiled and his eyes almost disappeared. His gums came down low over his teeth.

"Hello." Guy sidestepped him, not eager to make friends.

"Come on." The boy reached out his hand and took Guy's. "I want to show you something."

Guy knew he shouldn't go with strangers. His mother had told him that and he'd seen movies in school. He sidestepped in the other direction and said, "I have to go home."

The boy kept smiling and pushed back his greasy hair. "It won't take a sec, I promise. I've got something to show you, something you're gonna like."

He laid his arm around Guy's shoulders and steered him toward whatever it was he had to show.

Guy looked nervously over his shoulder. There was no one in sight, no one who would hear him if he cried "Help!" But it was broad daylight. Nothing could happen. He was safe.

There were two others, three in all. One had a mustache that looked like a little mouse lying asleep on his lip. The other one wore a black leather jacket with MONSTER written on the pocket.

Monster is right, Guy thought. And he longed for Isabelle. She'd know what to do. She'd fix their wagon.

The one with the gums said, "It won't take a sec, I promise."

"You already promised once," Guy said.

"Little wise guy, ain't ya?" Fingers tightened on Guy's neck. He pulled away. The fingers followed.

113

They were grouped around something Guy couldn't see.

"Looka that! Looka the little bugger!" cried the one with the mouse mustache. Guy heard a noise. It didn't sound like any noise he'd heard before. He thought maybe it was an animal caught in a trap. The sound the animal made sent chills up and down his spine.

The group shifted and Guy looked and saw what it was that had made the terrible sound. It was his dog. At least, he thought it was his dog. A tin can weighted down the feather duster tail. The eager amber eyes were dull. But Guy was sure he saw the tail wag feebly as the dog looked up at him. It must be hard to wag a tail with a tin can tied to it, Guy thought. He put out his hand. The dog tried to get to its feet and was shoved roughly back down.

The dog lay still, its sides going in and out, in and out. It was breathing. It was alive.

The boy with MONSTER written on his pocket lit a cigarette and held it dangerousely close to the dog's matted fur. The smell of burning filled the air.

Guy couldn't help himself. "Don't," he said, knowing it was a mistake. "Don't hurt him."

The cigarette touched the dog's fur again, and this time the dog howled.

"Gutsy little bugger, ain't he?" Did they mean the dog or did they mean Guy? Hard to tell.

Once again the dog thrashed on the ground, trying to get up. Guy bent down to help him. His hand was kicked away. Suddenly, it was cold. The sun had gone. "You like dogs, huh, kid? Little kid like you oughta have a dog of his own, right? You want this one? He's got no place to go. You want to buy him?" Their mouths stretched tight in joyless laughter.

"Yes," Guy said. "I'd like him."

"Well, whaddya know? The kid wants to buy our dog. How about that?" They widened their eyes at each other. "How much do you think this here dog's worth? A lotta bread, right? A whole lotta bread."

"I can get some money." The dog watched Guy. It tried once more to rise and got pushed down with the sharp point of a big stick one of them held. This time the dog closed its eyes and lay still.

"I'll go home and get some money," Guy said, through trembling lips. He tried to hold his mouth stiff so they wouldn't see he was afraid. He must be brave. If only Isabelle were here, she'd punch them all out, she'd holler and shout and run. Or someone would come.

"My father has some money."

They exchanged sly glances. "I don't know," MON-STER said. "This here is a very valuable dog. Worth a whole lotta bread, right?" The others nodded, their faces long, their eyes glittering. "I doubt your old man has that kinda bread. This here dog has his papers and all." At this, they went into gales of laughter, shouting, doubling over, thumping each other. "Papers!" they shouted gleefully.

Guy took a couple of secret steps backwards, toward the street. "How much?" he said. "Tell me how much and I'll get it."

The one with the gums said, suddenly calm, "A thousand."

"I'd say more like two." They all had ceased to smile. Their eyes were small and hostile.

"Maybe we better have a conference," the mustached one said, biting his fingernails.

"Yeah," the other two agreed. "But first, we better tie him up so's he don't get lost," the one with the gums said.

Tie who up? Him? Or the dog? Or both?

The rope was as thick as Guy's wrist. They meant him.

"Let's take him back in the woods and tie him to a tree," MONSTER said. "That way, we're sure he don't get loose."

They began to argue about where he should be tied up. When that was settled, they argued about who would do the tying. Their voices rose. They forgot everything else—Guy, the dog, everything. The stick was within reach, Guy realized. He put out his arm, remembering the girl on television, smaller than he, who had broken a bare board with her hands. This stick was his weapon, his only one.

"What is this? Will you looka the little tiger!" In a body, argument forgotten, they came at him. Guy swung the stick and landed a lucky, finger-tingling blow on the side of MONSTER's face. A string of swear words came from MONSTER's throat and he fell to one knee. Crouching, circling, the other two came at Guy, one to the right, the other to the left. In a panic, Guy kept swinging, not knowing what else to do. Once the stick stopped moving, he'd had it.

Thunk! He felt a terrible sharp pain. Something had hit him on the back of his head. He let out a yelp of pain, heard someone say, "What'd ya have to go and do that for?" and another voice said "Cops!" and that was all. That was the last he remembered.

Chapter Twenty

"Lucky the kid has a lot of hair."

Guy opened his eyes. His head hurt. Eyes as blue and shiny as two marbles stared down into his.

"You all right, kid?" The policeman held out a cup of water and Guy drank some. His head felt like a balloon with too much air in it—swollen, light, ready to take off and fly high.

A second policeman knelt to inspect the back of Guy's head. "Three to one and them big as any man, and they bean the kid with a rock." He shook his head.

Guy sat up.

"Where's the dog?" he said.

"In the car. He's a little shook up, you might say, but he'll be fine. He's only a pup. Is he yours?"

Guy shook his head. Something seemed to be loose in it.

"No," he said. "I wish he was."

"Try standing, son." The blue-eyed policeman helped Guy to his feet. "Anything broken?" He ran an expert hand over Guy to see if he was in one piece. "Can you walk?"

"Sure." Guy tottered a few steps. He felt like lying down again. Most of all, he wanted to go home.

"We'll run you home now," the other policeman said, as if he'd read Guy's mind. "Just check in so's your folks won't worry. Imagine they're already worried, you not home and it suppertime already."

Guy looked at the police car parked at the curb.

"Am I going home in that?" he said.

"What else? Hop in."

Guy smiled. He was going home in a police car.

"We'll drop you off, then run the pooch over to the Humane Society," the policeman said. "They'll fix him up good as new."

The dog lay on the back seat. Its eyes were closed. Its sides were moving as it breathed slowly, in and out. Guy got in the front seat, sandwiched between the two policemen.

"Where to, chief?"

Guy looked up at them. They meant him.

"Twenty-two Hot Water Street," he said. The car pulled out. They were on the way.

"Hot Water Street, huh?" the blue-eyed cop grinned. "They'll think you're in hot water for sure when they see you coming home in this."

Guy's heart hammered. That's what he hoped.

"Excuse me, sir, but do you think you could make your light go?"

"Sure thing. I can even turn on the siren, if you want."

Guy thought that over. "No thanks, just the light would be neat."

The patrol car turned into Hot Water Street. Guy closed his eyes tight. Oh Lord, please let them see me, he prayed. Let Becca see me. Please let a bunch of kids be hanging around. Let them all see me. Please, Lord. I won't ask for anything else if you'll just let that happen.

The Lord must've heard. Three boys whizzed by on bikes, then turned to stare as the police car slowed, blue lights flashing.

"Which house is yours?" the blue-eyed cop said.

"That one," Guy pointed. He saw Becca in the front yard. She and a friend were playing fairy princess. Becca had just made a deep curtsey when the car pulled up and came to a stop.

"Not just a little siren?" the policeman asked again. "Just to make 'em sit up and take notice?"

"Well, okay," Guy said. "But only a little."

The cop flicked a switch. The siren sounded very loud to Guy. Becca froze. Her friend clapped her hands over her ears and ran behind the big maple tree. The three boys on bikes stood on the sidewalk across from Guy's house, waiting.

First the driver got out. Then the other policeman. Then came Guy.

Becca's hand flew toward her mouth. Then she ran to the house, screaming, "It's Guy! It's Guy! The policeman brought Guy home!"

Becca had some loud voice. Guy had never realized how loud it was until now. He smiled, listening to her.

Across the street the three kids on bikes watched, their mouths hanging open. Up and down the block people came out and stood watching. It wasn't every day a police car, lights flashing, siren sounding, delivered someone to his front door on Hot Water Street.

"What's going on here?" Guy's father came to the door, glasses pushed up on his forehead, newspaper in his hand.

"Your boy got into some trouble, sir," the blue-eyed policeman said.

"My boy never gets into trouble," Guy's father said firmly. "He's a good boy. A very good boy. Never caused his mother or me a speck of trouble."

"He is a good boy," the policeman agreed. "And a brave one, too." Then he told what had happened to Guy. And the dog. By this time Guy's mother and grandmother were gathered around, listening. Guy's mother insisted on inspecting his head and then called the doctor to make an appointment to bring Guy to see him. The cut on Guy's head had stopped bleeding; it wasn't even very deep.

"Like I said, it's good your boy has such a fine head of hair," the policeman said. "Acted as padding when they walloped him." Then he took out his notebook and wrote down everything Guy could remember about the MONSTER, the one with the gums, and the one with the mouse mustache. That's the way Guy thought of it, the mouse mustache.

"All right, that's everything, then." The policeman put away his notebook. "We're going to run the pooch over to the Humane Society, see what they can find." He tipped his hat to the crowd. "I'll be in touch."

For the first time, Guy's grandmother spoke.

"What will happen to the dog?" she said.

The cop shrugged. "Hard to say. Dog's got no license, no identification tags of any kind. Probably a stray. Chances are they'll put it up for adoption. If no one claims it after a certain length of time, well . . ." The cop shrugged again.

Guy's grandmother, dark eyes gleaming, looked hard at Guy.

"I want that dog," he heard himself say. "It's like the dog I wanted all along. I think it's the one I wanted. It's a really nice dog. Just the right size. I bet he'd never make a mess or chew things or anything. He'd be a good watchdog too." Guy looked up at his mother and father.

"Well." Guy's father cleared his throat. "I guess that could be arranged. Thank you, officer. We'll call the Humane Society within the next few days, see how things stand."

The policemen tipped their hats.

"Good luck, son," the blue-eyed one said to Guy. By this time, quite a crowd had gathered, wondering what was going on. The policemen got back into their car and, lights flashing, drove away.

"Come in, Guy, let me have a good look at you," Guy's mother said. As he turned to go in, he heard Becca say in her loud voice, "Oh, it's my brother. He got into trouble and the police had to bring him home. His name is Guy. Yes, he's my brother. He's eight. Yes, his name is Guy. He's eight. He got into trouble. Yes, he's . . ."

Guy smiled. If Becca had anything to do with it, everyone in town would know who Guy Gibbs was.

Chapter Twenty-one

"So there I am, my father's driving me to school, and all of a sudden the radio announcer says, 'An eight-year-old boy fought off three hoodlums yesterday in an effort to rescue a stray dog the hoodlums were holding captive. The boy, Guy Gibbs of Hot Water Street, told police the dog was being tortured by the three and he . . . ' blah, blah, blah," said Isabelle, filling in for what she couldn't remember.

"So I said, 'That's Guy!' and my father says, 'Unh huh,' the way he does when he's not really listening.

When I got to school I told Mrs. Esposito and she said I could run down to Guy's room and check. His teacher said he'd be in later, that his mother called and she was taking him to the doctor. You don't think there could be two eight-year-old boys both named Guy Gibbs living on Hot Water Street, do you?" Isabelle said.

"I doubt it," Jane Malone answered. "Probably his mother had to take him to the doctor because he lost a lot of blood."

"Guy lost a lot of blood? My gosh, I can't believe it. That little weasel. Why wasn't I along? If I was there, I could've pinned their ears back. I could've helped Guy. I miss all the good things. Boy, they'll never call him a goody-goody again." Isabelle's eyes widened and she clutched Jane's arm. "You don't think Guy's gonna die or anything, do you?"

"Of course not," Jane said in her practical way. "I like that word 'hoodlum.' Hoodlum. It sounds just like what it is. Hoodlum." Jane was getting carried away by the word. Jane was a word person, always trying out new words.

"Isabelle," Jane said, "can you come—"

But Isabelle was distracted by the sight of Herbie, staggering under a load of books and papers. "Hey, Herb!" she hollered. Jane flinched and stuck a finger in each ear. "You hear about Guy getting rescued by the cops yesterday?"

"Guy?" Herbie said vaguely. As if he'd never heard

of Guy. "What happened? Did they have a shoot-out?"

Isabelle stopped moving. Hands, eyes, legs, arms, feet, all came to a dead halt. "A shoot-out?" she said. "My gosh, maybe they did. Maybe that's why Guy lost so much blood."

"He lost blood?" Now she had Herbie's full attention. "Maybe we oughta go down to the hospital and offer to give him blood. You know what your blood type is? Maybe it won't match Guy's. Maybe mine will."

Herbie screwed up his face. "I never gave blood. I'm scared it might hurt. How much blood did Guy lose?"

"Hey, slow down, Herb," Isabelle urged. "He's gonna be all right. He's at the doctor's now, but he'll be in school later on. You wanna fight at my house today?"

"I can't," Herbie said. "Got too much to do. My assistant editor is coming over after school. We gotta make plans. He—"

"Your assistant editor!" Isabelle's voice rang out. People turned to stare. "Your assistant editor!" she screeched. "I thought *I* was your assistant editor! What goes on?"

Herbie looked embarrassed. "Well, Chauncey called up and said he would be my assistant editor on account of he voted me into the job in the first place. So I said okay. So Chauncey's my assistant editor." Herbie looked at the floor, not willing to meet Isabelle's indignant gaze.

"Well, all right for you. That's the last time I offer to help you, Herbie. Fine pal you are. I said I'd be your right-hand man. All right for you, Herb."

Chauncey came chugging up to Herbie. "Meet me outside right after the bell goes," Chauncey directed, looking at his watch. "We have a tight schedule. I'm trying to line up a photographer. It's not gonna be easy, though. Remember"—again Chauncey checked his watch—"right after the bell rings. Outside." Chauncey chugged away.

"Boy, you got your work cut out for you, Herb. I'll say that. I bet you'll wind up in the booby hatch with that guy on your side."

"You're just jealous, Isabelle," Herbie said with dignity. "You're jealous because you're not the assistant editor."

"That's what you think!" Isabelle cried. "Next time you want somebody to fight with, try fighting with your assistant editor. That oughta be a barrel of laughs. Don't forget who your friends were before you were somebody. That's all I've got to say. Just don't forget who your friends were before you turned famous."

"Isabelle, can you come—" Jane Malone said. And stopped talking.

"Can I come where?" Isabelle demanded.

Jane looked around. "Are you listening to me?" she asked.

"Sure," said Isabelle.

"Well, my mother said I could ask a friend to come

to stay at my house for dinner and the night on Saturday," Jane said. "And I picked you. My father might take us to the movies and to McDonald's after. Can you?"

Isabelle was stunned. Never before had she been asked to Jane's house. "Can I!" she cried. "I would very much love to come to your house, Jane."

"That's good." Jane smiled. "Ask your mother when you go home today, all right? Then call me up and tell me."

"Sure." Isabelle punched Jane gently on the arm. "Sure," she said again, smiling at Jane.

I didn't even know she liked me that much, Isabelle thought. Jane is my best friend.

The thought warmed her.

Chapter Twenty-two

"Tell me what happened right from the beginning," Isabelle directed.

"Well, first, I went to Mrs. Stern's house and she wasn't home, so I hid in the bushes and watched when Philip delivered the paper and then—"

"I don't mean that beginning," Isabelle said impatiently. "I mean when the hoodlums got you. Start there."

So Guy told her about picking the violets and about the one saying "Hello, dere" to him and not letting go of him. About MONSTER and the other two. About the cigarette and the smell of burning and the tin can tied to the dog's tail.

"Then they said they were gonna tie me up while they planned how much money they wanted for the dog," Guy said. "And I thought about you and what you'd do, and so I started swinging the big stick, which was the only weapon I could find, and then they knocked me out."

"Why didn't you wait for me?" Isabelle wailed. "Oh, why didn't you!" She had missed the biggest excitement she might ever know.

"I did," Guy said simply. "You said you were real busy when I asked you if you'd thought of anything. But I waited anyway. When you didn't come, I decided to go to Mrs. Stern's by myself. To ask her about the paint."

He was right. She had said that.

"Guy," she said. "You know what?"

"No. What?"

"You did it yourself," she said. "You kept asking and asking if I'd think of a way to make them stop teasing you, calling you all those names and everything. And you did it all by yourself. Don't you see?"

A smile broke across Guy's face slowly. "You're right," he said. "I did."

"Excellent. Excellent," Isabelle told him, holding up the index finger on each hand and jitterbugging around him in a complete circle.

"Hi, Guy. You wanna come over my house after school? My cat had two more kittens. You can come see 'em if you want."

"Hello, Bernie. She did! Neat-o. Sure, I'll come."

"What's that on the back of your head?" Bernie asked. "You cut yourself?"

Guy looked at Isabelle. "I was in an accident," he said.

"That's my friend Bernie," Guy said. "He's in my class. His cat had kittens while he was eating a piece of toast in the kitchen."

"Jane Malone asked me to come stay overnight Saturday. We're going to the movies and to McDonald's after," Isabelle said.

"What're you gonna have at McDonald's?" Guy asked.

"I don't know."

"I always plan what I'm gonna have ahead of time," Guy confided. "If I don't, I get too confused when the girl asks me and I always pick something I don't like. So I write down what I want on a little piece of paper, and that way I know exactly what I'm gonna get."

"That's not a bad idea," Isabelle said.

"They said I could keep the dog," Guy told Isabelle. "He doesn't have a license or anything. They said if nobody owned it, I could keep it."

"Terrific. What're you gonna call it?" Isabelle said.

"Jake," said Guy, looking at her, eyes glistening. 'I'm calling it Jake."

"What if it's a girl?"

"If it's a girl," Guy said slowly, "I'm calling it Isabelle. I already decided."

"Isabelle?"

"Sure. It even sort of looks like you," Guy said.

"Cool," said Isabelle, without enthusiasm.

"Sure. It's got brown eyes and brown hair, like you."

"Yeah, but you hafta think about when it's out at night and you're trying to get it to come in. So you're out there, calling, 'Here, Isabelle! Come on in, Isabelle!' I don't think that sounds too hot." She'd been told she looked like lots of things, but never, not even by Philip, had she been told she looked like a dog.

"Besides, if you call it Isabelle," Isabelle said, trying to talk Guy out of it, "it'd sound silly. 'Here, Isabelle' "—she imitated Guy calling his dog—" 'Good boy, Isabelle! Supper's ready! Come inside, Isabelle, before your tootsies get all wet.'

"How would that sound?" Isabelle asked indignantly.

"So? I don't think there's anything bad about that," Guy said.

"What's bad is, you would sound exactly like my mother. That's what's bad."

"So what if I sound like your mother." There was something he'd forgotten, something important he'd left out.

"I know!" Guy remembered what it was. "You know how I got home? After they bonked me on the head?"

"No. How'd you get home?"

"In a police car," Guy said, in hushed tones.

Isabelle narrowed her eyes at him and scratched herself, knowing what was coming, pretending she didn't care.

"With the lights flashing?" she said, leaning down to pull up her socks so he couldn't see her face.

"Yup."

"How about the siren?" she asked, inspecting a hole in the toe of her Adidas.

Guy only nodded.

"I can't stand it," Isabelle said, clapping a hand to her head. "I cannot stand it!"

"I know." Guy couldn't help grinning. "And you know something else?"

She shook her head.

"I'm gonna be on the six o'clock news. Tonight."

Mary Eliza Shook came hurtling by at that moment.

"How's your little brudder?" she said sarcastically. Mary Eliza was always the last to get the word.

"Watch the six o'clock news tonight and find out," Isabelle said.

No actress ever had a better exit line. Mary Eliza stood there gawking at them.

"The six o'clock news?" she finally squeaked.

"Yeah, you can't miss it," Isabelle said, smiling sweetly. "It comes on at six o'clock."

There were so many good things about Guy's adventure and its aftermath that Isabelle couldn't pick her favorite. But certainly one of her favorites was telling Philip about Guy being on the six o'clock news.

"You're putting me on," he said scornfully when she told him. "Not that little squirt. I don't believe you."

She shrugged, knowing that for once she had the upper hand. "Okay, don't," she said. "See if I care."

And, although the rule was no television on school nights, Isabelle's mother made an exception.

At two minutes to six, the family gathered in front of the TV set. "It's Channel Eight," Isabelle said. Philip just looked at her. He was the official dial twirler.

"Good evening, ladies and gentlemen. Channel Eight here." The anchorman had a silly face, Isabelle thought. He laughed too much, too. The first story was about a suspicious fire set in a downtown hotel. The second story was about a group of concerned citizens picketing a proposed motel in the next town.

"If he's gonna be on, why don't they put him on?" Philip groused.

"If you don't wanta watch, don't." Isabelle sat on the floor and waited.

"Now for the last story, last but certainly not least," the anchorman said. "An eight-year-old boy became a hero yesterday when he stood off the attacks of three hoodlums who captured him and held him hostage against the release of a stray dog the hoodlums offered to sell to the boy for a thousand dollars."

The camera zoomed in and Guy stood there in his own front yard. He didn't smile but looked straight at the camera.

"Guy Gibbs," the person holding the microphone said, "how did you have the courage to do what you did?" The microphone waited for Guy to speak.

He opened his mouth, then closed it.

"The kid's lost his voice," Philip said.

Isabelle clutched herself around the middle with both arms, rocking back and forth, willing Guy to speak.

He cleared his throat as the camera ground away.

"It was Isabelle," he said, in a loud, clear voice. "My friend Isabelle."

"Isabelle?" the interviewer asked animatedly.

"She's my friend and she learned me, I mean, taught me how to stand up to things. So when they came at me, I tried to figure what Isabelle would do. And I did it." Guy's mouth clamped shut.

Isabelle's mother laid a hand on her arm, gently. Philip said, "Sheesh!" but that was all.

The camera zoomed in on a shot of Guy holding his dog.

"Just thirty seconds left now," the anchorman said jovially. "Tell us what your dog's name is, Guy Gibbs."

"Isabelle," said Guy. "I was going to call it Jake, but we found out he was a girl. So I'm calling it Isabelle."

A commercial about breakfast cereal came on. In Isabelle's living room there was silence.

"Well, that certainly is quite a testimonial," Isabelle's mother said at last, in a little choked-up voice.

"Not too many guys I know have a sister who gets a dog named after her," Philip said. The telephone rang. Isabelle ran to answer it. It was Aunt Maude.

"The strangest thing just happened," Aunt Maude said. "I was watching the six o'clock news and a little boy who looked familiar was on. He was getting some sort of award, don't you know, and he said his dog was named Isabelle. Was that the little boy who comes over every Sunday to fight or was that the little boy who said I looked like his uncle? It was one or the other. The strangest coincidence, isn't it? There he was on the television. He looked a little peaked, too. I really think his mother should've kept him in bed."

Aunt Maude sneezed three times: choo, choo, choo. Isabelle thought she sounded like a kitten sneezing.

"I must be coming down with something," Aunt Maude said. "Probably the same thing the little boy had. I couldn't make head or tail of it but just thought I'd call to let you know he was on the six o'clock news. Tell your mother I'll stop by after church on Sunday. I've got a new hat I want to show her. Good night, dear." And Aunt Maude hung up.

Chapter Twenty-three

"Well, I'm off." Guy's grandmother announced, suitcase in hand.

"I thought you were staying longer," Guy said.

"I've been here long enough. Time to go. Your room looks nice, Guy. I like the color."

"Mrs. Stern helped me mix it. How do you like the stars?"

"They're lovely. Look real."

"I'm sleeping out in a tent at my friend Bernie's house," Guy said. "He said I could borrow his brother's sleeping bag. His mother leaves the back door open in case Bernie gets scared." He looked at his grandmother. "Sometimes Bernie says he gets scared if a big animal comes along in the night and makes noises. Or if it starts to lightning and thunder. That's why his mother leaves the door open—so's he can get back in."

"That'll be fun," Guy's grandmother said.

"I told Mrs. Stern about you," Guy said. "I thought maybe you and her could be friends."

"That's nice, Guy. Maybe next time I come I'll meet Mrs. Stern. I'd like that."

A taxi beeped outside.

Guy's grandmother put out her arms. "How about a hug before I take off?" she said.

"Okay." He put down his books. "I'll miss you," he said. He put his arms around her and kissed her cheek.

"Well," she said, smiling, "that's better. Hugs are for everybody. Kisses you save for somebody special." She set her hat straight on her head.

"Give my regards to the paper boy," she said. And, "Good-bye, Isabelle," she said to the dog. Guy watched her go down the path and get into the taxi. Then he got down on the floor and rested his head alongside the dog's.

"I might call you Jake, after all," Guy said. Isabelle licked his face. "You look more like a Jake. Jake's a better name for a dog, anyway. Right, Jake?" Isabelle wagged her tail in agreement.

884434

F
GRE

Greene, Constance
C.

1722750

Isabelle shows her
stuff

$1

F
GRE

Greene, Constance
C.

Isabelle shows her
stuff

1722750

$11.95   884434

DATE	BORROWER'S NAME	
SEP 28 '88	Nancy &	4-P
OCT 7 '88	Kizzie L.	6-P
OCT 26 '88	Tressa. M	4-P

SEP 28
OCT 7
OCT 26
MAY 2 3
Sch De
NOV 2
DEC 14
MAY 1
SEP 24
OCT 1
DEC
DEC

15